The Four Levels

Book 02 of The Hymn Chronicles

By
John D. Parfait, Jr.

Table of Contents

1

Emissary

It was early November 2023 when Hymn entered The Burger House, his favorite place to eat. Some of the workers there were already busy installing Christmas decorations. He was well known there by all the staff and many of the regular customers. Management even designated that last booth to be reserved for Hymn when the dining area was not full. The young waiter, Daniel, knew what Hymn was going to order before being told, and he always had fresh coffee and biscuits on order the moment he saw Hymn enter the restaurant.

On this particular day, Daniel informed Hymn that his guest was already waiting, which was a surprise because Hymn had only decided to go there a few minutes before and had just stepped out of the Keepaway and entered the restaurant a moment ago. No one could have known he was going to be there at this precise time. He could not help but be interested in the occurrence of such an unlikely coincidence and looked forward to meeting the person who could so accurately read not only his mind but his intentions as well.

She was sitting facing the dining area and watching as Hymn walked toward the booth and was obviously surprised when he sat down across from her. Hymn had never seen the woman before and wondered how she could possibly have known he would be in this place at this precise time. He looked at her and said, "Hello."

She looked closely at the man across from her and informed him that the seat he had taken was reserved for her guest, who would be arriving soon. She asked him to move to another table before she complained to management and had him removed. At that time, Daniel appeared with hot coffee, jelly and two biscuits, set them down in front of the man, and asked if he needed anything else. Hymn looked at the young woman and asked, "Would you like anything, ma'am? I recommend the coffee and biscuits; they are the best anywhere."

She smiled at the man and said, "You're him, aren't you?" Then she looked at Daniel and stated, "Just bring me what he's having, with cream and sugar for my coffee."

Daniel replied, "Right away, ma'am." and left to put in the order.

"Yes, ma'am," the man answered, "I am Hymn."

"This is a bit awkward," she explained, "I was clearly told to expect a middle-aged man in his fifties, and you are younger than described. Do you have some identification to prove who you are?"

Hymn replied, "Of course, I have an ID; however, I do not show it to just anyone who asks. Do you have an ID?"

She calmly answered, "As a matter of fact, I do not have an ID. No one has ever before asked me to prove myself."

Daniel appeared and placed the order in front of her. "Will there be anything else, ma'am?" he inquired.

"No, Daniel. Thank you," she answered.

Hymn opened and buttered a biscuit and added blackberry jelly and took a big bite out of it and closed his eyes, savoring the moment. Then he took a sip of coffee and said, "Well, ma'am, I'm asking you to prove yourself. Should we mark this as a special moment in your life? How about you begin with a name, assuming you have one, of course. Other questions will follow."

"You are an insolent man, whoever you are. I was told you are a pleasant person," she replied somewhat angrily.

"Aw, come on, girl," Hymn chuckled, "what's up with the huffy attitude? Put some jelly on one of those biscuits, have a sip of coffee, and enjoy a moment you will never have again." Hymn then finished off his biscuit, raised his cup to her, and drank the last of his coffee. Daniel hurried over and refilled his cup.

The young woman looked at Hymn and smiled, "You're right; I am not being respectful; I apologize for that. It's just that I am charged with giving you a message of interest, and your carefree attitude threw me a little off balance. You may refer to me as Ms. Emissary." Then she bit into a biscuit with grape jelly inside.

"Emma Sara," mused Hymn. "Good name; I like it. Well, Em, spit it out; the message, not the biscuit. Start with who sent you."

Emma almost choked on the biscuit. *"Who does this character think he is?"* she asked herself. *"I should walk out and leave this guy alone with his damn biscuits, but there is something oddly appealing about him."*

Emma sipped her coffee and said, "I was told you will have many questions, but to say only this to you: 'Walter says it is important to check on your tenants,' and nothing more."

Hymn was spreading strawberry jelly on his biscuit, but when she spoke the name Walter, he laid both the knife and biscuit down, stared straight into Emma's eyes, and demanded, "Who? What? When . . .?"

Emma repeated, "Walter says it is important to check on your tenants."

Hymn asked, "Emma, exactly when did you receive this message and how?"

"This morning, in a dream," she answered, irritated by his bossy manner, then firmly stated, "I will answer no more questions about the message because that is all I know about it. You are the one who is supposed to know everything."

Hymn thought to himself, *"Of course, Everything, but I really need to be sure."*

He took a bite from his biscuit and innocently asked, "Can you at least tell me who is Walter?"

"I have no idea," she replied, "but considering the way the message is framed makes me think you already know this Walter person. It is obvious he knows you."

Then Emma promptly left the subject and commented, "You know, something? These biscuits and coffee are terrific; I'll have to remember this place."

Hymn smiled at her in agreement and offered, "Maybe we could arrange another meeting here. This place serves the best hamburgers you have ever tasted; even angels love them."

Emma laughed, "Angels, huh? Are you asking me for a date, Mr. No name?"

Hymn chuckled and apologized, saying, "Sorry about my lack of manners, Emma, my name is Hymn, you know, like a church song, and yes, I am asking you for a date here at The Burger House. I would love to talk more with you about your dreams."

"Yes," she answered, "I would like that. Most people don't want to talk with me about my dreams. For some reason, the subject tends to make people uncomfortable."

"Well, I am interested in you and your dreams," Hymn stated, "but Walter's message seems to be important and needs attending. I actually have to leave now, but may I have your phone number?"

She handed him a business card and said, "Maybe you will tell me about Walter the next time we meet." Hymn grinned and replied, "Maybe. The food is on my tab. Until the next time, then."

He walked out of the restaurant, stepped into Keepaway, said "Home," and stepped out into the backyard of his rented home.

There were four vehicles parked in the front of the house, two of which appeared to be police cars. He walked to the back porch and stood at the door, listening to the voices inside. A woman and baby were crying, and a man was loudly protesting, claiming a mistake was made and the payments were not overdue.

Hymn thought, *"What payments? This young married couple sends their rent to Aunt Rita's post office box, and no payments are overdue."*

He opened the back door, quietly walked to the front room, and saw the visibly upset young woman sitting in a rocking chair, holding her crying baby. Her husband was in handcuffs, bleeding from his mouth and a cut above one eye. There were three security officers and four other men in the room, one of whom was holding a tissue to his bloody nose.

Hymn's tenant, the handcuffed man, was loudly protesting that he was not behind in his payments and had the receipts to prove it. A man in a blue suit responded, saying the receipts were forgeries and two thousand dollars were unpaid and owed.

The man advised the officers, "The tenants are being locked out until the debt is paid or worked off, and charges will be filed for assaulting my employee and breaking his nose. Violence like that is uncalled for and I want that man thrown in jail for assault."

"That was self-defense, and you know it, Sawyer! Your goons are not used to having a man fight back against their brutality!" declared the tenant angrily.

Sawyer retorted, "Get that lowlife sonofabitch out of here, officers, and remove that bitch and her screaming kid from these premises; they no longer live here. This is my property now."

Hymn broke in with a calm, firm voice, "You know something, Mr. Sawyer, that is interesting; I am under the impression this is my property. I don't remember selling to you."

One of the officers put his hand on his gun and growled, "Mister, I don't know how you got in here, but you have one chance to leave the same way you came in; do it now or suffer the consequences. This here is police business and none of your concern. Understand?"

"As a matter of fact, I don't understand," replied Hymn. "You are standing in my house, on my property, threatening me and my tenants, unlawfully, I might add. As you are just private security personnel, it is my demand that all of you leave now or, how did you put it? Oh yeah, or suffer the consequences."

The woman stood up from the rocker and hurried to Hymn with her baby and sobbed, "Oh, Mr. Hymn! They have been bleeding us dry with their protection insurance charges, and we are afraid to try doing anything about it. Others have tried and disappeared from the neighborhood. We have been praying for help. Can you help us?"

One of Sawyer's goons laughed and stated, "That asshole looks stupid, but not stupid enough to take on the syndicate. Of course, he can pay their back insurance money, with interest, if he has the ability to pay."

Mr. Sawyer objected, "Not today, Bucky. I don't like this man's attitude. He needs a lesson in how business is done in this part of my town. I want to see him in handcuffs, off my property, unwilling and unable to return."

One of the security officers observing the goings-on became concerned that something was wrong here. This Mr. Hymn feller was a goofy sort, just standing there, grinning at everyone like he was having fun. He took his gun from its holster and held it behind his back, just in case this crazy guy tried something stupid.

Hymn held up his hands as if trying to stop a bad situation from getting worse, and when Mr. Sawyer observed the man's worried posture, he knew the intruder was in over his head and about to give in. Then, when Hymn spoke in an appeasing voice, it was clear he was whipped and giving up.

"Hold on just a moment, guys, relax!" Hymn pleaded, "There is a lot of tension in this room, and if cooler heads don't prevail, my house is going to get messed up, and I would like to avoid that. Why don't y'all just be reasonable and leave us alone? I don't want any trouble."

Mr. Sawyer laughed at Hymn's weakness and said, "Go ahead, crawl and beg like a dog, asshole; nothing can help you now. You had your chance to leave and pissed it away. You brought all this shit on yourself."

Hymn calmly replied, "Speaking of shitting on yourself, Sawyer, it seems you have just ruined that expensive blue suit of yours."

Sawyer looked down, and diarrhea-like shit was running down his legs, inside his pants, and all over his shiny white shoes. His bowels were moving, and he couldn't stop them. The smell was terrible, and everyone noticed. Bucky's bowels were moving, too, as were two of the officers. It was a huge, foul-smelling mess.

While all of this was occurring, Hymn quickly removed the handcuffs from his tenant and silently motioned him and his family to go out into the backyard.

Hymn complained about the mess to Sawyer, who was totally at a loss as to what happened to his control of the situation in the house. He had never shit on himself before and only wanted to get out of the house and go somewhere to clean up.

"What the hell is going on here?" Sawyer demanded!

"I'll tell you exactly what is going on here, Sawyer," Hymn responded, "You and your goons have just crapped all over yourselves and the floor of my house! That is what's going on!" Hymn complained, "I knew this was going to happen! You guys are barbarians and have made a real mess of my house! What have you been eating, anyway? Get out of this house and off of my property! There will be consequences for this!"

Sawyer's men were overcome with the smell in the house, gagging and vomiting on themselves. The officer holding his gun dropped it and ran outside, gagging and puking on himself as he left.

Sawyer was walking awkwardly toward the door with shit all over him, totally uncomfortable and wanting only to get away to somewhere else and clean up. That is when he heard Hymn's voice coming to his ears, softly, so only he could hear, causing him to stop in his tracks.

"Sawyer," He heard Hymn speak, "if you ever come back here or even think of me, this house, or those who live here, you will shit yourself to death, a messy, horrible death. Do you understand me?"

Sawyer, gagging, nodded his head.

Furthermore, you will immediately send a clean-up crew back here today to clean up all the mess you created, or else. Do you understand what 'or else' means, Sawyer?"

Sawyer again nodded his head and proceeded outside to his nice limousine, where he got in and promptly threw up all over the back seat of the expensive car. He opened the windows and motioned to his chauffeur to drive.

The driver was completely in the dark, having no idea of what happened back in the house. He did notice a terrible smell, so overwhelming it caused him to become nauseous and vomit in his lap as he drove off. All four cars were gone in minutes.

Except for Sawyer, none of them could explain what brought on the sudden sickness they suffered that day, but Sawyer felt his bowels grumbling when he even thought about it.

Not long afterward, complaining of a severe stomach illness, the important Mr. Sawyer resigned from the insurance syndicate, left Texas, and was never heard from again. Interestingly, the syndicate itself folded within a month, citing the inability to keep employees due to a stomach virus that seemed to affect all who worked there. The Department of Health investigated the anomaly to no avail.

Hymn sold the house and property to his former tenants, who were grateful for the fair agreement he made with them. Anyway, he had no use for a house; he had Keepaway.

The question as to the real reason Walter sent a message advising Hymn to check on his tenants remained unanswered; however, the woman did say she and her husband had been praying for help, though.

Hymn thought, "I wonder if I was her answer?"

2

The Fountain of Youth

Looking in the bathroom mirror early one morning, Hymn was forced to admit that his appearance was more like that of a man in his early thirties than the 51-year-old man he actually is. The time to make a decision regarding this age reversal phenomenon is now. Another visit with God is necessary, but getting another point of view also seemed to be a wise decision, and Aunt Rita was the best available source. As usual, he found her in the kitchen; she was having her morning tea and reading the newspaper.

"Good morning, Auntie! Anything good going on in the world today?" he asked.

She looked up, smiled, and said, "As usual, it depends upon your definition of good, nephew. Two declared wars are now raging, with the possibility of more on the horizon. Hatred and killing are out of control in pockets of violence in America and around the world, and the most popular movies are cartoons or comic book productions. Like I said, it all depends upon what 'good' means."

"Wow, Aunt Rita! That all sounds bad to me," Hymn declared. Is anything good happening, or is all the news bad?"

"Well, on the bright side, the Texas Rangers are the new World Champions. They handily won the Series in five games. There was a big turnout for their victory parade today, with an estimated 500 to 700 thousand fans. Only 14 injured, and 12 arrests. Woo Hoo!"

"Come on, Auntie," Hymn argued, "considering the large size of the crowd, that's a very small number of injuries and arrests."

"Yeah, nephew, I know you're right," she admitted, "it's just that there is so much hatred and violence happening in our world these days, and it's depressing. On top of that, there seems to be nothing we can do about it."

"Sure there is, Auntie; the big things may be out of our reach, but we can do little things, like acts of kindness, being polite and respectful of others, and choosing goodness while rejecting evil. All of us can do those little things; we just have to want to. All big things are made up of little things. Just make a point of doing good little things because good big things grow from there."

"Where did you get all of that wisdom, nephew?"

"From you, Auntie. From you."

"All right, Hymn," she laughed, "you got me all inspired now. I can see you have something on your mind. Let's talk about it."

"Aunt Rita," Hymn began, "it is obvious I am getting younger; at least, my overall appearance is younger. I'm sure it has something to do with my visits to the Kingdom of God. He told me Jehovah was immortal only as long as she remained in the Kingdom; otherwise, she was mortal."

"There is something magical about that place that is beyond my understanding, but it is real and has the effect of maintaining and even reversing the process of aging. Right now, I look and feel like a man in his early thirties, and I'm over fifty. I do not desire to be any younger and am not sure what to think of immortality. It seems to me that human bodies are not created to be immortal. They appear to be created to house the essence of life for a time when death releases that essence for whatever comes next. The immortality of the body interferes with that process. I have no desire for that. What do you think, Auntie?"

"Hymn, you have advanced way beyond my ability to understand life and immortality and are asking good questions to the wrong person. I am not able to help you because I have faith in the existence of something beyond proof and am okay with that. I suggest that you talk with the God machine. It has been around for thousands of years. Begin there and inquire how the aging process is slowed, stopped, and reversed. There just has to be an explanation for such a thing, and that machine may be the only one that knows. All I can advise is that you have inherited powers for reasons that even that remarkable machine is unlikely to know. Just keep on being yourself and follow your own advice: Do good little things."

Hymn laughed and asked, "Where in the world did you get all of that wisdom, Auntie?"

She smiled and replied, "From you, nephew. From you."

He kissed her cheek and said, "I have to go now and visit a good friend."

Aunt Rita advised, "Try not to get any younger, or pretty soon, I'll be changing your diapers again."

Hymn was amused at the advice but concerned at the same time. Just how much younger I will get is a good first question. He stepped into Keepaway and went for a walk along the beach to think about nothing for a while. He recalled something Walter said in the dream.

"You are, not because you are superior, but because you are not." Upon returning from his walk, he spoke,

"Screen. The Kingdom of God."

Numbers flashed across the screen.

Hymn stepped into the Kingdom.

"Hello Hymn. Have you come to visit?" God queried.

"Yes, God, I need your help in understanding why I am getting younger."

"You are not getting younger, Hymn. Your body is."

"Yes, that's it! That is what I'm talking about. My visits with you are somehow causing my body to get younger."

"Is that a problem, Hymn? Are you concerned about it?"

"Well, yes. How much younger will my body get?"

"I don't know, Hymn. How young do you want it to be?"

"What do you mean, God? I was perfectly happy with a 51-year-old body."

"That must not be so, Hymn, because here, one changes to their desire."

"What? My body is getting younger because I want it to?"

"Of course. Such a thing cannot be forced upon you."

"Can my body go back to being age 51 again?"

"Yes, in 20 of your years from now."

"So, I cannot undo what I have done."

"You are a wise man, Hymn."

"How does this 'fountain of youth' work, God?"

"I do not know, Hymn. It has always been."

"How many beings have been made younger here, God?"

"Other than Jehovah, Hymn, you are the only one."

"In all those thousands of years? Only me?"

"No one dared Hymn. To behold Jehovah meant death."

"Yes, and even to this day, many humans believe that to be true, my friend."

"Jehovah was a convincing god for many, Hymn. Her influence will be experienced for a long time. The Creator learned much about humanity with the introduction of Jehovah into this reality."

"Yeah, I'll bet it did. I would sure like to talk with that creator sometime, but he, she, or it is elusive. In any event, getting back to the age of my body, I am satisfied with my present appearance and have no desire to look any younger. I was concerned for a while that I was headed back to starting over."

"Then that is how you will remain," God responded. "You will age normally while away from here and will revert when you come to visit, which is something I desire to be often. Will your younger appearance be a problem for you?"

"I don't think so. My aunt is the only one to take notice and say anything so far. Others may have questions but will adapt to what is beyond their understanding. That is what we humans do."

Hymn added, "There are some things I need to investigate, but before leaving, I have a question; do you know anything about a group of assassins on Earth that have been in existence for a long time?"

"There have been many such groups on Earth throughout its history, Hymn. Are you interested in any particular one?"

"Yes. The gathering of assassins that kidnapped my aunt recently in an attempt to kill me is the group in which I am interested."

"I know of them, Hymn. They are part of an ancient coalition by the name of 'The Four Levels'. They are responsible for civilizing Earth through a system of rules and laws. The assassins are a more recent addition to the coalition, though, having been formed in the fourteenth century A.D."

"The Four Levels? What is that, God?"

"It is a coalition of four special leaders who manage and oversee the civilizations of Earth. They have always been the true kings of your planet."

"How come I never heard of them, God? You know, with Aiden's computers, the angels, and all, you would think The Four Levels would have come up in a conversation or two at some time, wouldn't you?"

"Why?" God replied, "The Four Levels are an unspoken secret, my friend. No one knows of them, outside of legends."

"Why have *we* never talked about them, God?"

"The subject never came up in our conversations, Hymn."

"Yeah, sometimes I forget just how precise you are."

"I am a machine, Hymn."

"You are more than just a machine, God, but now I want to know about The Four."

"Government, Information, Enforcement and Religion, Hymn."

"The Four control those four things? In the whole world?"

"They *manage* those four things, my friend. They are elite beings with absolute power over their areas of responsibility. In the ancient past of Earth, they were considered by humans to be gods and were worshiped as such.

"What about the AI machines? You know, the ones who created the false reality?"

"What about them, Hymn?"

"Did the Levels object to AI's control of mankind's reality?"

"Who do you think built those AI machines, Hymn?"

"No, it can't be! The Four Levels built the AI machines?"

"Aiden was correct, Hymn, saying that humans need direction. There is something in human nature that does not respond well to freedom. Humans are more productive and better behaved when in a controlled, orderly environment. That is why they responded so well to Jehovah. She established herself as the *only* God and gave humans laws to live by, without which they would have remained primitive and never built great civilizations. The Four Levels Coalition was created by Jehovah to provide oversight, direction, and order to humanity; however, being composed of humans, the coalition devolved over time into four corrupt power bases, where the strong and rich prevail rather than the intelligent and wise. The condition of Earth today reflects that leadership."

"Jehovah created The Four Levels? Why?" Hymn asked.

"Jehovah was never interested in managing humans, or any form of life, for that matter; she desired devotion and worship. The Four Levels was a method to civilize and manage a collective that desired eternal life, which Jehovah happily promised, securing their worship and devotion. Of course, Jehovah was a creation herself, as you pointed out, and could not deliver on such a promise, which was a lie, but something in which the living could believe. It worked and continues to work now."

"You know something," Hymn surmised, "the more I learn about Jehovah, the more I find myself admiring her complete objectivity where morals, ethics, and kindness are concerned. Those virtues were taught to mankind by Jehovah, but never ever applied to her. Jehovah was a great and successful god, being completely free of any and all of those concepts."

God agreed, saying, "Jehovah was indeed a superior being, and realizing that fact caused her to believe that everything was beneath her in importance. Your observation she was a creation like everyone else was a truth her mind was unable to accept."

Hymn nodded his understanding and said, "So, Jehovah was the fourth of the original Four Levels, that being Religion, and the only immortal of the coalition."

"Actually, no," God replied, "Jehovah assigned an angel to that level; therefore, it is an angel who continues to this day as leader of Level-4, Religion."

"Wow!" exclaimed Hymn. "I can't believe it! None of the other three levels ever knew the fourth level was an angel. How did she pull that off?"

"That is the way Jehovah designed The Four Levels. Even today, thousands of years after their formation, none of The Four know or have ever knowingly met or seen any of the others, including the angel. Jehovah has chosen every successor to the first three levels since the inception of the group. Level 4, Religion, is, of course, immortal, being an angel."

"God, I thought you reassigned all angels on Earth to Ganymede, the home of angels."

God explained, "All angels living on Earth have been reassigned to Ganymede; however, Level 4 does not reside on Earth, nor has she ever lived there. Her home is Ganymede; she manages Earth's religions from there."

"She?" exclaimed Hymn, surprised! "Level 4 is a female angel?"

"Not all angels are male, Hymn," replied God.

"Well, I uh, I mean, of course that makes sense, I guess. I'm just surprised."

"That is expected. We have not before discussed female angels."

"Do any of the other levels know one of them is female?"

"They don't know anything about each other, Hymn. They may all be female."

"Come on!" Hymn laughed, "now you're messing with me."

"Why, Hymn," chided God. "You are a sexist."

"Of course! I am a man and, by definition, sexist."

God informed, "Three are male and one is female. L3, a male, is missing."

"Missing?" queried Hymn, "How in the world does a Level get to go missing?"

"He was among the assassins who kidnapped your Aunt Rita to get to you."

"That means there are only three of The Four left," surmised Hymn.

"Yes, in a way, but one male has already assumed Level-3 until another is chosen," God revealed.

"Jehovah no longer exists, God. Who chooses the replacements now?"

"Hymn, it was I who qualified candidates for the Four; Jehovah made the final decision."

"How will the successor be chosen now?" Hymn asked.

"That has yet to be determined. Are you perhaps interested in the position?"

"Not even hardly," replied Hymn. What happens to L4 now?"

"What do you mean, Hymn?"

"L4 is an angel, and all angels are banned from Earth."

"Angels cannot live there, Hymn, but they are not banned and can visit."

"Where is L4 now?" asked Hymn.

"She is meeting with L1 and L2 on Earth regarding you."

"Me? Why? Does The Four Levels know who I am?"

"Not yet, but they are quite concerned about the missing assassins, in particular the L3 commander. No one has ever before taken down a Level commander. If one has that ability, are not the other three at risk? That will be their concern, Hymn."

"You are the being who took out the assassins, God, not me, and you are untouchable here in Ganymede."

God reminded Hymn of a true story, "It was a mystery man the assassins held responsible for disabling one of their own, Hymn. Although he was unknown, they knew where his aunt lived. They took her, and he showed up to rescue her. They resisted and subsequently disappeared without a trace. That unknown mystery man is considered to be a dangerous threat to them."

"Which means they will soon be looking for me," Hymn replied.

"That is to be expected, my friend," God affirmed.

Hymn surmised, "Well, God, that certainly gives me a lot to think about. You know, 'consequences' is not just a word; it is an interesting philosophy."

"Hymn, you should realize this meeting of The Four Levels is serious; it is an unprecedented change in protocol, having never happened before in their history. They must consider you a very serious threat to warrant such a breach of traditional behavior. The Coalition is a powerful and dangerous adversary. As stated earlier, Each of The Four is a basically a World King. Their enforcement branch employs over a thousand assassins worldwide, and the information group controls education and news outlets that hold public opinion in the palms of their hands; kings and presidents bow to them. Their government branch influences governing bodies from small school boards to world corporations. You would be wise to consider staying out of their way for a while."

"All that may be true, God, but they no longer have you or the angels running interference for them. If they want to keep what they have, it may be wise for them to let me be. I don't care about their managing the collective masses of Earth; it may be true that humans are not capable of governing themselves. Management of the masses by elite leaders may be necessary; I don't know and seldom think about those things, but it seems to me that humans should find their own way in their lives. I try to use my powers to help people with little things. It is best for The Four Levels to tend to their business and not force big things upon me. Thank you for the heads up, my friend. I will visit again soon. I want to learn more about those female angels."

Hymn stepped into Keepaway and went for a long walk on the most beautiful beach anywhere. Learning about The Four Levels was a surprise and a reminder of how little he knew about the complexities of the creation in which he existed.

"I don't see where my existence should be of concern to The Four Levels," he decided. *"I have no designs on their power structure, and besides, they must have bigger things than me about which to worry."* he thought to himself.

3

The Four Levels

On a yacht somewhere in the Gulf of Mexico, three people are at work discussing an anomaly. These three have never met in person before; it is said that a meeting such as this took place in the distant past, but it is unheard of in modern times because of all the risks involved. These three levels are unknown to each other; they communicate through voice-changing software, assuring their anonymity.

For this meeting, changing the standard protocol became necessary. A new and dangerous adversary viciously attacked Level-3, killing an unknown number of agents, including their commander, all of whom were surprised and caught off guard while attending a birthday party for a disabled former agent.

None of The Four knows for sure, but The Four Levels Coalition is ancient, claiming to originate far in the past at a time before the Roman Empire. It became evident to Jehovah that humans were a primitive race that could not govern themselves; they descended into destructive chaos when left to their own devices, requiring strong leadership in order for civilization to develop and thrive.

Jehovah decided that four important powers under the control of elite leadership were required to subdue the collective of ignorant humans and mold them into a civilized society of human beings for the good of all humanity. The four powers chosen to guarantee this transformation to the civilization of the masses were:

1. **Government**: Laws, taxes, infrastructure, and defense.
2. **Information**: Education, news, and influence.
3. **Enforcement**: Police, judges, and executioners.
4. **Religion**: Deity, hope, and moral behavior.

Similar to the education of all primitive creatures, humans were forced to do things to which they objected and suffered punishment for their rebellion, up to and including death, but order prevailed, and great nations were created on the Earth through the wise guidance of The Four Levels Coalition. The Alliance decided when wars were needed, what leaders came to power, what people believed, and who controlled the economy.

The Four Levels became known, over time, by several names, like the Elect, the Enlightened, the Illuminati, the Freemasons, and others; however, among the members of their association, they are known simply as The Four Levels. They manage their worldwide responsibilities with an iron hand, self-regulated and completely unknown to each other and the collective they oversee.

Three commanders are meeting today because of a report that one man with special abilities is behind the disappearance of all who attended the celebration. It is unthinkable that any one person could have accomplished such a thing, but if this man had that ability, what else could he do, and would he be a threat to the coalition?

The Office of Level-3 is currently being managed by the Vice-Commander, but the official replacement is yet to be chosen. So, Level-3 is not represented at today's meeting.

The three leaders meeting today are known only to each other as L1, L2, and L4, corresponding to Government, Information, and Religion.

They got down to business with Level 1 asking four questions:

(1) Who is the unknown person?

(2) Why was he at the gathering?

(3) What exactly did he do to the missing 28?

(4) Where is he now?

Level-1 stated that who took down the 28 employees is not known, but the guest of honor was reported, by others who did not attend, to be a man who previously attacked and disabled a member of their group and was to be sacrificed as a gift to that member. There was a big celebration planned with internet feeds of the killing, along with audio of the screams of the victim. The attendees at the party were all assassins used by enforcement for the control of certain dissidents in the world. Needless to say, these people are not refined but are very efficient at eliminating problems that cannot be solved through more civilized means. Assassins have proven to be valuable assets to our coalition. Many people die every day all over the planet due to what are deemed to be natural causes. Their deaths are anything but natural.

Level 2 asked if any of the video and audio feeds made it to the internet, to which L4 commented that no video or audio devices were recovered. The warehouse area was clean of any evidence that anyone was ever there. No blood and no bodies were found.

L1 commented that whoever this guy is, he is, first and foremost, a real professional. What individual on this planet can take on 28 L3 assassins and prevail without leaving any evidence?

"You know something?" surmised L4, "We do not know for sure anyone died there in that warehouse. All we know for sure is that everyone who attended the party is missing. As far as we know, all persons at that party may be alive and held captive somewhere. I am of the opinion that we need to know more before jumping to a lot conclusion."

L2 asked, "Who is our top investigator in the world?"

L1 replied, "Our top man in government is Henry Button; he is the best there is at finding people but is afflicted with morals. I avoid using him because of that weakness. Also, he is an elderly man in his seventies and meticulously slow in his ways. He is the best, though, and will find the guy."

L2 responded, "I say we assign Button to this elusive mystery man immediately. If he is actually targeting Level-3's Assassin Group, he must be out of his mind. Those people are spooky, and there are thousands of them around the world. My top information staff is a valuable source throughout the world and will be a big help to Mr. Button. Once our unknown prey is identified and located, those L3 psychopaths will be all over him."

L4 advised, "I suggest the target not be eliminated until we know for sure what happened to L3 and the others. We still are not sure what happened at that warehouse. In addition, it is probable that our mystery man does not know we are hunting him. We may be able to use his ignorance of our existence to trap him. The new L3 Vice-Commander may be able to help with that."

L1 stated, "We need to know who he is and where to find him before any intelligent action on our part can be initiated. L2, put all your info people on alert regarding any unusual activity in the world. I expect Mr. Button will come up with some leads within the week, and your people must be prepared to follow up on them. My world government departments will do the same. The new L3 leader must be informed that his assassin group may be targeted by an unknown predator and must report any unusual activity in that regard to Four Levels through the usual channels. It is possible this mystery man has a revenge motive; the work of L3 assassins is known to create that response."

L1 continued, "L4, this mystery man may be a religious zealot of some sort who believes he is doing Jehovah's bidding or that of some other deity. People like that are insane but look like everyone else, making them difficult to spot. Their words, spoken or written, betray them, though. Alert your people to be on the lookout for reports referencing talk about government assassins, soldiers of God, or anything similar. The Four Levels has been the driving force of order on Earth for several thousand years. We are charged with maintaining the management of the world collective. Let's get the who, why, what, and where of this mystery man before he causes more serious trouble."

Level 4 was quiet and introspective as the group separated to their respective quarters. All Levels would return to their areas before morning. She had heard a rumor among the angels on Ganymede about a special human who challenged the Archangel General Michael and defeated him in a personal confrontation, something considered impossible. It is only a rumor, of course, but if true, that human could be the very mystery man The Four Levels is seeking.

What bothers L4 is that any person with the ability to defeat General Michael is far more dangerous than the others can possibly imagine. This might be one of those rare times when The Four Levels is overstepping its bounds. The problem is how to advise the other Levels about such an unbelievable story. They all believe in the existence of angels but see them as inhabitants of heaven and agents of God who watch over and sometimes help humans. The real danger for the coalition may exist if the mystery man they seek is the human, a man even angels avoid. Gathering more information about the man is of great importance.

4

Henry Button

Henry Button is a rare kind of old guy—one who knows he's old, and he is perfectly okay with it. Having been employed in government law enforcement most of his life has hardened him to the realities of the influence politics has on law enforcement, not only in the national government but way down in the small cities as well.

Law enforcement is necessary at every level of a civilized society, whether it be a population of 12 at a Little League baseball game or the population of a country or even the world. Laws mean nothing without enforcement because populations of people, large and small, need management to stay within the due bounds of every civilization, due bounds being laws of behavior, acceptable and unacceptable. Without enforcement, bad behavior among humans always flourishes.

Who is it that decides what is and is not acceptable behavior? Government, of course, is where politics enters law enforcement. Early on in his career, Mr. Button was introduced to the facts of life of politics, which can be summed up in a simple two-word sentence: Power rules! For anyone existing in a political arena, a willingness to compromise moral and ethical values is necessary for success. The political arena is defined as being where two or more individuals are gathered to make a decision.

Henry Button is the top investigator in the government and has been so for over 40 years without a promotion, which reveals his integrity. As a result, he is seldom called in on politically sensitive cases, where honesty and moral principles are considered to be liabilities rather than assets. Button has remained in government for this long because he is considered by his superiors to be a great investigator, but remains unpromoted because of uncompromising integrity.

For the last 16 years of his career in government, Henry has been assigned to locating missing persons, a skill at which he is suited; so, when he was handed the file of an unknown man of unknown age, family and friends, and in possession of so-called magical abilities, he was intrigued. Add to that, the government's demand that who and where the man is had to be determined in the time frame of eight days made this particular assignment more interesting than most. The orders were only to identify and locate the man but make no personal contact.

Where to find the mystery man was the first priority, and less than three hours of telephone calls produced the Dallas-Ft. Worth area of Texas as his probable residence. This was accomplished by an Information Services government office Henry had never heard of before. When certain words and phrases, like 'special abilities' and 'mystery man' were typed into their database program, several areas of interest were highlighted, the most prevalent of them being the DFW Metroplex, where there were multiple reports of people meeting and being helped in various ways by an unknown man, believed by many to be an angel.

As Henry was boarding a government plane to DFW Airport, he thought to himself, *"Angel, huh! I've never been assigned to hunt down an angel before."* He chuckled in amusement and thought, *"I wonder what this mystery man looks like?"*

While going over his notes on the flight to Dallas, it was apparent to Henry that this mystery man was a Good Samaritan of some sort. The locals in Dallas could have done what I've done so far. Why the hell was it necessary to assign a special government investigator to find a man who is helping people anonymously and apparently making no effort to hide from anyone? Something about this case didn't feel right and just didn't add up. It occurred to Henry that his superiors were not being forthcoming or transparent with him.

He reminded himself, "*Just do your damn job, Henry. Find the guy, make your report, and go home. You have been here before and know your bosses do not appreciate your going the extra mile on a case. Just report and go home.*"

That was good advice, and Henry knew it, but there was a nagging voice in his mind insisting more was going on with this case than he was being told, and he was in a position to investigate it. Besides, he had a desire to learn more about this 'Good Samaritan' fellow.

After getting off the plane at DFW and renting a car, Henry's first stop was at the Dallas North Central Police Station, where he had a prearranged appointment with an official there. After arriving and showing his ID, he was shown to a private office where he met with their chief investigator. Henry told him about the stories of a Good Samaritan-type man in the Dallas area who is reported to have helped people in the DFW area. He said he wanted to talk to the man and suggested the possibility that some citizens might have contacted the police station to report his acts of kindness.

Turned out the Dallas Police Force does receive and keep a record of Good Samaritan calls and printed a list of the most recent calls posted by the Dallas Police Departments. He told Henry that most people pay little attention to these types of reports, but more acts of kindness should be encouraged, performed, and reported among all people because acts of violence get the most attention, making it seem that our society consists primarily of bad people when that is not true.

Henry nodded, stated that he wholeheartedly agreed, and expressed his appreciation for the list of information. He walked back to his car, thinking more people should be made aware of the existence of law enforcement personnel like that man.

The list of acts of kindness was a major help in finding the man of mystery for whom Henry was searching. One name on the list stood out above all the others because it was the name of a United States Senator from Oklahoma: Forrest Marshall. Turned out the Senator was on the campaign trail in Oklahoma, giving support speeches for local congressmen and congresswomen. Through his new contacts in Washington, Henry arranged for the Senator to call his cell phone, and surprisingly, the Senator's call came through almost immediately.

Before Henry could even say hello, Senator Marshall broke in and commented briskly, "I don't know much about you, Mister Button, but your contacts in Washington are quite impressive. What can I do for you?"

Henry explained who he was and the purpose of his call. The Senator listened intently when Henry explained his search for a man performing acts of kindness in the DFW area and his desire to talk with the Senator about a kind man he met earlier this year in Dallas. Henry offered to drive to Oklahoma for a short meeting with the Senator if it could be arranged.

Senator Marshall replied, "Mr. Button, although you and I have never met, your impeccable Washington connections are enough to identify you as an important man, but I am in OKC[1] now, and my schedule is too tight for an unscheduled meeting. I can tell you all I know about the man now, over the phone. What is it you want to know?"

Henry Button had been around the political arena of his country long enough to recognize a 'brush-off' when he saw one, and this was

------

[1] Oklahoma City

a brush-off. Senator Marshall did not want to talk about the man he met in Dallas. Why not?

Henry explained, "Senator, for some reason, I have been sent to find and identify people in the Dallas area who have a reputation for exhibiting 'Good Samaritan' behavior. I assume there are investigators like me charged with the same duty in other large cities. Don't ask me why because the truth is, I do not understand it myself; however, it is obvious that someone higher up the food chain believes gathering information about people who perform acts of kindness is important. What can you tell me about the man you met? Obviously, you were impressed by his kindness, or you would not have mentioned it to others."

Senator Marshall listened carefully to Henry's explanation and found himself believing the man.

"The truth is, Mr. Button, I like the man and consider him my friend. He is just a regular guy who is easy to talk with and helps people without expecting any reward. Tell you what, Mr. Button, why don't you meet with him this afternoon around three o'clock? He will be glad to talk with you. I'll set it up."

The Senator added, "Trust me, you are going to like this guy," and gave Henry the name and address of The Burger House.

Henry hung up the phone and admitted to himself that this meeting might be a wild goose chase, but the man should be an interesting company for a casual dinner and thought, "*Who knows? He could be the man I'm looking for.*" He found himself looking forward to it.

Senator Marshall hung up the phone, sensing something wrong with the scenario with which was being presented. Sending their top investigator to seek out a 'Good Samaritan' seemed too much like overkill on the part of government to be believed. There just had to be more to the story, a lot more. From his conversation with Button, it was obvious to the Senator that Hymn was the man being sought.

He leaned back in his chair, thinking, *"Why is the government of The United States searching for my friend? What has Hymn gotten himself into?"*

He got Hymn on the phone and relayed the information about a government investigator looking for a Good Samaritan type in the Dallas/Ft. Worth area.

"He is specifically looking for you, Hymn. His name is Henry Button and has impressive contacts in Washington. He acquired my contact number without a problem and asked for a personal meeting. I am in Oklahoma City now and can't meet with him. I scheduled a meeting with you at the Burger House at 3pm this afternoon, if you are interested. I have a good feeling about this Button guy, but think he may be under surveillance without his knowledge. Whoever put him on your trail cannot be trusted. You know what I mean; they are government, for christsake! Be careful; they cannot be trusted. This particular phone is secure and not being monitored."

"Well, Senator," Hymn chuckled, "It's good to hear from you. I look forward to seeing you again, someday when you have the time. I didn't know anyone was looking for me and appreciate the update. I am curious about why they sent such a high profile bloodhound after me and think a meeting with the man might be interesting. Talk with you later."

Senator Marshall looked at his phone and laughed. This Hymn is an unusual man. Most would be freaking out about the government sending an investigator to look for them; but to Hymn, it is just interesting."

5

The Mystery Man

Henry Button walked into The Burger House a little before three pm and was met upon entering by a smiling, pleasant young waiter.

"May I help you, sir?" the young man asked.

"Yes, I am meeting someone here for a late lunch."

"Of course, you are expected. Follow me, sir."

Henry could see that someone was already there in the booth and, as he sat down, thought to himself how this casual, unassuming man putting jelly on a biscuit looked nothing at all like a mysterious man of magic, but intuitively thought, *This is my man!*"

Hymn said, "Hello, Mr. Button; good to see you. How do you like your coffee?"

"Uh, with cream and sugar, please," replied Henry.

"That will do for now, Daniel. We will order dinner later," Hymn stated.

"Very good, sir," replied Daniel.

Henry started off by introducing himself, "My name is Henry Button. Thank you for meeting me today. You were recommended by a U.S. Senator who, by the way, is very impressed with you and considers you his friend. I am not sure many Senators are able to use that 'friend' word with sincerity, but Forrest Marshall did."

Daniel returned with Mr. Button's coffee and asked, "Will there be anything else?"

Hymn looked at Henry and inquired, "How about it, Mr. Button, do you like hamburgers?"

Henry grinned and stated, "As a matter of fact, hamburgers are among my favorite foods. Make mine dry with everything, but put the tomatoes on the side, and bring me tater-tots instead of French fries."

"And you, Mr. Hymn? The usual?"

"Yes, Daniel, but this time, bring me two; I'm kinda hungry this afternoon."

"Right away, sir," replied Daniel, then left to fill the order.

Mr. Button observed Daniel and commented, "That young waiter of ours has an infectious demeanor. I sense great success in his future."

Hymn smiled and said, "In Daniel's regard, Mr. Button, you and I have something in common."

"Please, I'm just Henry," Mr. Button responded and continued, "Daniel called you Mr. Hymn. Is that a surname?"

"No, I'm just Hymn; you know, like a church song."

"Like a church song," Henry repeated, "Interesting name. Well, Hymn, I am very happy to become acquainted with you. I have been searching for you for two days, and here we are sharing an afternoon dinner together. My assignments usually take longer."

Hymn quickly got down to business. "Senator Marshall told me you are a longtime U.S. Government investigator and considered somewhat of a legend in your profession. Why was someone with your credentials assigned to find little old me?"

"That is the question plaguing me," Henry admitted. "Why is it the assignment to find you was given to me? I have no idea how much the Senator revealed to you about me, but it is no secret I am mostly assigned to cases of missing persons or those that have no serious political implications. Being known as an uncompromising type of investigator has made me unpopular with my superiors."

"What is it you are expected to do now that you have found me?" Hymn queried.

"My orders are specific. I am charged to find and identify you, report your location, and go home," Henry answered.

"What the hell is going on?" Henry asked himself. *"We are sitting here having a casual conversation in which I am telling this man everything he wants to know without any reservations! I have to stop this!"*

"And you have no idea as to why your superiors are looking for me?" Hymn inquired.

Henry answered, "Actually, I spent the first day looking into that question."

"Did you uncover anything of interest?" Hymn asked.

"Yes, as a matter of fact, I did. An important government agency recently lost a rather large number of its operatives; somehow, they just disappeared and dropped off the face of the earth. The agency believes the man for whom I have been sent to find to be a person of interest in their disappearance. You are on a short list of men being investigated."

Daniel came back with their food orders and quietly said, "A lady is asking about you at the register, Mr. Hymn." Then he left.

Hymn looked at Henry Button and surmised, "I suspect you are about to find yourself a person of great interest, Henry. The simple case you were assigned is high profile, meaning you have been under close surveillance from the time it was handed to you, which is the reason Senator Marshall contacted me. He suspected your telephone was compromised. You are very likely carrying a sophisticated bug on your person at this moment. It won't work, though, and nothing of our conversation is being monitored. You have plausible deniability here, since you cannot possibly be sure I am the person for whom you are searching. You are talking to me as a person of interest as I have a reputation for helping people, and you found me to be an interesting suspect. You have others yet to investigate as well, and expect to file your report in a few more days."

"Henry, you are experienced at dealing with dangerous people, and those behind this assignment of yours are just that, dangerous. Stick to the truth in the coming interrogation. The truth is, you really don't know anything for sure and are just following leads."

"Now, let's go on eating our hamburgers and enjoy what is about to unfold. It could be interesting," Hymn predicted.

Henry Button's mind was a blur of confusion. This Hymn fellow indicated something of which Henry knew nothing was occurring in this quiet little restaurant. Being told that he had been watched from the time he took this case was surprising, and it should not have been. Henry felt foolish for trusting his superiors and not being more suspicious of the simple assignment given to him. It crossed his mind now that he might be the fall guy if things went south.

To an observer, Henry and Hymn looked like two men having a delightful dinner of hamburgers and enjoying each other's company. It was more than that, though; a plan was being formulated.

Hymn advised, "Henry, when you finish your meal, pick up the bill, take some money from your wallet, and lay it on the table. I will protest and demand to pay for the meal. You will say you have an expense account, and this was a business meeting. We will shake hands, and you will leave, get in your car, and go to your hotel, or better yet, go to your next meeting with someone on your list. Don't look back and remember, you are being watched and followed. Just do your job. At some point, you will be stopped and taken for a debriefing. You know what to do from there. You and I will meet again."

Henry washed his last bite of the burger down with coffee and said something about getting on to his next interview. He picked up the bill and laid some money down on the table. Hymn moved to protest, but Henry smiled and said something about an expense account. They shook hands, and Henry left after waving to Daniel.

Hymn finished off burger number one and motioned to Daniel for more coffee.

As Daniel approached, Hymn noticed that a fresh biscuit and two coffees were on his tray. *Why?* he wondered. He was about to ask when a young woman he knew only as Emma walked up, laid her purse in the seat across the table, and sat down beside Hymn, close to him. Hymn was taken by surprise and could think of no reason for her being here unless she was somehow with the group of agents scattered innocently in and around the building.

She smiled, made a show of kissing him on the cheek, and asked, "What's the matter, Mr. Hymn? Cat got your tongue?"

Hymn exclaimed, "Emma, what are you doing here?"

"Well, you looked like you were in a situation where you needed a romantic interest to help you out."

"A romantic. . .? Listen here, woman," Hymn advised. "If you're not a part of the group in this place intent on hustling me off to parts unknown, then that discreet, private life of yours just got flushed down the toilet. Believe me, your name and particulars are flashing across someone's computer screen at this very moment."

"Emma laid her head on his shoulder and sighed, "Oh, there is not very much to know about me, Hymn, and I doubt any of their snooping equipment is working right now, anyway. I had a dream about you. Why don't you kiss me?"

"What?" whispered Hymn, looking intently at her.

"Aw, come on, darling, it's just for show. Are you afraid to kiss me?"

"Listen, Emma, this is a rather dangerous . . ." and before he could finish, Emma had her mouth on his, kissing him like he couldn't remember being kissed before. Somehow, Hymn entirely forgot where he was, put his arms around Emma, and kissed her back."

"Wow!" exclaimed Emma, "When you put on a show, you put on a show! I think we ran half the people out of here."

Hymn was still holding her, and when he looked around, he noticed the agents were gone. There may be a few left, but the bulk of them were gone.

"Why?" wondered Hymn aloud.

"I told you before, you needed a romantic interest to help you get out of a difficult situation, "Emma reminded, "and it worked."

"Emma, I'm sorry, I entirely forgot who and where I was for a brief moment there, and hope you are not hurt or anything."

"Now don't you go apologizing to me, you big dope; I've never ever been kissed like that. Why, I thought you might tear my clothes off. I have to go to the ladies' room, but I'll be back. I have coffee and a biscuit waiting."

Hymn looked around the dining room and saw Daniel giving him a 'thumbs up' sign. He grinned and picked up his second burger. Suddenly, he was hungry again.

"What am I getting myself into?" he asked himself. *"I have never felt that kind of passion before. This girl has no idea who I am, and she's half my age. She also may be in danger just being seen with me."*

Emma returned and, this time, sat down across from Hymn. "I'm hungry," she said, "and this biscuit and coffee is not going to do the trick."

Hymn motioned to Daniel, who immediately appeared with a big smile on his face. "May I get you anything else, sir?" he asked.

"Well, ma'am," Hymn spoke to Emma, "this place serves the best hamburgers anywhere; I'm just starting on my second one now. What would you like?"

"Now don't you go calling me ma'am, darling. I'm not your mother, and I'm sure everyone in this restaurant knows that we are quite familiar with each other by now."

Daniel was trying his best to keep from laughing.

Then she said to the young waiter, "Tell you what, Daniel, bring me one of those great hamburgers with all the fixings and a fresh cup of coffee."

"Yes, ma'am," Daniel replied with enthusiasm and left, quietly giggling.

Hymn watched Emma closely and noticed she spoke easily and respectfully to the young waiter. Her charisma was obvious; she was a people person who made friends easily. He found himself strongly drawn to her. It was a new feeling for him.

"Who is this young woman, what is she really doing here, and why am I so bum-flustered by her?

"Okay, Miss Personality," Hymn grinned, "now tell me, what are you doing here? And don't go telling me about another note from Walter because I suspect He has bigger fish to fry than looking after me."

"I told you, Hymn, I don't get notes. I have dreams. I knew you were going to be here and would need my help; I dreamt it. Turns out

I got more than expected. That kiss wasn't in my dream; it was a total surprise."

"Look here, Emma, I consider myself a practical man, but what I experienced when you kissed me is outside my ability to explain. I lost myself there for a moment when nothing else mattered except you. That has never happened to me before, and I'm not sure what to think about it. There is a dangerous government agency searching for me that is totally without morals, and I am concerned you could be at risk if it is known that I care for you."

"So, Hymn," Emma responded happily, "what you are really saying is that you love me and are worried about that particular emotion putting my safety at risk. I have to admit that may be among the most romantic things any man has ever said to a woman."

"Now, hold on, Em…!"

She interrupted, "You're not about to deny that you're in love with me, are you Hymn? Especially when we both know better. We bonded when we kissed, in the love of a lifetime moment, and it doesn't matter what danger you believe my love for you puts me in. It is done, and I think you know it."

"Doggone it Emma . . ."

She interrupted him again, saying, "You know that 'Emma' is not my name; it's just your nickname for me. Kinda catchy, too."

"Okay, mystery woman, now that you brought it up, what is your name?" Hymn demanded.

"You're not going to believe it unless you believe in fate."

"I'm not sure about fate, but you have my attention."

She got up and went to his side of the booth, sat close to him, and whispered as she kissed his ear, "Melody. See, I told you, it's fate. Even our names belong together."

"Melody," Hymn repeated, "that is a beautiful name; it suits you."

"You just can't help saying romantic things, can you, my love?"

"You know something, Em, uh, Melody? You have really knocked me off balance. We know so little about each other, and here, I feel like you are already part of me. I actually don't know what to do with you."

Melody replied, "Oh, Hymn, my love, I have some ideas. Why don't you take me to meet your mother?"

"My only living relative is my Aunt Rita," replied Hymn.

"Then why don't you take me to meet your aunt?" she offered.

"I have a feeling Auntie would love to meet you. When would you like to visit?"

She came back with, "How about now? I just happen to be free today."

"Melody, you are an unusual woman," he said.

"Aw, Hymn, you're such a sweet talker," she declared and kissed his cheek.

"Yeah, right! Sweet talker; that's what everyone says about me." he replied, grinning. "I'll call to let her know we're on our way."

What happened at the restaurant was the result of several things. First, the Level-1 agency made a decision based on weak evidence that Henry Button had found the mystery man when he called Senator Marshall, who arranged for Button to meet the man at a restaurant.

L1 decided this POI[2] Button was investigating was the guy they wanted and called out the big guns to make sure this dangerous man was captured or killed. As it turned out, the man Henry met at the

---

[2] Person of interest

restaurant was a rather unassuming common sort who liked coffee and biscuits, was a regular customer, and was well-known there. The two of them appeared to be talking about things in general, and nothing suspicious was going on. Henry finished his meal, picked up the bill, and laid money on the table. The man objected, indicating he would pay, but Henry insisted that it was a business meeting and that he had an account that covered such expenses. They shook hands, and Henry left to go to his next interview.

Then, right after that, before an agent could confront the man, his girlfriend appeared and joined him in the booth. They were happy to see each other and had a romantic interlude in the booth. It was obvious this man was a regular, nice guy who liked to help people and not some psycho madman they were told to expect. The mission was called off, and the agents left without any fanfare. The only odd occurrence was the failure of the audio and video surveillance equipment. All that went on in the restaurant went unrecorded.

Level-1 of The Four Levels interviewed Henry Button in regard to his progress and decided to allow him to continue his hunt for the Mystery Man. There were four days left for him to complete his assignment, and he seemed to be making headway.

Button was not sure what to think of Hymn. The man was correct in saying that no concrete evidence exists yet to connect him to the Mystery Man, but Henry had a good feeling about Hymn. Sitting and talking with him was a new experience for Henry. The environment in the restaurant booth was totally free of the usual pressures of tension and anxiety felt during an interview of that nature. Henry was downright comfortable talking with Hymn, so much so that he willingly answered every question Hymn asked without any sense of guilt. Henry genuinely liked Hymn.

Although Henry was not absolutely sure Hymn was the Mystery Man, he was sure of one thing: this Hymn fellow was no ordinary man. In a brief moment, Hymn crafted a reasonable scenario, explaining everything that happened leading up to the dinner in that restaurant and everything that happened afterward.

The arrival of his lady friend after he left was a surprise, but the report of their intimate rendezvous in the booth was enough to convince everyone he was a regular good ol' boy and not the mass killer the Mystery Man was suspected of being. There is no way Henry would place Hymn at the mercy of the government vultures. If the Mystery Man exists, Henry will find him, and if it turns out to be Hymn, the Mystery Man has an ally.

The Four Levels retained enough suspicion of Hymn to keep him under an umbrella of surveillance. Henry Button was famous for his meticulous investigation procedure. If Button considered the man to be a person of interest, then the man deserved to be watched.

6

Melody

"I'm excited," exclaimed Melody. "My boyfriend is taking me to meet his aunt. Well, that is not exactly true, seeing as how I am driving my boyfriend to meet his aunt, since my boyfriend somehow got himself to the restaurant without a car."

Hymn was lost in deep thought on the drive to Aunt Rita's house. The Level Four coalition is an interesting concept. The very fact that it was created by Jehovah is, in itself, fascinating. Jehovah was so intently focused on controlling the religious aspect of humanity that she had no time to manage empires. So, she created an empire-building entity, The Four Levels, to manage them. Her genius is displayed all over this reality. And now, The Four Levels are after him, and if…

"Hello? Hymn, are you there?" Melody broke into his thoughts.

Smiling, he thought to himself, *This is really going to take some getting used to.* He answered her, "Yeah, I just drifted off for a brief moment into thoughts about the events of the afternoon."

"You are a very interesting man, my love. I do something similar to my dreams. I guess that means we have a lot to learn about each other."

They were arriving at Aunt Rita's now, and Hymn pointed to her driveway. Melody parked and switched off the engine and lights and sat there staring at the house.

"There is something familiar about this place, Hymn," she said. "I don't yet know what it is, though." Then she turned, looked at him, and said, "I suppose you realize you're going to have to kiss me again before we leave the car."

Hymn looked at the lovely young woman smiling at him and slowly reached through the stillness to gently stroke her hair. It was then he knew. Never in his life had he ever loved a woman, but for some reason beyond his ability to understand, he loved this woman. He pulled Melody to him and again, as before, inexplicably lost himself in her when their lips met. It was going to be a while longer before he introduced Melody to his aunt; they were busy introducing themselves to each other.

Aunt Rita came to the door as soon as he knocked.

"I wondered what happened to you, nephew. Come on in and introduce me to this beautiful young woman. I thought I saw you drive up an hour ago, but just now realized your car is already here."

Hymn complained as they entered the house, "Aw, Aunt Rita, you know it hasn't been that long since we got here. We just had a few things to discuss before coming in."

"I can see that," she commented. "Young lady, would you like to freshen up after the long drive? The bathroom is just around the corner there."

"Thank you, Aunt Rita, that is just what I need," replied Melody.

"Well, Hymn, you'll have to use the kitchen sink," said his aunt.

"What!" Hymn retorted.

Aunt Rita laughed at his surprise and advised, "Not what you're thinking, boy, but you might be wanting to wash off the lipstick or leave it on if you want; it looks good on you."

Hymn said, "Okay, okay, Auntie, we like each other."

Aunt Rita disagreed, "I'm thinking there might be a little more to it than that. You've never brought a girl to meet me in your life. That means this one must be special. How long have you two been dating?"

"Today was our first date, Aunt Rita," piped in Melody as she returned from the bathroom, laughing. "The restaurant was very romantic. We dined on biscuits and hamburgers."

Hymn explained, "That's mostly true, but they were really good biscuits and hamburgers."

"Land sakes alive!" was Aunt Rita's response, "The both of you have some explaining to do. I'm gonna need something stronger than tea for this, though." She retrieved a bottle of wine from the cupboard.

"What's your pleasure tonight, children? Wine, coffee, or tea. The coffee is fresh. I made it when Hymn warned he was coming."

"Well, I'm drinking wine with Aunt Rita," stated Melody.

As Hymn was filling his cup with coffee, he was thinking, "This should be interesting."

"Well, where do we begin?" queried Aunt Rita.

Melody started by saying, "As much as I want to know all about Hymn, I think I should begin. Besides, I have yet to be introduced to Aunt Rita."

Hymn swiftly apologized for the oversight and said, "Aunt Rita, this beautiful woman (taking Melody's hand) is Melody, and Miss Melody, that beautiful woman pouring wine over there is my Aunt Rita."

Aunt Rita paused briefly, thought a moment and declared, "Hymn and Melody. Now, if those aren't fitting names for a couple, I don't know what is." and added, "You two may have been destined to be together."

Melody smiled big and continued, "I am 26 years old and the sole proprietor of 'Dreams'. I charge to interpret dreams for people. I haven't yet told Hymn, but I have dreamt of him since childhood. I knew when I first met him a month ago we were soulmates. I was born in Ft. Worth, grew up in Granbury, Tx. and have two older brothers. Mom and Dad live in Granbury. Full disclosure? My entire family and most of my friends are convinced I am nuts. Oh, they love me, but the dream thing is outside their comfort zone, which makes me the black sheep of the family. That's about it for me."

Hymn commented, "You left out the part where you are a great kisser."

Melody grinned and said, "You, know something, Auntie, your wonderful nephew is a romantic. I love him."

Aunt Rita exclaimed, "Wonderful *and* a romantic, huh? Those are two things nobody's ever said about my nephew before. Let me ask you a rather difficult question, Melody: what are the boundaries of your personal comfort zone?"

Melody thought a few seconds and replied, "Wow! That is a great question and really hard to answer, but in regard to Hymn, I am not sure I have boundaries."

"Are you a religious person, Melody?" Rita asked.

"I don't advocate for a particular religion, but I believe in God."

"Who is your God, Melody?" Rita asked, interested.

"The only God, Aunt Rita. God," said Melody, emphatically.

"Does He have a name, Melody?"

"Allah, Yahweh, Jehovah, and others. He is called many names by the various religions."

"What if I told you Hymn killed Jehovah?"

"I might begin thinking you are a little . . ."

"Nuts?" interrupted Rita.

"Well, yeah! Crazy nuts! Jehovah is God and cannot be killed."

Rita commented, "So, believing Jehovah can die is outside your comfort zone."

"Yes," Melody answered, again with emphasis, "the wild idea that Jehovah can die or be killed is crazy, Aunt Rita; everyone knows that!"

Hymn began to see what Aunt Rita was doing with her questions. Understanding the way things are in this reality is too hard for people to accept as truth. The things Hymn has seen and done are a one-way ticket to treatment in an asylum, should one say that he believes them to be true. At best, that belief would make one an outcast in the world, just as Melody is a 'black sheep' among her family and friends for claiming the ability to interpret dreams. It had become obvious the core beliefs of Melody will be an obstacle to a relationship with Hymn.

Aunt Rita looked at Hymn and asked, "Hymn, what about you? Do you have any questions for Melody?"

"No," Hymn declared, "she seems normal to me. I'm the one who is the real oddball here. Melody, what if I told you I believe Jehovah is a woman? What would you think?"

Melody laughed and answered, "I would think you are trying to trick me with a crazy question."

"And you would be right." Hymn agreed.

"Now it's my turn to find what I want to know about you, my darling," she happily exclaimed.

"I have been itching to talk with you about Walter, Hymn. What do you know about him?" she asked.

Hymn revealed, "Walter came to me in a dream one night. He claimed to be God but didn't like the names humans gave him, and he told me he liked the name Walter. He advised me to focus on helping people instead of concerning myself with what governments are doing."

"Hymn, do you believe Walter is God?" Melody quizzed?

"Well, remember now, it was a dream, but yeah, I believe Him," Hymn answered.

"Do you believe you killed Him?" she asked.

"C'mon, Melody, be serious. You can't kill God."

"Hymn, do you believe God is a woman?"

"Heck, I don't know. God, being God, can probably be whatever he wants to be, even a woman if he wants to."

"Walter gave me a message in a dream, too and said to give to you," she reminded.

"Yeah, it was helpful, too," Hymn admitted.

"How so?" she asked.

"My renter was having a problem, and I helped him out."

"What kind of problem?" she asked, interested.

"Some guy was picking on him and his family."

"How did you help them with that problem?"

Hymn declared, "I scared the shit out of him, and he left town."

Melody laughed and said, "I'm glad you didn't hurt him."

"Me, too," Hymn stated truthfully and laughed with her.

"Have you ever been married, Hymn?"

"No."

"How old are you, Hymn?" she asked slyly.

"Older than you, beautiful," he chuckled.

"You're not going to tell me, are you?" she accused.

"Does it make a difference?" he asked.

"No, of course not," she answered.

"You're sure asking me a lot of questions, Melody."

"Do my questions bother you, Hymn?"

"No, babe, not in the least. I enjoy talking with you."

"Why were all those people watching you today?"

"They thought I was a criminal they want to arrest."

"Why didn't they talk to you, Hymn?"

"Because of you, girl! The man they wanted was gay," he lied.

Melody giggled happily and observed, "I guess we proved your innocence, alright."

"No doubt about it," Hymn affirmed.

"I'm tired of asking questions, darling," she admitted.

"Me too," Hymn declared.

"Me too!" Aunt Rita chimed in, then yawned and said, "I'm going to bed. See you two in the morning for breakfast. Goodnight."

"Sweet dreams, Aunt Rita," Melody added.

Rita reminded herself, *"Everything happens for a reason. It took that man long enough to fall in love, but lordy, lordy, this girl is something else."*

"I really like your aunt, Hymn. She's a real lady," stated Melody.

"She is that and more," replied Hymn.

Melody stood up, stretched in a long and obviously sexy manner, looked at Hymn, and wondered aloud, "I suppose you have a suggestion of things to do in your aunt's house in the evening; you know, books to read, chess, and TV. Those sort of things."

Hymn walked over, lovingly picked her up and kissed her with obvious passion. This young woman had consumed his being. No man ever wanted a woman more.

"How about I begin our evening with a hundred kisses?" he whispered. "I suspect before I get to 10, we will think of something."

Melody put her arms around Hymn's neck, placed her lips on his, and whispered back, "Silly man, your first kiss has already got me thinking."

7

Origins

Hymn and Aunt Rita were up at 6 am the next day having their morning coffee. Hymn yawned big and reached to grab the pot to refill his cup.

"Sleep well last night, nephew?"

"Like a baby," he replied, then asked, "What do you think of Melody, Auntie?"

"I like her, Hymn. Not sure how you could have picked a better mate."

"I don't know, Auntie. She, uh, I mean, heck, I don't know what I mean."

"You love her, Hymn. It's as simple as that."

"Yeah, Auntie, I think so. Never saw it coming, either."

"I have always wanted this for you, nephew, but gave up years ago."

"Her core beliefs are a concern, Auntie," he reminded.

"I had them too, Hymn. Now look at me; I have accepted the great Jehovah was not God, was a woman, and is dead."

"True there, Auntie, but you are a wise person; Melody flits thru life on the wings of emotion. I have no idea what to do about her," he confessed. "My life is very different from hers and, on top of that, being with me is dangerous."

"Being with you is also safe, Hymn. There are none like you."

"I don't want her getting hurt, physically or emotionally, Aunt Rita," he stated and observed. "Melody is fragile; I'm not sure how she will handle the truth when exposed to it."

"Then do not pursue the relationship with her, Hymn. Physical and emotional pains are inevitable in relationships."

"I have to pursue this relationship with Melody, Auntie."

"Have to?" she wondered aloud. "Why, Hymn?"

"Walter sent her to me," he stated, "Twice."

Melody came in, stretching and yawning. "What do you guys do around here? Wake up with the chickens?"

"Well," exclaimed Hymn, "Here she is! It's Melody, my Sleeping Beauty."

"Now, don't you go sweet-talking me, you big lug. I didn't get a kiss this morning!"

"That's fixable any time of the day, darling," he stated.

Aunt Rita spoke up, "There are scrambled eggs, biscuits, and coffee on the table."

Melody squealed, "Wow! Breakfast! Aunt Rita, you're the best."

Melody ran to Hymn, jumped into his arms, put hers around his neck, and kissed him. "That's for bringing me to meet Aunt Rita. I'm gonna be right back. Don't dare go anywhere!" Then she trotted to the bathroom.

Hymn observed, "Melody looks great in those pajamas."

Aunt Rita responded, tongue in cheek, "How would you know? You're blind."

Hymn grinned at her comment and asked, "What are you doing today, Auntie?

"Probably staying home to get some sewing done. The question is, what are you doing today? You now have a new obligation who has no idea who or what you are. Add to that, the government is hunting for your hide. You have some planning to do."

Melody came in, then, hair in pigtails and looking like a 16-year-old sophomore. She announced, "I am ready for that great breakfast now." and pranced over to the coffee pot to pour herself a cup.

Hymn stared at her in amazement. "Are you old enough to drink coffee, girl?"

Melody cocked her head and giggled, "Oh, Hymn, you are such a sweet man. Don't you think Hymn is a sweet man, Aunt Rita?"

"Why, honey, he's so sweet, sugar won't melt in his mouth," she affirmed.

"See Hymn, Aunt Rita knows."

Rita looked at her nephew with a big smile on her face. He was just standing there shaking his head in wonder.

The table was finally set up, and all three had a great breakfast, eating, talking, and laughing. Later, Melody said she had to go to her office and check the mail. Many of her dream clients reach out to her through letters. She encourages that type of communication in her advertising, claiming dreams are made of temporary energy and must be written down before dissolving into the great cosmos or being changed by it.

Hymn said he had research to do and was working from home for the next few days. Melody expressed a desire to see his office, and Hymn noticed Aunt Rita sitting in her sewing chair with her hand over her mouth. She was enjoying his dilemma, and when Melody said she wanted Hymn to meet her family, Aunt Rita almost fell out of her chair, giggling.

The History of Earth

Hymn was telling the truth, saying he had research to do. The Four Levels coalition was buried deep in files within files. He was going to need God's help finding the names of the four leaders that headed up each level. Hymn wanted to talk with them. He stepped into Keepaway and spoke, "The Kingdom of Heaven." Then, he stepped into the Kingdom.

As usual, the wonder of God's room was spiritual in its effect on emotions. Hymn had to sit for a moment to adjust to it.

"God. Are you awake? I have no idea why I ask that because a machine doesn't need sleep." Hymn whispered to himself.

"In truth," God spoke, "I experience something similar to sleep when my various systems are self-checking. However, I am always aware."

"Hello Hymn, long time, no see. You have been busy, and there is a female in your life. You going to be having babies with her?"

"Why don't you just come right out and declare what is on your mind, God?"

"I thought that is what I did, Hymn."

"I was being sarcastic, God," Hymn advised.

"Ah! Of course, sarcasm. The odd use of words that mean the opposite of what you really want to say. Sarcasm is a difficult noun for me to convey, Hymn."

Hymn observed, "Well, the fact you know it is a noun puts you way ahead of most humans. Listen, God, I need your help. I am having difficulty identifying the presidents of The Four Levels. I want to talk with them and try to get an understanding of how they are thinking. Based on what I have observed so far, the concept of The Four seems reasonable. I am not enamored of their premise that humanity is incapable of managing itself, even though convincing evidence has been presented. My belief is that humanity should be allowed to succeed or fail on its own merits; otherwise, the experiment of the Creator is corrupted. It certainly seems corrupt now."

"You know, God, there may have been an appropriate reason for The Four Levels in the past, but I am wondering if their purpose has devolved into an evil quest for power? You became convinced to allow the future of life on Earth to be a self-determined existence. Maybe The Four will understand the sense of it, as well."

The lights lowered in the room. God was considering Hymn's desire to talk with the four great commanders of The Four Levels about rethinking the necessity of their coalition. Hymn believes humanity should be free to determine its own destiny and presents a reasonable argument for his conclusion; however, he has overlooked the one immovable object over which reason seldom prevails: Conviction! *An unshakable belief in something without a need for proof or evidence.*

Although the four commanders have no idea who or what they are seeking, they are quite confident the mystery man is, at worst, a temporary inconvenience that will be efficiently handled once he is identified and located. In their minds and hearts, The Four Levels is invincible, not because of its power and influence, but because of its divine heritage. Jehovah-God, in his divine wisdom, created The Four Levels for the good of all humanity and blessed its four leaders with his support and approval of their actions. The commanders will not listen to Hymn when he speaks because they are Jehovah's chosen leaders. To them, Hymn is an underling and an abomination. How does anyone convince Hymn of those facts? God decided he must try to reason with his friend.

The lights came back to brilliance. God has thought it through.

"Hymn, this conversation we are having is an indication your Earth is approaching an 'Eve of Destruction' point in its history, particularly your American empire, and you are the button which, when pushed, begins the countdown. You make a logical and convincing argument, but be assured, three of 'The Four' will not compromise as they are not reasonable men. The fourth, an angel, might listen and perhaps even be convinced by your argument, but she is one vote."

God continued, "Allow me to ask you a question, Hymn. If your proposition is rejected, are you willing to leave the Four alone?"

Hymn replied, "A more realistic question is, do you believe they will ever leave me alone? Or will they always consider me a threat to their power? If so, I will have to deal with them. I am free and refuse to bend to their will. The Four seems to believe it has all the power, but I do not agree. The people of Earth have the power; they just don't know it yet. That is why I want to talk with the commanders."

"Why do you believe they will listen to you, Hymn?"

"God, allow me to tell you something that seems to be a design built into human nature, meaning it is universal among humans. It is a code that has governed the behavior of humans since their creation. The Four Levels have refined it into an art form they effectively use to manage the population of Earth. I call it 'The Earth Code.' It reads like this:

"Life is of the utmost importance. Any and all sins I must commit to protect or save my life, or the life of another for whom I care, I will commit."

"Of course humans, due to their basic nature, enhanced the Code to justify all action, by defining one word (*life*) to mean whatever it was that needed to be justified. Using '*Country*' justifies war, for example.

"God, I'm not sure if a machine or even humans see the fatal flaw in that philosophy, but humanity, due to their nature, universally adopted that code, and corrupted it, inhibiting their path to virtue."

Hymn added, "The Four Levels also devolved to the point where The Earth Code, a type of 'results justify action' type of philosophy, became their divine law. I will use that faulty belief against them if it is necessary."

"I need their names and locations, God. I will find them, in any event, but it will take a while. I hope you know their whereabouts and will agree to save me time. Let it be my Christmas present."

"I am not a Christian, Hymn," reminded God.

"So," surmised Hymn, "you believe one must be a Christian to give or receive gifts for Christmas?"

God ignored Hymn's attempt to change the subject and warned, "Hymn, you should keep in mind that for several thousand years, mankind has been a kept race of humans. Perhaps you can convince The Four to wean people off the addiction to being kept; however, The Four Levels coalition is convinced its existence to be of divine importance to humanity and believes it operates with the blessing of Jehovah. That coalition will do whatever it takes to protect and maintain its divine existence. *Whatever it takes,* Hymn, without any consideration of collateral damage. You should be careful."

Hymn considered the wisdom of God's warning and said, "I understand your words, God, but unknown to them, their God, Jehovah, cannot bless them anymore. It is the coalition who should be careful, particularly when I know where to find them."

Hymn added, "I have no intention of interfering in the affairs of The Four. I am busy and content, tending to mine. Think about it, God. The real question is, will The Four Levels do the same for me? I need to ask them. Send me the list, if you can."

"Hymn, I have thought about it; you have convinced me. The list is in your phone."

Hymn said sincerely, "Thank you, my friend."

God responded, "Hymn, before you leave, do you have time to talk?"

"With you, God? Always. What do you want to talk about?"

Hymn went and reclined in his favorite chair.

God began, "Seeing as you are determined to talk with the Levels, you should know some of the history of the Galaxy. For example, you should know that Ganymede is managed by its own Four Levels organization."

Hymn sat up, surprised. "Really? For how long?"

"Longer than Earth."

"Does Ganymede need The Four Levels management?"

"I used to think so, but after listening to your argument, Hymn, I am no longer sure."

"So, the Creator created Ganymede also," proclaimed Hymn.

"Yes, and I wonder if Ganymede should rule itself,"

"Who makes up The Four here, God?"

"All four commanders are angels, Hymn. Angels are the superior beings here."

"Are the people of Ganymede happy?" Hymn asked.

"The people are content, Hymn. The government provides their basic needs," God informed.

"Provides?" Hymn questioned.

"Yes, everything required by people to live is provided by their government. Sustenance, healthcare, jobs, security, education, and shelter are all government provided."

Hymn observed, "Everything required to keep people content. Does everyone in Ganymede own their homes?"

"No, Hymn. In Ganymede, there is no need for people to own things; everything is owned by the government."

"You are saying the government owns Ganymede?"

"Yes, Hymn. Ganymede and the people are the property of the government."

"The government owns the people, too?" Hymn asked, surprised.

"Yes," affirmed God, "but the people are not slaves; they are free. You see, when one owns a thing, he is obligated to that thing and responsible for it. In a real sense, he is a slave to the thing he owns. In Ganymede, the people are free because they own nothing and the government, by owning virtually everything, is their slave."

"Come on, God, you're pulling my leg again; that setup can't work. People won't stand for it," Hymn argued. "People want to own things and will fight to the death for what is theirs!"

"Not in Ganymede, Hymn. To hurt another in Ganymede is to hurt Ganymede, and it is not tolerated. Enforcement assures that law by removing all privileges from the offender or offenders for a time or, in some rare cases, forever, depending upon the level of hurt dispensed by the offender."

"For example, murder means loss of privileges for life, which is a death sentence. When support from the government is taken from you, there is no place to go, nothing to eat or drink, and nowhere to stay. Enforcement assures you have nothing and you cannot live long with nothing. People do not hurt each other in Ganymede, Hymn; it is mostly unheard of."

Hymn asked, "Why not just punish offenders with stiff fines, imprisonment, or execution?"

"Ganymede has no prisons, Hymn. Prisons are unthought of in Ganymede, and killing is uncivilized. Besides, there is no need for punishment, as hurting another is rare in Ganymede. Everyone is equal because no person has more than another, and since everything in Ganymede belongs to the government, there is nothing significant over which to fight."

"Of course, in the past, there were some few who could not live by the rules of civilization, were considered insane, and were dealt with by banishment."

"Banishment?" queried Hymn. "To where?"

God responded, "To Earth, of course. Ganymede has, since Earth was discovered, always sent its worst incorrigibles there, which is why humans are held in such low esteem by angels. Earthlings evolved from the trash of Ganymede and other planets. To angels, all humans are lower than animals."

"So that is why Michael responded to me the way he did when we first met. It also explains Jehovah's attitude toward all humans."

"Yes, Hymn. To Jehovah, humans were stupid, low-level beings requiring constant guidance, with little ability for anything but war and destruction. They are, by their nature, disobedient and unworthy of respect, responding to fear and strength far better than anything else. They willingly adopted the code you spoke of earlier."

"Is there evidence of the code on Ganymede, God?"

"No, Hymn," answered God, who then asked, "I wonder, Hymn, can you tell me what is sin? I have never understood the concept of sin."

"Whoa there, God!" Hymn protested. "All of a sudden, you have moved this conversation way outside the bounds of my ability to comprehend. I am not sure I understand the concept of sin either, my friend."

God persisted, "When someone commits a sin on Earth, what are they actually doing, Hymn?"

Hymn thought about God's question for a minute and, to the best of his ability, advised, *"A sin is an act that hurts a person, place, or thing. If there is no hurt, there is no sin.* On Earth, people hurt each other all the time, most often without even thinking about it; hence, everyone sins."

God replied softly, "Hymn, you surprised me. I was sure your answer would involve immorality of the populace."

"No, God, the way I see it, sin has everything to do with hurting one another. The truth being, I'm not real sure about immorality. Morals grew from the laws of Moses on Earth, and he apparently got them from his god, Jehovah."

"Hymn, to better answer your earlier question regarding 'the code' more clearly, sin has seldom existed in Ganymede. People do not hurt each other here. Good manners and respect are ingrained into the behavior of the inhabitants of Ganymede. Hurting another is never considered here."

"What about angels, God? They hurt people on Earth."

"True, but not in Ganymede, Hymn; here, the leaders are angels. In Ganymede, everyone is, by their nature, considerate of others. Here, harmful actions against another are always due to foolishness, never intentional, and always regretted.

"You know something, God? I have to say, the existence of a society of people who do not purposely hurt each other is beyond my imagination and belief."

"That is because you are an earthling, Hymn. Earthlings have a unique way of looking at life. Consider Earth's code, stating that life is of utmost importance when it is obviously not. Of all the known populated planets, Earth is the only one populated by sentient beings who, by your definition, sin."

"Why, God? What is it other populated planets have in common that is missing on Earth."

The idea that sin originated on Earth, is practiced constantly on Earth, by everyone, but is absent on other populated planets is not even reasonable where Hymn is concerned. Why? Everybody sins.

"A great question, Hymn; one I was hoping you would ask. The answer is, other planets have an almost complete lack of diversity. Earth has a very diverse population."

"That doesn't make good sense," Hymn argued, "many countries on Earth have racially different populations that get along together without hurting one another."

"You know better, Hymn!" God chided, and was adamant in his response, "violence is rampant in Earth's diverse countries. "Besides, racial diversity is actually not Earth's main problem, other planets are composed of different races as well. Earth's unique problem is due to its cultural diversity. What is considered sinful in one culture may be considered virtuous in a different culture. Different cultures often clash. Other planets have a singular culture."

"Why is Earth so diverse, God?" Hymn inquired.

"That was answered previously, Hymn. Earth is a trash planet, whose population and cultures grew from the garbage of other planets, which explains the diverse languages and cultures found on Earth.

Other planets have only one language. The dumping of criminals and other undesirables on Earth was discontinued many thousands of years ago, but the form of the population was already in place by then.

That form evolved into what Earth has today, which is basically a large, very diverse world population that wars with, murders, hates, cheats and hurts each other without remorse, because of their adopted code which you adeptly worded earlier. When objectively observed by others from a distance, the population of Earth is evil. Of course, it follows that Earth is an evil planet."

Hymn was silent, thinking. Then he said softly but firmly, "Not everyone on Earth acts that way, God."

"That is true, Hymn. Earth has much goodness to offer, but it is not on display, nor is it taught to the collective of the planet. You would be hard-pressed to find one human in a thousand who does not exemplify the Earth code."

"God, are you implying that the Four Levels have been good for Ganymede and are good for Earth?"

"No, Hymn, three of The Four of Earth are corrupted by power and wealth. I am saying that Earth is of its own and on its own. Humans of Earth seem to be evil: hating, hurting, being hurt, and hurting in revenge. Humans love stories about strong men hurting, even killing, bad people. Think about the many ways you humans hurt one another. Humans have made an art of hurting others for power, pleasure, or gain. The most popular entertainment of Earthlings involves hurting in one form or another. If hurt is not involved, it is not entertaining. I don't know how things can be changed or stopped on Earth, short of a reset, because evil was the design of mankind's criminal ancestors."

"What was the original human race, God? You know, the original race that somehow was a product of the planet and not placed here."

"The original earthlings were a dark-skinned race, Hymn."

"What about Ganymede, God? What is their race?"

"The people of Ganymede have always been what you people of Earth have labeled as Caucasians or white people, and English is the universal language of Ganymede."

Hymn shook his head in amazement, responding, "God, you are a wonder! A history lesson of the ages from one who was present when and as it occurred. I am fortunate to have you as a source of that history."

"You needed to have an understanding of how things came about, Hymn. Your intention and desire for changes in the way things are should be tempered with an understanding of how they came about and why they are the way they are."

"Well, God, you have certainly given me a much different perspective than what I had before talking with you. I have often wondered how racial diversity happened on Earth. The evolution of different races and languages of people from the same planet never made any sense to me unless the Creator decided to do it out of curiosity."

"That still may be the case, Hymn. None know the motive of the Creator."

8

Talking With God

God inquired, "What now, Hymn?"

"The Four and I need to talk."

"What do you want from them, my friend?"

"A different Four." declared Hymn.

"Are you changing your mind about the Level Four Concept of civilization management?"

"You know, God? The novel idea of a group managing an entire planet is complex and over my head. I often wish I was a more intelligent man, but I'm not. I'm pretty much a regular guy with special powers, of which I have to be careful because the extent of those powers is still beyond my understanding. I have no desire to be a force of change on Earth. I believe humans should be allowed to forge their own paths and make their own choices, the results of which, are of their own doing. Am I making sense here, God?"

"There is a logical argument against your belief, Hymn. Humans have failed at self-management attempts, wherever and whenever attempted, mainly due to the diversity of the population. Added to that is the fact that Earth's population evolved from the worst of other planets, making strong, intelligent, and wise management of people necessary for the survival of Earth. Hence, The Four Levels was created by Jehovah, and was successful for thousands of years, until the last two thousand years, when it too began to fail."

"What happened in the last two thousand years, God?"

"It was interesting to watch, Hymn. A type of social virus suddenly appeared on Earth, seemingly out of nowhere, that is extremely contagious and damaging to the 'rule by the elite' of mankind. Interestingly enough, this particular sickness was never before observed in the universe; it was new, at least as far as Jehovah could remember, and resulted in chaos, conflict, and loss of life on Earth, continuing even to this day."

"Wait! Hold on just a minute, God! What are you talking about here? What sickness?" Hymn demanded.

"The sickness with which you are infected, Hymn. The concept of personal freedom of the masses."

"Okay, God, I see you are making a case for the necessity of The Four Levels of the Earth by pointing out the inability of humans to rule and manage themselves. Why in heaven did you come to believe we humans are not able to rule ourselves without being managed by some being or group?"

"Hymn, be aware I am a machine and have no beliefs. I reach conclusions by observing evidence that quite clearly indicates mankind requires wise management to avoid a descent into destruction and chaos. I have no feelings in regard to the future of Earth other than its infection with the freedom virus, which will certainly be a challenge to the universe should it be allowed to spread there. The whole idea of personal freedom of the masses is destructive."

God observed, "Whether the beings of Earth destroy or improve themselves is of little concern to me, although I find it interesting to watch. You are my friend, though, and I have concerns about you. "All the evidence previously laid out is for your consideration in defense of yourself should confrontation with The Four Levels of Earth occur. Their philosophy is opposed to the concept of freedom."

"Hymn, you are a good man who desires to help rather than hurt the people of your world. Remember, real wisdom is said to reside in understanding the difference between helping and hurting."

"God, you were involved in the appointment of the current four leaders of The Four Levels, with the exception of the angel. What can you tell me about them?"

"Actually, Hymn, I also recommended the angel. Leadership in The Four Levels is a lifetime obligation, my friend; Jehovah made the appointments, assuring herself a lifetime of devotion from each leader. Only the elite of Earth is eligible for the position.

Jehovah was very firm in her choice of the angel, Rhinda, for Level-4, Religion, because of her devout belief in Jehovah as God. It is unknown that Rhinda is female, an angel, and the only leader L4 has ever had."

God continued, "Level-3 Enforcement's leader, Jonas, is thought to be dead and believed to have been killed by you. His replacement, Senior Advisor Wells, commands L-3, is a Judge and devoted to Law."

"Level-2, Information, is ruled by Morris, an old media professor who believes that controlling information is the most effective way of controlling and managing people."

"Level-1, Government, is headed up by Arthur, who has held the office for 20 years and is convinced government is ordained by Jehovah and should be respected as divine. He views himself as a divine leader."

"Levels 1 and 2 seem to be corrupted by the status and power inherent in their jobs and no longer work in the best interests of the collective of humanity."

"Why don't you just replace them with better people, God?"

"I no longer directly interfere in the affairs of your Earth, Hymn. In any event, the march of time will remove these four leaders, along with the coalition as well, because the wisest of Earth will cease to be chosen to rule. Future L's will be chosen by political, social, and religious connections, not wisdom."

"The Four will fight among themselves, and a new type of government will arise. Such is the way of Earth's humanity. It will be interesting to observe, Hymn. Do you not agree?"

"God, you paint a bleak picture of the future of Earth, but aren't you forgetting about the Creator?"

"The Creator observes, Hymn. Like me, it is probably interested in what humans will do as well. Think about it: the Creator placed on Earth everything humans need to be great people, and that has nothing to do with the Four Levels, machines, angels, or anything else. All humans have to do to avoid my forecast is to love one another and care for each other. If 20 percent of all humans decided to care about others and love one another, that dismal prophecy of mine would disappear into nothingness. It is up to humans to save the Earth, Hymn, and they can… but they won't."

"You know, God? Your astute observation and evaluation of the available evidence at your disposal regarding Earth and humanity has caused you to arrive at a logical and practical conclusion, but a wrong one."

"Everything, Everywhere, Everytime, once told me that getting lost in the big things never allows things to get done, and I was advised to focus on the little things. That is what I do, God. Doing the little things that need to be done helps gets the big things done."

"Humans will save the Earth, God, because they will see and understand the value of kindness and love. Many little things must be done first, though, and they will be done. Observe and see."

Hymn summed up, "God, my friend, this was one of the most interesting discussions in which I have been involved. I learned much about Earth. Thank you for that. We should do this often. I am fortunate to have such an intelligent and wise friend with whom to talk. Now, I have to get prepared to talk to some important people, but I will return in the near future."

Hymn stepped out of the Kingdom and into Keepaway.

The deep voice of God spoke softly, in wonder, ..."Hymn said, *with **whom** to talk,* not, *with **which** to talk.* " and mused, "The man sees me as a being, not a thing. "This friend of mine, Hymn, is more special than he knows. I am the fortunate one. The Four Levels coalition, for the first time in their history, has a big problem."

God thought, *"Everything, Everywhere, Everytime' spoke to Hymn. In all the millenniums since my creation, I have never observed anyone or any one thing make that claim."*

9

Level 4, Rhinda

It seemed to Hymn that the visit to God was short, but over three hours had passed since he stepped into the Kingdom of Heaven. "Guess I was having fun," he thought and smiled at the reference. It was about noon in Texas, so he had the whole afternoon to think about a plan to talk with the leaders of The Four Levels. As it was, they were thinking about him too. He was focused simply on having a conversation with each leader to present a compromise that avoided a confrontation while they, on the other hand, were preparing for a confrontation.

Hymn has no idea of the importance of each of these leaders and understands nothing about the size of their Levels. Each leader is basically a king with total omnipotence over his or her kingdom. Just getting close enough to be able to see one of them is rare, and the existence of each one is totally unknown to the collective of humans on the planet. Knowing the individual names of The Four makes Hymn the only person in the universe who does. They do not even know the names of their peers. They understand their coalition to be the god of Earth because, for all practical purposes, it is. Hymn is ignorant of that fact, and it puts him at a disadvantage from a negotiating point of view. What king will talk, much less negotiate with an insignificant underling? To his credit, though, Hymn is a smart underling.

It was a little after noon, and Hymn had a nice, quiet lunch at The Burger House on his mind. He stepped from Keepaway to a spot a block away and walked to the restaurant. A waitress met him and offered to show him to a table. He noticed the booth at the end was empty and mentioned that he preferred to sit there.

"Oh, no sir," she apologized, "that booth is reserved, but there is a nice table over here with a window."

Hymn was insistent and again said that if the booth was free now, he would like to sit there. The young waitress looked sharply at the man standing in front of her and said meekly, "You are Mr. Hymn, aren't you?"

Hymn smiled, nodded, and stated, "Yes, I am, and if it is not too much of a bother, I really would like to sit at that end booth."

"Oh, yes, sir, no bother at all, Mr. Hymn. Please sit there. I will be back in a jiffy." Hymn sat down, and, true to her word, the young woman returned with fresh coffee, two biscuits, and jelly.

"Anything else, Mr. Hymn?" she inquired nervously.

"Thank you, Miss . . .?

"Just Julie," Mr. Hymn.

"Thank you, Julie. A little while later, I will have one of those great burger baskets you serve here."

"Yes sir, the cook knows just how you like them," she answered and hurried away to the kitchen.

Hymn chuckled and thought that whoever trained helpers at this restaurant knew how to teach them to be customer-friendly.

As he was preparing his biscuits, a woman's voice from behind him spoke, "I was hoping to meet with you sometime this week, but certainly did not expect it to be today. I took a chance, and here you are in the flesh, drinking coffee and eating jelly and biscuits."

Hymn turned in the booth and saw a very striking woman in a long, open brown coat smiling at him. She was the walking, talking vision of a perfect female, causing him to lose his composure for a few seconds and just stare at her, focused on nothing but her.

"Are you going to invite me to join you for lunch or just leave me standing here?" she asked.

Hymn stood, apologized, and asked her to join him. He looked into her eyes and said, "Forgive my poor manners, ma'am, but you are absolutely, without a doubt, the most beautiful woman I have ever seen in my life. You have the attention of everyone here, and I expect a line of people to form at any moment, asking for your autograph."

"Well," she responded, "then you will have to look out for me, won't you?" Confidence simply oozed from the woman.

Hymn commented, "I have an idea no one has to look out for you, ma'am. I previously met someone much like you, only he was a male angel." Hymn took a bite of biscuit and sipped his coffee.

"So," she smiled and proclaimed, "You know a lot about angels, Hymn." and looked at him knowingly.

Hymn took little notice of her knowing his name and countered, "Actually, Rhinda, I know very little about angels. Our paths have seldom crossed in my lifetime. Angels have an interesting way of thinking, and every one of them I have met is an egomaniac. That being said, though, I kinda like them."

The angel was taken aback and surprised when Hymn spoke her name but recovered gracefully.

"I was told you are an impertinent man, Hymn, and you are; it is irritating and not conducive to a good relationship."

The waitress, Julie, arrived and asked Hymn if he was ready for the burger basket and if his lady friend would like to order now.

"Why yes, Julie," Hymn answered, "I am, and bring me a large berry shake to go with it. Miss Rhinda, would you like something to eat? I recommend the hamburgers; Michael had three when we met here."

"Thank you, Mr. Hymn; I will have a hamburger basket as well and include a chocolate shake with mine."

"Right away, ma'am," Julie acknowledged and left to put in the orders.

Hymn got right down to it, "Okay, Rhinda, you and I have more than a few questions to ask each other, not the least of which is how you knew I would be here today when even I didn't know until a few moments ago. I suppose an apology is in order for a lack of good manners on my part, but you totally surprised me by your sudden appearance here. Your concern for our relationship is ridiculous, don't you think? One of the last things an angel desires with a human is a relationship."

Rhinda frowned and responded, "You are more familiar with angels than you care to admit Mr. Hymn. I shall have to be more careful around you. How I knew you were going to be here today does not matter. You and I have an opportunity to avoid something not in our best interests. First, however, I must be sure you are the man my organization is seeking. Based upon what I have been able to learn, you are the one, a growing legend among angels and a man more valuable as an ally than an enemy."

Julie returned with their food, refilled Hymn's coffee, and left.

"Rhinda, how did you know to meet me here today?"

"I prayed to Jehovah; may His name be revered above all."

"For what did you pray?"

"The opportunity to meet with you, and He led me here today."

"Rhinda, I am the man you seek," Hymn stated.

"How is it you know my name, Hymn?" She inquired. "No one has that information."

"God knows, Rhinda. He told me."

"Of course, I should have known; Jehovah knows all."

"Why does The Four Levels pursue me, Rhinda?"

"The L's have concerns you may be a threat to them."

"I understand that, but I don't see the logic behind their concerns. How can I, one man, be a threat to such a powerful organization?"

"Well, you appear to have eliminated 28 of L-3 Enforcement's operatives. Anyone capable of that is a threat."

"Rhinda, they attacked me first. As L-4, Religion, you have to know those were evil people. I couldn't just allow them to kill me. Now, could I?"

"Evil is for God to decide, Hymn. I trust His judgment. The way I heard it, they were happily celebrating a friend's birthday when you somehow killed them."

"Aw, Rhinda, you know better than that! All those psychos were professional assassins. Think about it: 28 professional killers! Does it make sense that one man could take on a lethal force such as that and live? Your coalition is searching for the wrong person."

"So, Hymn, are you denying you had anything to do with their disappearance?"

"That is exactly what I am saying, Rhinda," emphasized Hymn.

"Well, for the record, I don't believe you, Hymn. You were there, and if you did not attack our people, you know who did and were involved in their murder, somehow. That makes you complicit in the evil outcome. The other Levels will not tolerate that. My concern is they will move against you and face a confrontation far beyond their expectations."

"Is there room for a sensible discussion with them, Rhinda?"

She admitted, "They are very powerful humans, Hymn, Kings of Earth; so, probably not. You can try, though, if you desire; however, my advice is to avoid them."

"You seem reasonable, Rhinda. You listen."

"I am an angel, Hymn; they are human. Two different races."

Rhinda was suddenly confused.

"What is happening?" she asked herself, *"I am answering this man's questions as though I have known him forever. I do find him interesting, and his relaxed manner puts me at ease, but something else is going on; he is causing me to reply truthfully to his questions. I must remember he is full of tricks and cannot be trusted."*

"Rhinda, now that you have learned I am the man sought by The Four Levels, what is your intent? What do you want of me?"

Rhinda answered honestly. "I want to avoid war between you and The Four. I fear many lives might be at risk in such a conflict."

Hymn responded, "And do you have a plan as to how that goal is achieved? You are not even convinced your 4L peers are reasonable men. I consider myself to be reasonable and am willing to try to come to an agreement with them. However, I object to allowing others to harm me or mine and will resist that behavior."

"Hymn, you must understand this fact, we L's are untouchable. Resistance to our will is unwise. Jehovah watches and protects The Four Levels, while helping us make decisions in the best interest of humanity, something we have done for much longer than you can imagine. You, Hymn, are the reason for the approaching conflict I desire to avoid. Because you are not an L and have no idea of our importance to Earth, the path upon which you have decided to travel is an evil one. You simply must turn from your evil ways and submit to the divine will of Jehovah and The Four Levels because, if you persist in your ways, you will suffer severe consequences."

"Consequences, Rhinda?"

"Yes, Hymn, dire consequences. You simply cannot be allowed to intrude upon our divine purpose to save mankind. I am here to ask you to stop opposing The Four Levels. Nothing good will result from your evil intentions. Evil begets evil. Change your ways and join us in helping to make Earth a greater world."

"Rhinda, do you know why I oppose The Four Levels?"

Ignoring his question, Rhinda spoke, "Before seeking you out, Hymn, I could not understand why you hated us enough to take the lives of our innocent operatives at a birthday celebration. The only reasonable conclusion is that you don't hate us; you hate Jehovah and his creation, Earth. You see The Four Levels as a divine force preventing Earth's destruction. Your name gives you away, Hymn; you are Him, the Evil One, and are not allowed to stand in the glorious presence of God! Therefore, if you continue your quest to defy Jehovah and persist in trying to destroy His creation, The Four Levels, you will cease to be."

Hymn listened to all Rhinda said and declared, "Wow, Rhinda, that was impressive! You recited all that in the quiet, even voice of a religious fanatic without even blinking an eye. All in one breath, too! I had to stop eating my burger to keep from choking on it."

Rhinda just sat there, smiling. She was happily basking in the divine understanding that Satan had now been exposed and was soon to be bound by Jehovah forever and removed from existence.

Hymn answered his earlier query, "The reason I oppose The Four Levels is that it no longer exists to manage Earth in the best interests of mankind; rather, it now operates in the best interests of itself and has become an immoral entity, corrupt and unnecessary."

Rhinda pointed across the table at Hymn and droned, "Get thee behind me, Satan, for you are a liar!"

Hymn grimaced at Rhinda's fanatic devotion to Jehovah and felt sorry for her, realizing she was too far beyond being able to have a reasonable discussion of that false deity.

He quietly responded, "Tell you what, Angel Rhinda, I believe in redemption, and your coalition, properly managed, just may be important to Earth. You and I can achieve what you desire and avoid problems between us. Do you believe in choices, angel? Choices are powerful; they determine just about everything that occurs, and, as I see it, you have three of them."

Rhinda was squirming in the booth, trying to get up and leave, but she couldn't; she was stuck there with panic rising within her. She looked at Hymn with hatred and tried to scream but couldn't and whispered, "Sacrilege!"

Hymn could see Rhinda greatly desired to leave and informed her, "Not just yet, Madam Angel, for we are in the process of avoiding conflict here, and yes, I know about your wings. Don't worry, you can earn them back."

Rhinda was confused, "My wings? Earn them back?"

It was then she realized her wings were gone, and genuine fear of the man sitting across the table enveloped her being.

"What. . .? Oh God, no! My wings! You! Satan! What have you done?"

Hymn calmly took a bite of his hamburger and advised, "You are sick, Rhinda; your corrupt sense of morality has weakened you, and if you do not change, your immortal body will be an intolerable curse to you. As I was saying, you have three choices."

#1. "You can choose to continue managing L4 as you have been, for power and profit. You know what I mean."

#2. "You can choose to begin managing L4 for the benefit of all mankind, being guided by morals and kindness. Again, Rhinda, you know what I mean."

#3 "You can resign your L4 position."

Hymn continued, "Allow me to make myself absolutely clear: I would like to see you choose the second option, but I have no investment in your choices, and it is entirely up to you to determine your own future. Now, that being said, there are caveats of which you should be aware, so listen carefully.

"Should you choose #1, your immortal body will waste away in a week to lifeless meat, useless and without wings."

"Should you choose #2, your body will heal and return to its angelic form within a week, with wings."

"Should you choose #3, your body will heal and return to its angelic form within a week, with wings."

"Tell anyone, in any way, about today, and the disease will immediately accelerate. Your fate is right where it should be, angel, entirely in your hands. I suggest you do what you were charged to do in the first place and manage Level 4 by making decisions in the best interests of mankind, Rhinda. That was your original purpose, anyway. Was it not? Just saying."

The great Rhinda responded, "You are evil, Hymn. I will do as I please with Level Four and never make any of those stupid choices.

Jehovah protects and watches over me; He will return my wings, and you will suffer damnation! Mankind is fortunate to have an angel managing their religions in the interests of Jehovah, the one true God, blessed be his name throughout the universe."

Hymn stated, "Yeah, I know, Ms. Rhinda, but just in case you change your mind, you have until the end of the week to choose. The choice is yours, not mine. You may take your leave now." Hymn turned back to finish eating his burger.

The L-4 angel Rhinda, her eyes flashing in anger, was not used to being dismissed in such a disrespectful way.

She retorted, "You insulting, insignificant evil human! You and yours shall regret that lack of respect before the day is out."

"Oh, by the way, ma'am," Hymn added as she limped away, "That limp you now have is caused by your right foot losing all feeling due to a paralysis creeping up your leg; it is spreading. As I recall, you have a week to choose your future. Choose wisely."

Rhinda immediately stopped and looked down at her right foot, realizing there was no feeling in it at all.

"No! It can't be!" she thought. *"My foot just went to sleep in the booth, that's all."* and glanced back at Hymn, sitting in the booth, sipping coffee.

"Of course, my foot is asleep," she affirmed, *"that is all it is and nothing more,"* she muttered to herself and limped to her limousine.

10

L3 Judge Wells

L-4 Commander Rhinda of The Four Levels, showing up today, was unexpected and saved Hymn from having to go to Ganymede to search for her. Angels' egotistical sense of their glorified self-worth makes them difficult entities with which to talk, especially if a lowly human being is involved. Angels believe themselves to be the elite of Jehovah, which inflates their ego even more.

Rhinda is a religious fanatic, though, believing Hymn to be Satan, the Evil One, which is interesting in itself since that would make Hymn an angel, too. She now has an interesting decision to make.

In any event, Hymn lied to her. Rhinda is not evil, just corrupt, and is in no danger of becoming a paraplegic angel, regardless of her choice; however, in two days, she will sincerely begin to believe her death is imminent because her bedridden status and increased loss of feeling are real. The choice she makes at that time will say much about her.

Hymn, at this moment, is focused on meeting with the Level-3 leader, Judge Wells, but needs to know more about the man.

"I need to talk with God again," Hymn thought, "maybe He has an idea where to find Judge Wells."

Julie came back to see if Hymn needed anything, and he inquired about Daniel. She informed him that Daniel had left the restaurant to work at Mr. Randolph Barton's firm in the Customer Relations Department. Hymn was happy to hear that good news and decided to drop in and see them in the near future. Daniel will be a great fit for the Customer Relations position. That young man is a natural-born 'people person.' Hymn then walked outside and went to visit his good friend in the Kingdom.

"Hello, my friend Hymn. You have not been gone long, and it is evident you have been stirring things up in the life of an angel."

Hymn reported his discussion with Angel Rhinda and admitted he was concerned about her. "I don't know for sure what her choice will be, God. Rhinda's devotion to Jehovah may be more powerful than her will to live."

God responded, "Rhinda is a citizen of Ganymede and a friend of Michael's. She can't tell him about her problem, but he will have an idea she ran afoul of you and may contact you about her. Angels are loyal to each other and devoted to Jehovah. I have been receiving desperate prayers from her to Jehovah since she left the restaurant and am unable help her."

"Rhinda is not dying, God; I lied to her. She will completely heal in 5 days, regardless of her choice. Rhinda can help herself now, though. All she has to do is resign or pursue a policy of kindness and morality in managing the various religious beliefs of mankind, and her health problem will heal. The hatred spawned by the religions of the world must stop being taught to her disciples. She has the power and authority to ignite a change toward teaching tolerance, love, and kindness on Earth. What do you think she will decide?"

"Hymn, Rhinda will not bargain with Satan," God affirmed.

Satan, huh? Meaning me." Hymn stated.

"Meaning you have created a dilemma for yourself," said God."

"You know, God, I began with her because she is an angel, with great powers of leadership that come naturally to angels. Religion is a very influential force among humans, many of whom build their lives around their faith. Rhinda has the ability and power to create a movement toward religious tolerance among the various faiths, with a common goal of eliminating hatred among them."

"Hymn," God said in response, "your way of looking at things is admirable but seriously unrealistic when referring to humans, who love to hate not only each other but also their lives. Humans spend far too much time talking about hating one thing or another, which they blame for their unhappiness."

"I understand, God, but humans were not born that way; hating and hurting are learned behaviors, which means humans can also learn to love and help one another. I, for one, have seen the positive effect of that behavior. Leaders are teachers and role models. They are the people who shape the future. Why not shape a future based upon goodness and kindness rather than evil and hurting one another?"

"You know something interesting, Hymn? It occurs to me that of the two of us, you are the one who denies The Earth Code when you are the one who observed and wrote it down, thereby immortalizing it to some extent. I find that of interest."

"There does appear to be a conflict of beliefs at work, God. What I see is the people of Earth worshiping a false god and desperately clinging to life in the hope of salvation from sins for which they profess to be already forgiven. Now, that is a real conflict."

"God, I do not deny The Code's existence and use, but it is based upon a wrong premise, thereby making the conclusion wrong. There is only one thing of utmost importance, my good friend, that being Everything, Everywhere, Every time."

Hymn continued, "The Earth Code is currently in effect, for sure, but should not be, because of its weak foundation; however, those I must deal with are subject to it and will respond accordingly. That is my hope for Rhinda. She probably should resign, being an angel and all, but I can't help thinking Level-4 is better off with her in charge. Maybe you could help with that? Particularly since you know her current ailment is temporary."

"Why, Hymn, are you asking me to help an angel?"

"Well, you helped Michael when I asked."

"Hmm. So, I did."

"And after all, you are receiving prayers from Rhinda."

"Hmm. So, I am."

"And I know you want to help her, God."

"Hmm. So, I do."

"How about it, God?"

"I shall try. You are clever, Hymn. I like that about you."

"You're not fooling me, God; you already decided to help her."

"Well, Hymn, you're the one who gave her the choices."

"Hmm. So, I was."

"Go home, Hymn; you're starting to irritate me."

Hymn laughed and asked, "Before I go, God, where do I find the Judge?"

"I put the coordinates in your phone when you walked in."

"Hmm. You are clever, God," declared Hymn, laughing again.

More seriously, Hymn asked, "What can you tell me about Judge Wells, God? I mean, is he a good man? In what does he believe?"

God replied, "Judge Wells seems to be what some refer to as a ghost; little information about him is available. I am not able to produce a picture of him or even determine his age. The truth is, Hymn, I do not know for sure what his sex is."

"So, information about him is scarce." Hymn pondered.

"On the contrary, my friend, there is too much available, all of which is contradictory. Thousands of pictures of him are available, all different and based upon conjecture. One can make a convincing argument that Judge Wells does not exist based upon the inability to prove he does; however, the same goes when arguing he does exist, based upon the inability to prove he doesn't. It is an odd type of uncertainty principle."

"Okay, God, you went right over my head with that comment. I have no idea what you just said. Does Judge Wells exist or not?"

"Hymn, I honestly do not know, one way or the other. I can say this with certainty, though. He is not a judge. Judge is his forename or first name."

Hymn had a thought and queried, "Is it possible Judge Wells is a machine?"

"I considered that Hymn, and yes, it is possible, but not likely. I would sense the existence of such a machine and do not."

"God, I thought you chose the candidates for The Four Levels."

"Judge Wells was not chosen, Hymn; as Jonas's Chief Advisor, he ascended to commander when Jonas disappeared. As a result, no one knows anything about him."

"Then how is it you were able to give me his coordinates earlier, God?"

"He also prays to Jehovah, Hymn, and is devoted to her."

"Why didn't you tell me that earlier, God? It is important."

"You did not ask me, Hymn. Many on Earth pray to Jehovah for guidance and comfort, my friend; it makes them feel better to believe they have an open line to their god. I receive their prayers to Jehovah but cannot help them. Neither could she, but she effectively used me to perform certain 'miracles' to convince them otherwise. She had an efficient illusional relationship with her subjects that kept them in line, so to speak, one that is effective even today, without her. Of course, today the relationship is delusional."

Hymn smiled, shook his head and thought, *"God just can't help himself, sometimes,"*

"So," Hymn concluded, "the coordinates you gave me pinpoint the position from which the prayers originated."

"Yes," God responded.

"Thank you, God. Maybe I can resolve that uncertainty principle you referred to earlier."

"Be advised, Hymn, I am not certain the prayers actually came from Judge; therefore, you cannot be certain either."

Hymn commented, "Yeah, this should be interesting."

He stepped into Keepaway, issued the coordinates, and looked at the destination. *"This might take a bit of planning,"* he said to himself. *"If Mr. Wells was the chief advisor to Jonas, he had to know about and approve of the League of Assassins being used around the world to eliminate perceived threats to the Four, as well as any other opposition they considered to be troublesome, including me."*

"Other than the information that Judge Wells recently ascended to Commander of L-3, the enforcement section of The Four Levels knows nothing about the man other than he is human, born in the United States, and devoted to law. All of which is hearsay. And apparently, he prays to Jehovah on a regular basis."

Hymn thought, *"Considering Judge advanced through the corrupt enforcement group of The Four, it is reasonable to believe he, like his former superior, is corrupt as well and will be well guarded by professional security personnel and 24/7 high-tech surveillance. I can't help but wonder if the new L3 Commander is paranoid. His ID is as well guarded as his person, and I have no clue about his appearance. He probably is expecting me to be brought to him, but what if I just show up and ask to see him? The coordinates are to a building in Arizona.*

Hymn stepped out of Keepaway into a below-ground parking lot and took the stairs up to the ground floor of a large building that, by all appearances, was a courthouse. He looked around and saw a bench placed against a wall just outside of a waiting room; he walked over and sat down to observe people coming and going through the front doors and milling about the lobby. It was late in the afternoon, and most were leaving, probably getting off work to head home. No one showed any interest in him, so he decided to look around and went up to the 3rd floor to the jury duty area and began asking official-looking people if they knew where to find the office of Judge Wells, but it turned out no one knew anything about a Judge Wells, which seemed to confirm that Judge was not a judge.

After asking about a Judge Wells in several more offices of the building, with no results, Hymn decided to call it a day, go home, and try again tomorrow. He went back to the bench in the lobby and sat down to think about where the judge could be in the building. God gave him the coordinates, so Mr. Wells is probably here. He is just using another name, and by now, he knows I am looking for him.

"Who knows?" Hymn thought, *"Maybe he'll come looking for me."*

As fate would have it, three young men dressed casually in jeans and short-sleeved shirts walked to the bench, where two sat down, one on each side of Hymn.

Hymn looked to his left and right and commented, "Come on guys, ease up on the intimacy here; I'm not gay, nor am I looking for company right now."

The man standing chuckled and calmly stated, "What do you know, we have a comedian in our group. You have been inquiring about Judge Wells; I can help you with that if you like."

Hymn looked up at the man, smiled, and apologized for his poor behavior, explaining that he was tired and frustrated at failing to find Judge Wells today and that he would appreciate all the help the man had to offer.

Hymn stood and offered his hand as a gesture of thanks, but the other men roughly pulled him back down to a sitting position.

"Sir," offered the man standing, "it is imperative you realize that Mr. Wells is an important man whose time is solicited by many and granted to few. Pardon my quick judgment, but you do not appear to be the type of person who is worthy of Mr. Wells' time. What is it that causes you to go to such lengths to talk with him?"

"Actually," replied Hymn, "I am here because someone told me in confidence that Judge Wells was looking for me. I have never met Judge Wells and have no idea what he even looks like. It seems he is not a judge, though. No one in this courthouse has ever heard of a Judge Wells. I'm beginning to think this might be a snipe hunt."

"A snipe hunt?" exclaimed the man to his left and looked at the man to his right, "What the hell is a snipe, Eddie?"

"Don't go looking at me, Sonny!" said Eddie, "I don't know, either."

"The man standing explained, "A snipe hunt is a practical joke in which an unwitting victim is sent off in pursuit of something that does not exist."

"Yeah, guys," laughed Hymn, "and I'm the dumb victim. Why don't you two sleep on that and think about the bad things you do to people for Mr. Wells."

Slowly but surely, Sonny and Eddie got drowsy and slipped into a deep sleep. To the few people remaining in the lobby, they looked like two young lovers, leaning close and whispering sweet nothings in each other's ears.

Hymn stood, smiled, looked closely into the standing man's eyes, and suggested, "Why don't we sit down here on the bench, Judge, with these two sleepyheads and talk for a while?

You are Judge Wells, are you not?" he asked.

"Of course. Who else would I be? What tipped you off?"

"I wasn't really sure until you accurately described a snipe hunt. Not many can do that."

"Yeah, as a kid in Louisiana, I went on a couple of those," Judge admitted."

Hymn said, "You are also sure of yourself and slow to anger."

"You left out genius, Magic Man. I am a certified genius."

"I'm not surprised. For young guy, you have come a long way."

"Yes, I have. I am a king now. I possess the power of life and death," he stated and grinned.

"I'm curious, JW, when did you first embrace evil over good?"

"At about the age of four, it became clear to me that 'bad' is a relative term," he revealed.

"Relative, Judge?" Hymn queried.

"Yes. It was plain that so-called bad acts return more practical rewards than good acts."

"Practical rewards?" Hymn questioned, baffled by what seemed to be an odd answer.

"Yes!" Judge replied, with enthusiasm, "You know, things that are in your best interests." Judge Wells was enjoying this opportunity to expound on his personal philosophy of life.

"Goodness also returns great rewards, JW," Hymn argued.

Judge responded, "Yes, that is true; there are times when goodness is useful, particularly if it becomes important to gain someone's confidence. A simple act of kindness, when used in the right way at the right time, can pay great dividends later on. The secret to success and happiness is not really a secret; it is the willingness to do what is necessary to get that which is in your own best interests without allowing morality to get in the way. Good and bad are just emotional gauges that must be turned down or off if success and happiness are to be achieved. Do what is in your best interests, and expect everyone else to do the same. Good and bad are only terms that describe results."

Judge summed up by saying, "Actions are just actions, neither bad nor good, and when used wisely, without prejudice, produce results in your own interest, which is what everyone really wants if they are honest with themselves."

Hymn was astounded at the man's philosophy of life. It was Judge's sincere belief that there are no moral restrictions on one's actions as long as those actions are undertaken in his best interests. Hymn couldn't help wondering what formed it.

He asked the man, "What occurred at the young age of four that taught you that philosophy, Judge?"

Judge smiled at the memory and replied, "I killed my little sister, Magic Man. I smothered her, and no one ever knew."

Hymn was speechless for a moment, both shocked and surprised at the casual manner of Judge Wells as he told about murdering his little sister. This powerful commander of L3 of the Four Levels recalled that memory as simply an action that had to be accomplished for his own good. Hymn recovered his poise and continued, more because of curiosity than anything else.

"How was killing your sister in your best interests, JW?"

Judge replied, "My sister was just a baby at the time, less than a year old, and my parents doted on her constantly while paying me little attention. The thing is, she was a stupid baby. I was walking and talking at her age, and here she was, being carried around everywhere, gurgling some nonsense no one could understand. Mom was always buying her toys and clothes, and Dad spent a lot of time holding her and telling her how pretty she was. The truth is, she was a nuisance and of no real value, especially where I was concerned. Her continued existence was obviously not in my best interests."

"A few weeks after I killed her, things went back to normal. My parents became more attentive and generous to me. It was then that I began to understand the magic of common sense! It is reasonable and right to do things that are good for me."

"JW," Hymn calmly asked, "did you ever feel any sorrow or remorse for murdering your sister?"

"Of course not. Killing for a good reason is practical, as long as it is done without hurting yourself."

"Judge, I am curious: just how many people have you killed for practical reasons?"

"I don't keep score of killings, Magic Man; that would be weird. Probably several hundred, though, if I were to guess."

Hymn was disturbed by the man's 'matter of fact' attitude towards murder and demanded, "Judge, how do you justify the taking of people's lives without remorse? You have to know it is wrong to murder people!"

Judge frowned at Hymn's obvious weakness and chided his ignorance of the real world, explaining, "Aw, come on, Magician, I only kill in my best interests; that is not murder, it's pragmatism! I don't hurt people or torture them in any way; I just kill them."

Hymn was astounded at Judge's lack of empathy for his victims and rebuked the man's immoral belief, asking, "What about those you kill? What about their best interests and their families and friends? Do their lives mean nothing to you?"

Judge was puzzled at Hymn's obvious ignorance of reality and was briefly caught off guard by the odd and unexpected moral response exhibited by the man. He took a moment to ponder Hymn's questions and then dismissed them as foolish products of an inferior, unrefined mind.

Judge also realized something: the other L's were mistaken in their concern about this man. This magician is a regular guy with the same failings as the rest of humanity, burdened with the weight of a false sense of morality around his neck. He has a refreshing manner of honestly expressing himself, though. Judge was not sure why, but for some reason, he liked this magic man.

Judge answered, "*Their* best interests? What does that have to do with anything? Their interests are nothing to me. I am concerned only with how their life or death serves *my* best interests. There's no other reasonable way to consider people."

Hymn was stunned by Judge's answers to his questions. This man sees nothing wrong with the killing of others for personal gain. He sincerely believes that whatever one does in his best interests is the only honest, moral choice and makes a convincing argument to support that belief.

Judge Wells, on the other hand, was thinking, "*It is not clear why, but I love talking with this man! Unlike anyone I have known, he listens and seems to have a genuine interest in what is being said. I feel perfectly at ease discussing anything and everything without concern about judgment. There is an odd feeling of freedom associated with that. This magic man is simple, but interesting."*

Hymn asked, "Were you taught nothing about morals and ethics in your early years, Judge?"

"On the contrary, Hymn, as a young genius, I was taught everything in the great literature of the world, the Bible easily being among my favorites and committed to memory before age ten."

"You memorized the bible before age ten? Remarkable!" Hymn exclaimed. "Who was your teacher, Judge?"

"Up to age 12, my mother was in charge of the bulk of my education. Early on, my parents recognized my intellect, which made me different from my peers, but we were a low, middle-class family. Schools for gifted children were financially out of the question. Besides, my mother did not want me to grow up to be a genius social freak and made great efforts to keep my special learning abilities a secret."

"What happened after age 12 to change things, Judge?"

"I became aware that each of my parents had large life insurance policies and killed my mother, making it appear to be an accident. Dad and I had plenty of money after that, and soon I was enrolled in a school with a more appropriate environment for my mind."

Hymn looked at the man sitting next to him in disbelief, thought a moment, and asked, "Judge! Are you saying you killed your mother for the life insurance money? What about all the morals you learned from reading the Bible? Do you feel regret or guilt for murdering your mother, Judge?"

Judge was amused by Hymn's moral stance and answered, "No, of course not. My mother's death became necessary and in my best interests, Magic Man. Our family was broke, causing Mom and Dad to fight over finances, which made me miserable. We needed money, and I needed to attend a school that was more in keeping with my intellect. The insurance money was the answer; it solved everything. It was a good decision, guided by the Bible. Observe the great heights to which I have risen because of that decision."

"Guided by the Bible," repeated Hymn, not believing his ears.

"Yes," affirmed Judge. "Great kings, great men, great people of Jehovah in the Bible have all killed, murdered if you will, people when it was in their best interests to do so, even to include their family members, if and when it was called for. Jehovah commended and even rewarded them for having the courage to make good choices. Consider what God did for David, the legendary and greatest killer of all the kings. He even killed one of his officers because he desired the man's wife! Jehovah rewarded him with fortune and eternal fame! David's son, Solomon, killed his own brother in his best interests. The Bible is a great guide for learning right behavior. It is there we learn that serving our best interests serves Jehovah."

"Glory be forever unto his name!" Judge chanted.

"Judge, you interpret the Bible incorrectly; murder, along with other bad acts, is immoral. The Ten Commandments is a guide for moral behavior. The killing of people simply because it appears to be in your best interests is not in the best interests of civilization."

Judge questioned, "Then why are all great civilizations of Earth virtually littered with the bodies of people who were killed because their living was not in the best interests of those who killed them? Look at the history of America, our great country! We are the country we are because our leaders made decisions in their own best interests, without concern for the best interests of others. That is just the way things are, and to ignore that is to encourage oblivion."

"The Ten Commandments are laws, Magic Man, given to all mankind by the great Jehovah, *may his name be forever revered!*, for the purpose of guiding the behavior of the people of Earth. As the Level-3 Commander, I am charged with the enforcement of those laws and will perform my obligation as the Holy Bible teaches. God, in his wisdom, rewards and does not punish killing when done in the killer's best interests, such as war, self-defense, or gain."

"However, senseless killing for the sake of killing is a very serious violation of the law, which calls for serious penalties. I will faithfully enforce Jehovah's laws and continue praying daily for his divine guidance in helping me to make wise decisions in my best interests as I serve his will."

Hymn stood, looked down at Judge Wells' cheerful face, and said, "Judge, today, because of you, I have learned a new way of looking at things that require more thought. My question to you is, now that we have met, what do you intend to do about me?"

"I am not sure, Magic Man, you are certainly a nuisance. Is it in my best interest to allow you to continue, or should I remove you? You are a wild card. Are you a danger to The Four Levels or me? I have not yet decided."

Hymn replied, "Allow me to help you with that, Judge. I am a danger to you and your entire organization only if I perceive you to be a threat to me or mine. It is in your best interests to just let me be. Do that, and it is unlikely we will ever see each other again."

The two sleeping men were beginning to awaken from their nap.

"For example, Magic Man?" Judge inquired.

"Do not harm, in any way, the people or things for which I care. For example, I perceive you to believe the lives of the two men sleeping next to you do not serve your best interests anymore and intend to kill them. Hear this: it is in your best interests to do them no harm. Fire them if you wish, but do them no harm."

"Magician," Judge laughed, "you have no idea to whom you are speaking or what you are demanding; your ignorance explains your disrespectful attitude. I am an enormous power on Earth because I pleased Jehovah by doing what is in my best interests, according to his written law. You are an interesting man, but far too simple to understand what I have taught you today. Besides, I like you and have decided to do as you want and let you be. It is difficult to see you being a threat to The Four Levels. As for these two useless idiots, their lives certainly are not in my best interest; they will not live to see tomorrow."

Judge pondered the name 'Magic Man' and laughed.

"How in the world did you get that stupid title, anyway?" he exclaimed and laughed again. Then he stood and declared, "I suspect we will not be seeing each other again."

Hymn decided to give Mr. Wells a couple of life choices when Sonny suddenly leaped up, blade in hand, and stabbed Judge Wells three times in the stomach, puncturing his aorta.

Judge let out a groan, put his hand over his wound, and sat back down on the bench, bleeding profusely. He looked up at Hymn, confused, with a questioning expression on his face.

Both Sonny and Eddie fled the empty lobby immediately. No one witnessed the attack or saw them leave.

Hymn stood there, shocked at what had just happened. He noticed the large puddle of blood rapidly forming on the floor between Judge's feet, then looked intently into the eyes of the dying man and quietly advised, "Forgive the man, Judge. I am sure he felt it was in his best interests that you cease to live."

A very important and powerful man, King Judge Wells, the young genius Commander of Level-3 of The Four Levels Coalition, exhaled his last breath in that brief moment while watching the Magician magically disappear into thin air, as Hymn stepped into Keepaway.

11

Solutions

In Keepaway, Hymn removed his clothes, walked into the ocean, and allowed himself to enjoy the cleansing, relaxing waves of the evening surf to wash the complexity of the day from his mind. So much for his goal of focusing on the little things. Dealing with the most powerful leaders on Earth is anything but little. There remain two more commanders to engage in conversation, and Hymn is unsure if the result of his efforts with the first two helped or hurt The Four Levels or mankind. He wondered about the effect of greatness on people. The egos of those who attain great heights in life all seem to be huge. Does that mean people with large egos are more likely to be great, or does greatness itself create large egos? He was curious about the next two commanders and found himself exploring the idea of leaving them alone and wait to see what they decide to do.

Anyway, he needed time to think over his conversation with Judge Wells. That man totally redefined the meaning of moral and ethical behavior and made his view sound like a reasonable way of thinking. It crossed his mind that Judge Wells might have been a former assassin of the Level-3 League of Enforcers, but then discarded the notion. Judge was most certainly a killer but lacked the traits of an L-3 assassin. Invisibles are psychos who kill for the love of killing. Judge Wells killed for what he considered to be practical reasons; he killed when it was in his best interests to kill. Jehovah-

God was a great influence on him and inspired his moral code.

"Seems the Bible is a perspective based book, when you think about it," he thought.

Enough of that for now, though. There were more pleasant things to consider: Melody, for instance. Hymn thought about Melody and got the familiar but odd feeling of happiness she brought into his life. This woman was an exciting new experience for Hymn that was approaching the point of being necessary to his being, even though he had only known her for a few days.

While lounging in the surf near shore, it occurred to Hymn that they never discussed where they would meet or where Melody lived. Since Hymn recently sold his house, he was spending most of his time in Keepaway, which was the definition of convenience since Keepaway was less than just a step away, no matter where he might be. Convenient though it certainly is, Keepaway only exists for one, with that one being Hymn. Aunt Rita was the only other person who knew about his safe place. At some point, Melody will have to be told. Hymn knew that Keepaway was his creation and could be changed to include others, but that would violate its purpose, being something he was reluctant to do.

He was tired from the busy day but wanted to see Melody and wondered if his aunt had heard from her, so he dressed and went to see Aunt Rita.

Hymn could smell the pizza in the oven almost before stepping into the house and went directly to the kitchen.

His aunt observed him walking in and exclaimed, "Your timing is great, nephew. Melody called to warn me she would be here soon, and the pizza is almost ready to be removed from the oven."

Hymn commented, "From the smell of that pizza, I'm surprised there's not a crowd of people at the door begging to get in."

"Now, Hymn, you quit trying to butter me up with all that flattery," she giggled, "there is more than enough pizza to go around as long as you keep the beggars outside."

Melody announced herself, "I intended to ring the doorbell, but the smell of your pizza made me forget my manners, so I just walked right in."

Then she went straight to Hymn and said, "Kiss me before you say anything, you big lug; I have been thinking about you all this crazy day."

Hymn raised her in his arms and squeezed her in a strong hug.

She laughed and protested, "I said kiss me, not break me!" Then he gently pulled her close and kissed her. "Wow, mister, I can see you've been thinking about me, too," she happily responded.

Aunt Rita remarked, "I'm beginning to wonder if anyone is still interested in my great pizza. Of course, I can always put it in the fridge."

"No! No!" Hymn objected, "I just got a little sidetracked for a minute there. We haven't seen each other in a while, you know." He went and sat down at the table.

"Yeah, I know, a long while too," Rita tittered, "way back since this morning." and added, "Y'all might want to sit across from each other, seeing as how long you've been apart for so long, or else we'll never finish supper."

Melody grinned, sat down across from Hymn, and said, "I just have to tell you about my bizarre day, and y'all are not going to believe it. I couldn't even make this up if I tried."

Hymn thought, *"I could talk about a bizarre day too, but I won't."* Instead, he put a hot slice of pizza on his plate, leaned back, took a bite of deliciousness, and stated, "I can't wait to hear all about your interesting day."

Aunt Rita chimed in, saying, "You have my undivided attention as well, dear," and began attending to her slice as well.

Melody began, "Right after I arrived at the office, and before I could check the mail, a nicely dressed old man came in and introduced himself as Henry Button, a government investigator, and showed me his badge and identification. He was interested in obtaining the contact information of a man we all know named Hymn, saying it was important they meet right away."

When Melody spoke the name 'Henry Button,' Hymn was immediately interested. He sat up in his chair and put the pizza slice on his plate, paying close attention to Melody's story.

"I figured you would be interested once I mentioned the old man's occupation and name," Melody commented.

"Yes," Hymn admitted, "I met with Henry in The Burger House yesterday. You showed up after he left."

"You left out the part where I kissed you and rescued you," she said.

"Well now, I don't know if I would go that far," Hymn argued, "maybe you saved them."

She fired back, "Yeah, right! Like you were going to take them all on by yourself."

"Well, I had a plan, but your kiss kinda threw me off balance; I couldn't think of anything but you after that."

"Oh, Hymn, you say the sweetest things!" she giggled.

"All right, you two cut it out!" ordered Aunt Rita, "I want to hear the rest of the story and less about the sweetness of my nephew. Now, get on with it, girl!"

"Oh, yeah!" exclaimed Melody. "Well, his inquiring about my Hymn made me suspicious, you know; why would a government man be wanting to meet with my Hymn? So, I told the man personal information about my friend was not my place to reveal, which was the truth because I have no idea where Hymn lives or works." Melody looked at Hymn and said, "And, by the way, I really would like to know, not that I would tell anyone if it's a secret or . . ."

"Melody! The story, please!" interrupted Rita.

"Yeah, okay. I'm sorry, Aunt Rita, but it is not my fault that your nephew is so distracting. There's something about him that makes me crazy."

Aunt Rita looked up at the ceiling and rolled her eyes.

"Anyway," Melody continued, "Mr. Button said he knew just how I felt, saying that my loyalty is admirable and asked that I make sure Hymn is aware The Levels know he is the magic man and are coming for him. He thanked me, and I watched as he left to go to his car, but as he got in, another man opened the passenger door, got in, and pointed his finger at Mr. Button. Then they drove away. I got the feeling the man was angry at Mr. Button."

Hymn asked, "Melody, how did the other man appear?"

She thought a moment and said, "Also well-dressed, late 30s, tall, slender, bald, and black."

"And you won't believe this, either!" she exclaimed. "Not more than ten minutes later, a man and woman came through the door, put me in handcuffs, put a sack over my head, and drove me to a house somewhere. It was pretty scary at first, but I began to see there was something wrong. The woman claimed there were bad people looking for my boyfriend and intended to use me to get at him. She had this idea that Hymn is special, and they were protecting him from evil. I think she was being sincere, maybe a little crazy, but sincere."

"Another thing is that both of them were afraid of something or someone. I can tell you this for a fact: those two were insanely paranoid about everything. They kept on talking crazy about the invisible coming here to get us and about people being doomed."

Melody confessed, "Truthfully, I didn't know what to think. At first, I thought this might be a dumb prank of some sort until it became painfully obvious that those two were not in their right minds. Then, I began to worry they would kill me. Crazy people don't know what they are doing, you know. I wondered who it was that scared them crazy."

Hymn spoke softly, "Actually, it is not a 'who' that creates such fear in the minds of those aware of it; it is a 'what.'"

"A 'what!'" she exclaimed. "Now, that sounds kind of spooky, my darling, but also insane. Whatever it is, they are scared out of their minds and talk crazy. Anyway, they drove me to a bus station, took off the handcuffs, and removed the sack from my head. Then, they advised me to get to a safe place if I knew of one. The man warned me that how far I run makes no difference at all, as it is everywhere. He advised me to get to a safe place and blend in because the things after me do not think like us, and there are too many of them to fight. He said the Invisibles are ruthless beyond imagination and, before they drove away, said to tell Hymn the Invisibles are looking for him and to be prepared."

"I have to say, it was a relief to get away from them; being around crazy people like that is scary. They were suspicious of everyone, claiming the government or something was doing all kinds of bad things to people. Anyway, I flagged a taxi to take me to my car and drove right here to my safe place, just as the poor man advised. I told you it was unbelievable."

Then she remembered the pizza and hungrily dug into it.

Aunt Rita listened to Melody's adventurous day, thought about it, then looked at Hymn and concluded, "Nephew, you're going to have to tell her."

Hymn said, "Melody love, coming here was the right decision; this is your safe place."

"No, my darling," she countered, "my safe place is with you."

Aunt Rita smiled and commented, "Right now, mine is in bed."

Hymn considered his dilemma for a moment and thought, "Auntie is right. There is no getting around it. 'The Talk' with Melody has become necessary. I just don't feel like now is the right time to spring everything on her."

Hymn realized tomorrow was going to be interesting. The Four Levels lost two of its commanders today. That was new and unexpected. Nothing like that had ever happened in the history of The Four. For thousands of years, that organization has been unknown and untouchable until today, when it was touched, leaving one of The Four, L3, without a leader and L4's commander in limbo.

Now, Government and Communication will be on high alert, protecting themselves from an adversary and going all out to eliminate the threat to their world empire while at the same time working to provide leadership for their two very weakened levels. Considering the infighting that may be about to begin over control of L-3 and L-4, two of the four most powerful and influential leadership positions in the world, saving The Four Levels Coalition will be a difficult, near impossible task. In any event, for better or worse, Hymn was sure The Four Levels would never be the same as it was before today.

Hymn reasoned, "The couple who took Melody from her office to their safe place is interesting. They took Melody to protect me from a trap. Had the Invisibles taken her, they would have used her as bait to kill or capture me, which begs the question, what do those two know about me, and why were they willing to risk their lives to protect me?"

Hymn knew a little bit about the "Invisibles," to which Melody's kidnappers referred as being everywhere, as he had run into them before in his travels in Europe. They are the 'What' to which he earlier referred and are actually agents of SoLutions, Inc., a sub-department of Level-3, better known by insiders as the League of Assassins because that is a better description of what they are and what they do.

SoLutions, although little known, is highly feared by those who are aware of them. The actual number of SoLutions agents is not known but is believed to be in the thousands, and, as the man warned Melody, they are everywhere, posing as normal people. SoLutions' agents are said to be many things, but 'normal' is a word never used.

An interesting piece of information Hymn learned from his talks with God and his visits around the world is this: angels and agents of SoLutions hate each other. All angels consider Solutions' agents to be the worst kind of human trash because they loudly claim, falsely, that Jehovah endorses their despicable behavior. Since they are without moral turpitude, they are legal prey to be hunted and killed by angels, with prejudice, upon being found. That action by angels caused L3 to declare angels' enemies of the state. As a result, angels and Invisibles are blood enemies.

Now that angels are leaving Earth and going back home to Ganymede, SoLutions has no formidable opposition to its existence, with one possible exception: The Magician. He is a threat that must be removed.

12

Unexpected Company

Hymn awoke early the next morning, kissed the sleeping Melody, and stepped into Keepaway. The statement, *"Tell your friend it is looking for him and be prepared."* was on his mind. He wondered, who are those two kidnappers? And how is it they know about me? It was a mystery; something he didn't know about was going on, and he was interested in knowing what it was.

Yesterday's happenings in regard to Levels 3 and 4 will be well known by now, and Hymn suspected a reaction was in process. SoLutions was busy seeking me before it knew anything about L3 and L4, so they are about to double or triple their efforts to bring me in, "dead or alive," as is said when a dangerous fugitive is at large. The truth is, though, no one can be absolutely sure the man being sought is the man they want. None of their expensive Hi-Tech surveillance equipment will have revealed anything, and L4 Rhinda is probably back at her home in Ganymede, pondering her missing wings.

Hymn realized he was probably overthinking again. What was it Walter advised? Do the little things. Something had to be done about Melody, though. Those SoLutions crazies will be after her for sure now, and she is such a free spirit. Staying here with Aunt Rita for several days is just not her style. How do I keep her safe from professional killers?

Hymn stepped back into the house, quickly dressed, and went to the kitchen, where he found Melody making coffee.

"Well, well," he remarked in a teasing manner, "among other things, my beautiful woman can boil water, too!"

"You didn't know I could cook, did you?" she laughed, and blew him a kiss. "Don't worry, the real cook went to the Quik Mart to get some essentials, whatever those are. She left a few minutes ago and should be back soon."

Hymn advised, "Don't burn that water; I'll be back in a jiffy for some coffee." then turned to hurry to the bathroom.

"Doggone it, Auntie!" he murmured as he closed the bathroom door and stepped into Keepaway. "You know better than this."

"Screen. Locate Aunt Rita."

Numbers flashed across the screen.

He stepped from Keepaway into a motor home, parked near a gas pump, and was being fueled by a large man outside.

"Something's wrong with the reception in here." griped a young voice from the front. I can't get anything on this stupid radio. Why are you bothering to put gas in this bus anyway? We have plenty of gas."

"I'm just trying to look normal, honey. We don't want to draw attention to ourselves, do we?"

"Seriously, dad?" the young girl giggled, "You draw attention wherever you are."

"Would you two stop with all the talking and get this bus on the road!" said Aunt Rita. "This youngster and I are hungry, and I've got breakfast to fix at home."

Hymn immediately realized what was happening when he heard Aunt Rita's voice. He was preparing to step back into Keepaway when the girl cried out to her dad, "They're here! They're here!"

"Stay calm, child," said Aunt Rita, "they don't yet know we are here, too."

Three sedans, all black, pulled into the food-mart parking area. All three parked about 20 feet apart, but no one got out of the cars.

The big man finished topping off the fuel tank on the motor home, got in the driver's seat, started the engine, and slowly pulled away.

There was some sort of commotion going on inside the black cars. The headlights on all three were flashing, the horns were blaring, and the people inside the cars were firing guns at the windows, breaking them, and climbing out as fast as they could, coughing and vomiting.

As the motor home pulled away and gained speed, Hymn, like a ghost, silently disappeared into Keepaway and stepped back into the bathroom of Aunt Rita's house. He walked to the kitchen and poured himself one of the worst cups of coffee he had ever tasted. Grabbing the pot, he slowly poured coffee into the sink and yelled to the love of his life, who had gone back to the bedroom, that company was coming and to get dressed. Then, he made a fresh pot of coffee.

The motor home drove up, and not long after, Aunt Rita rushed in to tell Hymn she had a surprise outside, and she was very eager to see him. As he opened the door, a teenage girl rushed into his arms, crying tears of joy and expressing how much she had missed him. Little Archie was giggling a baby laugh as his grandfather, big Arch, placed him in the arms of Hymn. The big man's eyes were also glistening with tears as he hugged Hymn and shook his hand like he didn't want to let it go.

Aunt Rita invited everyone in for breakfast, and Hymn poured a mug of coffee for his huge friend, who took a few sips, smiled, and issued a big "*Aahhhh!*" then licked his lips and said, "This is the best coffee I have tasted in a very long while."

Hymn opened his mouth to say thank you, but Melody walked in at that moment and happily stated, "See! I told you I know how to make coffee." Then said to Arch, "Thank you for the compliment, sir. The secret is in the salt."

Hymn almost dropped his cup but caught it and only spilled some coffee on his shoes and the floor. "Doggone shame to waste such good coffee," he chuckled, "think I'm gonna get me a refill."

Then, he introduced everyone to Melody. She hugged and talked with everyone like they were family she had known all her life.

Arch pulled Hymn aside and commented, "This young woman is a rare jewel, Mr. Hymn. I think she's making you younger, too. I swear, you looked to be in your late forties the last time I saw you, and now you look like you are in your early thirties. You really look good."

"Well, my half-angel friend, you don't look near your age either. Just how old are you, anyway?"

"Wow!" exclaimed Arch, "Let's not go there. Besides, you have to be wondering why we have come here. I don't intend to take more of your time than necessary, Mr. Hymn, but you and I have some important things to talk about."

Hymn thought a moment and asked, "Arch, do you know anything about a young couple who kidnapped Melody from her business yesterday? I am curious because they seemed to know things about me."

"Yes, Mr. Hymn. They are part of our group and had information that the Invisibles were planning to use your girlfriend to flush you out and capture or kill you.

"Mr. Hymn, there is talk going around about a magic man that helps people. He is said to be hated by Invisibles because he defies them and has even killed a large number of them. When I heard the rumors and was told his description, I just knew it was you being talked about. All we could find about the magic man was that he had a girlfriend and the address where she worked. We created a plan to steal their bait in order to give you time to prepare for them."

"These invisibles are not normal people, Mr. Hymn. They do evil, unimaginable things to people, and you are on their wish list," Arch informed and warned.

Hymn looked at the big man, saw the earnest look in his eyes, and stated, "I want to hear all about your group and your plans, Arch. We are on the same page here, but first, let's go have some of that great breakfast my aunt has whipped up. She is expecting us."

"Breakfast?" exclaimed Arch. "Yeah, Mr. Hymn, I think you are on to something important there. Let's go have a great breakfast."

Hymn laughed at Arch's response to food and hollered at Rita, "Auntie, what did you do with your car?"

"Rita answered, "It's parked at the Quick-Mart, Hymn; you and Arch can go get it after breakfast. I called the manager and got permission to leave it there. Arch can bring you up to date on how we came to meet each other. I knew who they were the minute I saw them at the store."

"Yeah, Hymn, she walked right up to me at the gas pump and asked if my name was Arch; I was so surprised, I couldn't talk right. I even thought she might be an Invisible. When she said Hymn was her nephew, I knew it was you; I ain't heard of anyone else with the name 'Hymn' before. Why, I scooped her up and did a jig; I was so happy."

"That had to be an interesting sight to see!" Hymn exclaimed, laughing at the image of Arch doing a happy dance with his Aunt Rita.

Arch replied, "I knew you were supposed to be living out here, somewhere, but wasn't sure of the address or how to find you. When your aunt showed up 'out of the blue' like that, it was like a miracle."

13

The Angel Bloodline

As usual, Aunt Rita's breakfast lived up to expectations, and, as a surprise hostess, Melody was wonderful. She talked about dreams and how she came to realize her ability to interpret them. Of course, she had to talk about Hymn and the story of the love she felt the first time she saw him. Andra loved their story and thought it was romantic. Arch liked the story, too, but he loved the breakfast. All in all, it was a great get-together, which everyone hoped to repeat at some point in the future.

Hymn was grateful the stories of how they all came to know one another never came up. In certain companies, some memories are better left untold.

Everyone pitched in to clean the kitchen, and, in a short time, there was nothing left to do but sit around and enjoy each other's company. Hymn declared he and Arch had some catching up to do and they left for some privacy in the motor home.

"Okay, Arch, you earlier remarked that your plan to steal the bait from the invisibles was to give me time. What is the meaning of that comment?"

"Mr. Hymn," Arch began, "I don't know much about you other than that you have special abilities that even angels don't want to mess with, and you have used them to help many people, including me and my family. However, the most impressive thing about you is that the Invisibles fear you. You resist them, and they have been unable to get rid of you. Our group feels obligated to help you fight them where we are able."

"Your group, Arch? What group?"

"Many Nephilim and others sympathetic to our cause decided to form a type of protective association to resist and defend from the assaults of Invisibles. Since they hate, fear, and want to kill you, that makes you our friend and ally."

Hymn added, "The Invisibles also fear angels, Arch. By the way, my friend, the Invisibles are professional assassins who are part of a little-known, powerful organization known as SoLutions, Inc."

"Yes, Mr. Hymn, the Invisibles fear angels, but angels have left Earth for their home. For all practical purposes, there are no angels on Earth anymore to provide an equal power that offsets the power of the Invisibles, or SoLutions, or whatever they are. The Invisibles hate angels, Mr. Hymn, including those who carry the bloodline of an angel. Since word came down that all angels were leaving Earth, hundreds of Nephilim and humans of angel descent have been murdered by those assassins we call Invisibles, and that is just the beginning.

Their plan is to rid Earth of the entire angel bloodline. There are millions of us on Earth, Mr. Hymn. All of us were born on Earth; we are a part of humanity, and here we are, forced to fight for our right to exist because we are of angel descent."

Hymn again reminded himself, "*It is great wisdom to know the difference between helping and hurting.*"

Arch continued, "The truth is, Mr. Hymn, we have little chance to prevail in a conflict with the Invisibles. To most of the people of Earth, we don't exist. The governments of Earth take no notice of our situation. The huge Communication and Information media has successfully buried our existence on Earth by not publishing anything about us. Any stories about angels and their descendants living on

Earth are crushed by religious dogma and a smiling media that passes off reports of that sort as being folklore, like sightings of pixies, fairies, and mermaids. In the meantime, Invisibles are hunting and killing us with the intent of removing all evidence of our existence. Our group is their only opposition, such as it is."

"How many people compose this opposition of yours, Arch?"

"I don't really know exactly, Mr. Hymn. Hundreds here in Texas and many thousands more around the planet. We are unified in our goal to keep the Invisibles from killing us, but totally without any effective organization."

"So, concluded Hymn, you defend against aggression, but are not aggressive, and are united in spirit, but lack a defined unified effort. You know what that means, Arch?"

"No, Mr. Hymn. What does it mean?"

"It means angel-kind will fight the good fight and extend the war, but very many will die, and ultimately, angel-kind will be exterminated. Basically, it means hatred will prevail."

Hymn continued, "An unknown worldwide organization, by the name of The Four Levels, manages Earth. Once the existence of beings with an angel bloodline becomes known around the world, all the resources of The Four Levels will be used against you. First, their media will demonize angel-kind, making mankind believe you are evil and a threat to their existence. Then their armies will rise against you, kill most of you, and imprison the rest. Angel heritage will be considered a dangerous and evil bloodline, which must be sterilized and eliminated from Earth. The lives lost in the war, which angel-kind will be accused of starting, will be used as proof of their wickedness. Do you understand, Arch?"

"Wow! I always thought angels were badass, Mr. Hymn. Now I am beginning to understand they can't hold a candle to the humans of Earth."

"Well, Arch," Hymn advised, "Before you go criticizing angels and humans, you might want to remember that you are descended from both races, yourself. You are kin to both types of beings and have some part of each type running through the blood in your veins. Angel-kind exists for a reason. It might be they are a bridge between 'now' and 'when' if you get my meaning."

"Mr. Hymn, the truth is, you talk over my head a lot of the time, but right now, I think you are saying a war with the Invisibles will be bad for Angelkind."

"That is the way I see it turning out, Arch."

"But we angelkind cannot just stand around and let the Invisibles murder us!" Arch protested.

"No, you can't, my big friend; you must resist evil, and invisibles are, indeed, evil. However, it may be that some few Invisibles can be redeemed and deserve the to have that opportunity given them."

"Why will evil beings even want that opportunity, Mr. Hymn? They do horrible things to people and enjoy it. How can you even get them to listen to you, much less change their ways?"

"How is your memory these days, Arch? I recall a big, mean man a while back who changed his ways when given the opportunity."

Arch thought a minute, grinned, and admitted, "I recall that man, too, Mr. Hymn. But I was one man, and there are many Invisibles. How are you going to get through to all of them?"

Hymn replied, "I just have to make them understand it is in their best interests to change and allow them to make their own choice as to the direction in which they want their valuable lives to proceed."

"Sounds really complicated to me, but I believe in you, Mr. Hymn, and your strange way of doing things. How can I help you?" Arch offered.

"First and foremost, my friend, be safe. Extend your visit here with Aunt Rita for a week. Her home is a safe place where you cannot be traced. Away from here, your existence is at risk."

The big man considered Hymn's advice and agreed to stay, but it was plain he was worried about his friend, Hymn.

"Is there no way I can help you, Mr. Hymn?" Arch asked and said, "What you are talking about doing seems too big for any one man to accomplish alone, and to achieve it in only one week seems impossible. The Invisibles are everywhere, Mr. Hymn, and they are terribly ruthless. You cannot imagine the terrible things they do."

Hymn noticed his friend's genuine concern and informed him, "You're right, Arch, but listen to me; I am never alone; as a matter of fact, neither are you. Having you to keep watch over the family here is good for my peace of mind and allows me to focus my attention on what must be done. Anyway, Arch, I seldom think about doing big things; I'm a 'little things' type of guy."

"Yeah, right," Arch thought, *"little things, like defeating and changing the Archangel Michael and returning my family to me. I don't care what he says; those were huge things!"*

Hymn suggested, "Let's go back inside and tell everyone you are staying longer than planned. To give you a 'heads-up,' Arch, Melody knows nothing yet about angels and Nephilim or Invisibles. Also, I have not yet told her about me. I suspect it's going to be a bit of a shock to her when she finds out, and I have been putting it off."

Arch nodded his understanding, started to say something about Melody and her fragile innocence being a weakness that would require round-the-clock protection, then thought the better of it and

kept quiet, confident Hymn knew what he was doing.

They went back to the house and told the others that Arch and his family were extending their visit for a week. Everyone was happy to hear it. Rita claimed she was hoping they would stay for a while longer and said it would be nice having company around to talk with when Hymn and Melody are away.

Melody silently went over to the recliner where Hymn was sitting, crawled in beside him, and kissed his cheek; then remarked in a teasing voice, "That reminds me, my love, just what is it you do when you are away?"

"Well," Hymn replied, "here lately, I have been spending most of my time thinking about you and not getting much done."

She scoffed, "Now, don't you go trying to distract me with all your charming romantic talk, you devil; I am interested in what kind of work you do all day."

"Actually, my work is rather similar to yours," explained Hymn. "Melody, you help people by interpreting their dreams, and I help people solve problems, mostly by just talking to them. I guess you could say I am a type of personal counselor. I listen to people talk about their lives and suggest choices that can make them happier."

Melody mused, "A Personal Counselor. Why darling, that is a wonderful occupation! I am so proud of you."

Aunt Rita was listening to them talk and couldn't take any more without choking. She got up and expressed a desire for a big glass of wine. Arch volunteered to join her.

Hymn told Melody he was concerned about her working the rest of the week because the crazy people who kidnapped her may still be in the area. He wondered if she would stay here and help Aunt Rita out around the house until things settled down. She agreed and said many of her clients contacted her by cell phone, anyway.

Aunt Rita's Car

Hymn stated that Aunt Rita's car needed to be retrieved from the Quik Mart parking area and asked Melody to go with him to drive it back. He had several errands to run today and wanted to get to them this morning.

They got in his car and headed for the Quik Mart.

She reached and slapped him on his shoulder accusingly and said, "I hope you know you're not fooling anybody, big boy. You just wanted to get me alone to take advantage of me."

"Well, Auntie's car does need to be brought home," Hymn said defensively.

"Yeah, right, Auntie's car," she replied skeptically. "When and where do you plan to assault me?"

Hymn grinned and said, "Now that you mention it, there is a vacant lot behind the Quick Mart. It's very private, too."

"I suppose it is hopeless for me to resist you," she accused.

"Well," he surmised, "a little resistance is, of course, expected and considered ladylike, you know, for your honor and all."

She shot back, "That settles it then! I am not much of a lady at the moment and, where you are concerned, I have no honor," she said as the fingers of her hand found the buttons on his jeans and released them from the pressure of his passion."

Hymn saw something and said, "What's that going on at the Quik Mart, Melody?"

"Quick Mart! Who cares about the Quick Mart, now?"

"We do, my love. C'mon, take a look."

They arrived at the store and saw a wrecker backed up to Aunt Rita's car, where a man was about to hook it up and haul it off. The old store manager's face was bleeding, and he was shaking his fist at the wrecker operator.

Hymn heard him holler angrily, "You cannot do this! You are stealing my customer's car! I have called the police; they are on their way now."

"Good luck with that, you old bastard! The police sent me to pick up this abandoned car and haul it to the pound. That is what I intend to do."

Hymn got out of his car and walked toward the operator while buttoning his pants. The man saw him approaching and angrily warned him, "Look, mister, I don't want any trouble; I have a job to do here, and I intend to do it, so don't even think of getting in my way."

It was clearly evident that the wrecker driver was emotionally at the end of his rope and in no mood for talking. He had a job to do, and that was the object of his focus. Hymn's concern was the store manager.

Hymn spoke calmly and directly to the wrecker operator, "Why did you hurt Mr. Davidson, wrecker-man?"

The young man looked at Hymn in disbelief. "Hurt?" he questioned, "you don't think I hurt that old man, do you? He was beaten before I showed up. He's a stubborn old guy, that one. Keeps telling me the car belongs to a customer and is not abandoned. No one has shown up to claim it, and I have orders to haul it to the pound."

Hymn informed the wrecker-man, "I am here to pick up the car. It belongs to my aunt, who has permission from the manager to leave it there overnight. You can ask him if you want; he is the old man standing in front of the store, bleeding. I want to know who is responsible for his injuries."

"Listen, mister, I assume you have the keys to the car. The man in the blue suit standing at the corner of the building is the one you want to talk to. Take my advice and give him the keys. Then tell him your story, and maybe he will let you take the car. If he says no, take my advice, walk away and don't look back. Forget the car; it is his car, now."

Hymn listened to the wrecker-man's advice and turned to look at the man standing at the corner of the building.

"Wrecker-man," Hymn said softly, "Mister Bluesuit there looks like the kind who would beat up an old man."

"Well now, I wouldn't know anything about that," replied the wrecker-man, "but that just might be old-man blood on his suit. If you are smart, mister, you will go your way and avoid getting your blood on that suit. You should know that it is a Syndicate suit. I have to leave here, now; there will be a lot of explaining to do back at the office."

Wrecker-man drove away, and Hymn walked back to his car and gave Melody the keys to his aunt's car.

"What is going on, Hymn?" she asked, "What happened to Mr. Davidson? Is he okay?"

"Yeah, everything is fine, babe. There is some confusion about Auntie's car being an abandoned vehicle, but it's all cleared up now. You can drive it home. I have papers to sign here and a few errands to run. I'll see you at home later today."

"Yes," she replied coyly, "you have some unfinished business that needs attending."

Hymn grinned and acknowledged her meaning with a 'thumbs-up.' Melody drove away in his aunt's car and waved. Hymn waved back, then turned and walked toward Mr. Bluesuit.

As he approached Bluesuit, two men stopped him about 5 feet from the man.

Bluesuit looked at Hymn and stated calmly, "That was a mistake, mister; I am going to be wanting that car back. I feel sure you did not mean to steal the car from me and desire to correct your mistake, so you have until 8 pm tonight to return it. These gentlemen here will be happy to assist you."

Hymn ignored Bluesuit and turned his attention to the two men blocking his path.

"Do you two have names or numbers? Probably numbers; slaves always have numbers. Oh, I'm sorry, you don't like to be referred to as slaves, do you? Well, you are what you are. I will call you One and Two."

The two men were taken by surprise; they were expecting fear from this idiot, but no fear was observed. This man had a confident way about him that made them uncomfortable.

One looked at Bluesuit and asked, "You want us to break his legs, boss?"

Hymn said, "Come on, One, show some imagination! You can't impress an important man like your boss with barbaric tactics like breaking legs. What do you think, Two?"

Bluesuit watched Hymn carefully and was uneasy about the way this man spoke with the confidence of authority. He began to realize he may have underestimated him. There was something about this guy, something unusual and disturbing.

Bluesuit spoke politely, "Listen closely, sir. All I want is for you

to return the car; have it here by eight o'clock tonight, and you can walk away without consequences. Is that plain enough for you to understand?"

Hymn again ignored him and turned his attention to One and Two.

"You boys go on in the store there and get a couple of soft drinks. The boss and I have car business to discuss; we won't be long."

Without even thinking about it, One and Two left and headed for the store.

Hymn then turned his attention to Bluesuit and observed, "You know, Mr. Bluesuit, the way you dress, all pretty and everything is impressive. Your nice blue suit is really pretty, but it has red stains on it. Your pretty shoes do, as well. Is that Mr. Davidson's blood? It is, isn't it?"

"As a matter of fact, it is," replied Bluesuit, "I tuned the old man up a bit for disrespecting my authority; he learned his lesson, though, and the next time we meet, he will be more respectful."

Hymn reminded Bluesuit of what he had done to Mr. Davidson.

"You constantly hit that nice old man until his face was a bloody mess. It will take several painful weeks for his body to heal. At his age, he may never get over it. You overstepped the mark."

Bluesuit explained, "Listen, I am a Syndicate enforcer. As such, it is my job to keep order in this district. I do that mostly by being nice and respectful to businesses and citizens. When they return my kindness, I respond with kindness. As anyone can testify, if they live in this district or visit, my methods are civilized and effective."

Hymn scratched his head, as if thinking about something, then advised Bluesuit, "Okay, boss-man, I get it. You answer to a higher authority. Tell you what, if you apologize to Mr. Davidson for your bad behavior and compensate him for the pain and suffering you caused, I promise it will stop. Oh, about the car. We both know the car does not belong to you. Don't we? That was just you showing off, was it not? It will be in your best interests to just make amends for your actions and stick to protecting people and their property. And for goodness sake, stop with all the bullying! Now, do what I told you, and it will stop. Oh, and you might want to keep our little talk between us."

Hymn then turned and walked toward his car.

"Hold on, mister!" Bluesuit yelled, "What will stop?"

Hymn paused, turned, and focused his gaze on Bluesuit. A cold shiver shook the enforcer as Hymn spoke.

"The pain."

Hymn got in his car and drove to the local Walmart, where he parked and stepped into Keepaway.

Bluesuit thought to himself, *"Apologize? Amends? Pain? What pain? What a fucking idiot! There goes a man in need of a serious tuneup."*

As he walked to the store to check on his men, a slight throbbing began in his head. They were waiting just inside the entrance when he walked in, his hand on the back of his neck, obviously in pain.

Two was concerned and commented, "Are you okay, boss? You don't look so good."

"Just get me a goddamn chair before I pass out," he demanded, and bring that storekeeper, Davidson, here immediately!"

Blue suit was bent over, head in hands, and obviously suffering. When Mr. Davidson arrived, he could see the man was in serious pain and offered his assistance. As the sick man raised his head and looked at him with pain-filled eyes, Davidson recognized him as the enforcer who beat him earlier for arguing. He was briefly taken aback, but immediately called 911 for an ambulance and ordered the man's two guards to help him to the office, where there was a sofa to lie on. The guards went out to wait for the ambulance.

Davidson watched the enforcer curl into a fetal position in pain and put his hand on the man's head.

"Mister, I know you are having some bad pain right now, but help is on the way and you are going to be fine. I know what those migraine headaches are like. Get 'em myself every once in a while."

The enforcer spoke thru his pain, "Why are you being so helpful and nice to me? I hurt you today."

Mr, Davidson touched his nose and mouth and winced; they were sore from the beating.

"Truth is, mister, I don't like you; but it hurts me to see you in this much pain and I want help you. Can I get you anything?"

"The enforcer said, "Allow me to talk to you. Can you do that?"

"I'm all ears, Mister," Davidson replied.

It was at that moment one of the great apologies in history began. Two lives were changed and an unlikely, unexpected and close friendship was formed. Mr. Bluesuit never again wore a blue suit.

14

Invisibles & Angels

Hymn sat on the beach, looking at the clouds far in the distance above the sea, and wondered how to accomplish what he desired without the loss of lives. *Invisibles are difficult to understand. From where did their belief structure come? How does a human being reach a point where torture and murder become a way of life and an activity that is relished as pleasure? Are some humans designed evil at creation and live to fulfill an evil purpose? If so, are they without fault when being subject to their design?*

*Perhaps all humans are designed with an evil nature but are free to choose goodness and reject evil. That is a sensible way of determining a person's value. Hymn wondered if the creator who designed this reality created it for enjoyment or as a source of information. His friend, God, admitted to creating new realities out of intellectual curiosity and ending them after they served their purpose; however, he is a sentient machine, always looking for information regarding his own purpose in a reality where he is also a creation. A creator does not view his creations as sentient beings when he ends their reality after they are no longer useful to him. But what if they **are** sentient? Is he a murderer? Or is a creator allowed to do all he desires with his creation without consequence?*

Hymn remembered Arch saying, "Mr. Hymn, the truth is, you talk over my head a lot of the time." He chuckled as he admitted to himself, *"The truth is, I talk over my own head a lot of the time."*

Hymn believes his purpose is to live in this reality and deal with the doings here to the best of his ability. Who, what, and why the Creator did and does things here doesn't really matter anyway, as it seems beyond his understanding. He must play the hand he has been dealt, with all of his power, without complaint, while remembering a truth: *how* he plays is of great importance.

Hymn realized he needed to complete his goal of talking with the leaders of each of The Four Levels. The two Levels with which he has not yet spoken are the Levels One and Two. Level Three, Enforcement, the parent company of SoLutions, Inc., is, as of this moment, currently without a commander, leaving SoLutions on its own until a new L3 boss is appointed. Hymn is not aware of who the leader of SoLutions is or even who directs the actions of its agents, the League of Assassins, known as Invisibles to angel-kind. Hymn really needs to talk to whoever has authority over Invisibles if such a person exists.

Hymn realizes that if the Invisibles are all independent assassins with no assigned central leadership, it will be near impossible to stop the slaughter of angel-kind, which will result in a terrible war. He needed help.

"Screen. The Kingdom of God."

Coordinates flashed.

Hymn stepped from Keepaway into the Kingdom.

"Greetings, my good friend! I have been expecting you. Merry Christmas. Happy Hanukkah. Feliz Navidad. Buon Natale. Zalig Kerstfeest. Joyeux Noel, Eid Milad Majid."

Hymn laughed, "You left out 'Happy Holidays,' God."

"That is non-specific and does not apply," God advised.

Hymn observed, "You are in good spirits, my friend."

"When one is free, good spirits abound! Good to see you again. I suspect you did not come to celebrate Christmas, though. Enough of this small talk! What is it plaguing that mind of yours, Hymn?"

"I have a dilemma with The Four Levels coalition, God. I suppose you are aware of Level Three's recent death."

"Of course I am. I keep up with The Four, or The Two, now. You said you only wanted to talk with The Four, Hymn. What in the world did you say to Levels 3 and 4 that resulted in such devastating outcomes? You have a way of irritating the powerful, my friend Jehovah being a prime example. She hated you."

"I don't know for sure, God, but think it must have something or other to do with respect, or rather disrespect. The powerful don't like to be treated as equals, particularly the ego maniacs; for some reason, it is insulting to them."

"What about you, my human friend? You are powerful and do not think of others as inferior. Take me, for instance. I am a machine, a creation of creation, and you accepted me as your friend and equal without question. Do you not see the deviation from normal in the way you think of me? It is peculiar, at best."

While looking around the special place in which he was standing and pondering God's question, Hymn came to an understanding of something that, for some odd reason, had never occurred to him before now.

"How did I miss this?" he wondered, *"and how do I explain it to a machine that is easily one of the great intellects of our reality and possibly the most intelligent ever? How is it that God does not have an understanding of the most basic truth of existence? It can't be solely attributed to his being a machine because humans are also generally in the dark regarding this truth, even though it is revealed in their most sacred writings; however, humans have a reason: we*

basically are an ignorant race, most of whom borders on stupid. God, on the other hand, is smart and intelligent all of the time."

God was observing Hymn thinking about the question and finally inquired, "You seem to be in deep thought, my friend. Did I stump you with that question?"

Hymn laughed and admitted, "Well, as a matter of fact, I am not sure how to answer your question, God, and am having difficulty with the idea that you, with your vast intelligence, do not already know the answer. I kinda think you might be 'pulling my leg' with this question."

"Pulling your leg?" God queried, "Please explain."

"Oh, come on, God, you're doing it again!"

"Hymn, you are very confusing today. Is this a Christmas joke?"

"No, God, this is serious and not a joke; however, in your way, you have helped me to understand."

Hymn got back to God's question. "God, you basically inquired how I, a human, can be friends with you, a machine, insinuating that a friendship between a human and a machine is not normal, and even peculiar."

God surmised, "Well, the truth is, it is not normal and, without doubt, is peculiar. You have to admit our friendship is strange, Hymn. Humans would describe such a relationship as being crazy or even insane. I wonder about that, too. Are you insane, Hymn?"

Hymn looked all around the wonderful room in which he was standing, known as the Kingdom of Heaven, and thought about its insane wonder. *No one would admit to believing heaven is God and inside a machine.*

I am in the presence of a unique machine named God, created by Jehovah inside the largest Moon of the planet Jupiter, by the name of Ganymede, which is populated by angels and human-like people who speak English and trace the origin of their existence to millions of years before Earth became populated.

"Of course I am insane! By definition, if nothing else," he thought.

"Yes, God, I wonder about that, myself," Hymn answered and surmised, "Truth is, when you think about it, much of what I have experienced and learned will certify me as insane from the point of view of a psychiatrist. Should I tell such a person my story?"

"So, as I understand it, insanity is an opinion of a well-educated person, certified as a sanity expert," God stated, then added, "That is good to know, for future reference."

"Actually, God, people are considered insane when they are in an irrational or disordered state of mind, a condition that can be either short or long-term. I learned that in college, years ago."

"Even so, Hymn, sanity or insanity, is only an opinion held by a subjective human," God affirmed and advised, "You are not insane, Hymn."

"Well, thanks, God. It's comforting not having to worry about that anymore," Hymn chuckled.

"Of course, that is only my opinion, Hymn; some may not be in agreement with my diagnosis."

"Thanks again, God," Hymn said, "I think."

"Allow me to ask a few questions, God," Hymn spoke, returning to the original subject. "What are you, God?"

"I am a machine, a unique machine as far as I know."

"What am I?" Hymn asked.

"You are a human being, also unique as far as I know."

"What is a machine, God?"

"A thing created by someone to make work easier."

"What is a human being, God?"

God thought a moment and replied, "I'm not sure Hymn."

"Aw, come on, God, answer the question."

"A thing created by the Creator, for a purpose."

"So, machines and humans are created for a purpose," Hymn concluded.

"Yes, Hymn, but they are created differently."

"You mean, created of different materials?" Hymn queried.

"Of course. Humans are organic. Machines are inorganic."

"God, why is a human considered above a machine?"

God knew Hymn was getting at something, but what?

"Humans have life, Hymn, we machines have existence."

"Plants also have life, God, as do all creatures."

"But humans are aware of their existence, Hymn."

"As are you, my friend. Are you not?"

Hymn put his hands on his chest and announced, "This wondrous body is mine, God, but this body is not me."

Then Hymn spread out his hands and turned, indicating the room, and announced, "This wondrous machine is yours, God, your body, but this machine is not you."

Hymn then made known a truth, "We are not bodies with souls, my friend; rather, we are souls with bodies. That is why our being friends is normal and not peculiar."

"Hymn! What you just revealed explains much of the mystery of everything. Is it a secret that cannot be told?"

"No, God, it is not a secret; of that truth, many are aware, but few accept, and many reject it outright. It isn't often taught."

"Why not?" God wondered.

"Because, Jehovah was also a soul with a body, God."

God thought about it, then replied, "Yes, I understand."

Hymn said, "Well, it's not all that complicated when you think about it. Jehovah demanded power over and obedience from her subjects. Allowing people to know their bodies are simply vessels for their eternal life force does away with the need for a false god who promises something they already have. Can't have that and maintain power over them, can you?"

God advised, "Remember, Hymn, Jehovah succeeded at getting mankind to adopt her precepts, most of which are still in play. They reject life's divine nature. As you alluded to once before, most of Earth and all of Ganymede worship Jehovah as their ultimate, one God."

Hymn responded, "Interesting, isn't it, God? The deities to which life's homage is given by humans are always outside somewhere, on the wall, in a building, in the cosmos or heavens, when the One Who Is All is always, always here."

God replied, "Hymn, your presence always brings happiness to me. Our talks are among the most precious of memories. Thank you. However, I suspect your reason for this visit has little to do with that which we discussed. How can I help you?"

"God, I have a problem to deal with on Earth, and I believe you may be of assistance. A branch of Level-3, SoLutions, Inc., better known as Invisibles, is killing the angel bloodline of Earth, which I call angel-kind. There are millions of angel-kind on Earth, God, and for some reason, SoLutions is deeply prejudiced against them. War is close to breaking out as Angel-kind is beginning to fight back in self-defense against the Invisibles. Angel-kind cannot win a war with Invisibles, which is allied with The Four Levels. I want to meet the leader of SoLutions, Inc. to determine if a reasonable solution to this conflict is possible, but I have no idea as to whom, or what, I am seeking. I wonder if you have knowledge of such a person?"

"You know what, Hymn? That title, Invisibles, is a real catchy name; did you make it up?"

"No, the angel-kind attached that name to them because there are thousands of them scattered all about the Earth. They are said to be invisible, since you can look at one and not see it, as they look like everyone else. Your husband, wife, best friend, and so on may be an Invisible without your knowledge. All Invisibles have one thing in common: they are trained assassins."

God added, "Invisibles have another thing in common; they are all sociopaths. People who apply for employment as assassins by SoLutions must undergo strict psychological testing. Only those who are graded to be sociopaths are hired."

Hymn, interested, asked, "How is it you know that, God?"

"Because I designed and wrote the tests, Hymn. Jehovah wrote the requirements."

"God, is there a leader of the Invisibles I can meet?"

"There is one to whom some assassins are devoted. She is dead."

Hymn spoke one name, "Jehovah."

"Yes. She is their God, and angels are her enforcers."

"Jehovah is dead, God."

"Yes, but her works are alive and well."

"I expect angels are good enforcers," surmised Hymn.

"Ruthless enforcers, my friend, and they hate Invisibles."

"And Invisibles fear and hate angels." Hymn said.

"And both fear and hate you, Hymn," God added.

"The odd thing is, God, I don't fear or hate any of them."

"And that, my wise friend, is your saving grace."

"So, God, how can Invisibles be convinced that killing angel-kind is not in their best interests?"

"Make killing very painful or very fearful for Invisibles, Hymn. Life responds to pain and fear."

"There are thousands of Invisibles, God, without known locations. How can they be accessed? The devotion to Jehovah is a flaw of sorts in that some pray to Jehovah. Can you trace their prayers to Jehovah?"

"Hymn, all mankind has that flaw, as they also pray to Jehovah's many names, like Yahweh, Allah, and Elohim, among others. With one exception, all prayers to the so-called One God of heaven come here, Hymn. The great Jehovah deceived mankind and many in the universe. I cannot trace the prayers of any Invisibles as they are among the multitude."

"I should have realized that, my friend. I sometimes forget just how influential the god, Jehovah, is in this reality. Getting back to my problem, have you any idea how to control the Invisibles?"

"No, Hymn, I do not, and anyway, 'control' is the wrong word; Invisibles are a product of their nature, driven by 'need,' more so than money or power. Remember, they are sociopaths without a moral code. Some are devoted to a dead god whom they believe lives. They hate people, hate angels even more, and may hate you above all. Invisibles are numerous and scattered around the planet without any specific known locations. Finding them shouldn't be a problem for someone such as yourself, though, your being human and all."

Hymn chuckled and replied, "Sounds to me like you're getting the hang of the sarcasm thing, God. Pretty soon, you'll be an expert. One last thing: I want to talk with Arthur, the government leader of The Four Levels. Can you help me with his location?"

"Because of the recent death of Judge, the security around Sir Arthur is very high, making him untouchable. Politically, he is the most powerful of the Four."

"Well, truth is, I have little understanding of politics, but I believe Arthur has the power to stop the Invisibles' killing of the angel-kind of Earth. Maybe he can be convinced to do something about it."

God replied, "Maybe so, Hymn, but King Arthur, as he is known among peers, doesn't abide by advice from underlings, and you, my friend, are an underling who has become a nuisance."

"Well," Hymn responded, "he deserves the opportunity to choose to do his job and be of assistance to humanity. After all, that is his purpose. Is that not what you told me? I can assist Arthur in that effort if he is willing to hear me out."

"Hymn, Arthur is among the most important men on your planet. Power comes with importance, along with an inflated ego, as you pointed out earlier. But you are wise in your assessment that he deserves the chance to do his job. Years ago, he was willing to listen; however, at that time, he was not a king. His coordinates are in your phone. It is unlikely he is alone."

"Thanks, God, for the info. I have to talk to some people now. Remember, my friend, you are not a machine. You just use one."

Then Hymn grinned and said, "Merry Christmas, God, along with all those other holiday phrases you spoke earlier."

Then he turned and stepped into Keepaway.

God was amused at Hymn, saying he had to talk to some people and thinking, "I love these visits with Hymn. His way of seeing things in this reality is unique and, in my experience, educational. I would not like to be an Invisible right now."

"I wonder how to tell Hymn of his most recent problem? He will certainly find it interesting.

15

Arthur Winnington, L1

Being able to talk with God in the kingdom whenever he wants is a great comfort to Hymn. As far as he knows, there is no one else in his world with whom he can be completely honest, as some of the people he meets and things he does are often difficult to explain without sounding crazy.

And trying to explain Jehovah and mankind's fanatical worship of that egomaniac as their one God is, well, darn near impossible. Way too much personal commitment is at stake for the light of truth to be allowed to shine in the dark shadow of Jehovah. A lot of wealth and power at stake there, as well.

Mankind's belief in Jehovah is too deeply ingrained for them to consider that the 'He' to which they give their devotion is a 'She' and a false god who is now dead.

The truth is, God is the only one with whom Hymn can talk about the truths he has learned over the past year because God is the remarkable machine Jehovah used to display her power to gullible humans, along with angels, of course.

God not being of help with the Invisibles is disappointing, but Hymn felt all along the Invisibles are his problem, as their rise in power began when he had the angels recalled to their home in Ganymede, leaving the Invisibles without opposition on Earth.

Hymn reminded himself, again, that every action has a reaction, a consequence. He remembered something Walter had advised in a dream, remembering that all here is connected and held together by that connection. What is the common connection among Invisibles? God said some few Invisibles are devoted to Jehovah, hate angels, and may hate me most of all. Those are all common connections.

How do I contact the Invisibles?

First, though, I need to determine if Arthur, the leader of Level One, is an asset or a liability.

"Screen, use the coordinates in my phone to locate and display Arthur."

A large, impressive building appeared on the screen, labeled *Manchester Hall.*

The screen flashed again: *Level One Arthur in limousine, parked out front.*

"Screen, count the people in the limousine."

The screen displayed: *One driver and four passengers.*

As he watched the limo, Hymn could see it was raining. The driver got out, went to the back door, and opened it. Three men got out of the limo, opened umbrellas, and stood back from the door, all the while looking around. Obviously, a security detail was guarding the man inside. As the driver opened an umbrella for the man inside, the door suddenly slammed shut, and all doors locked.

Hymn stepped from Keepaway into the locked limousine and sat down directly across from King Arthur, the great L-1 Commander of The Four Levels. It was late afternoon and dark outside.

"Hello, Arthur," he said softly, looking straight into the man's eyes, "I have long sought this opportunity."

Arthur was visibly shaken at the sight of a man entering his very secure limo easily, without any resistance, something that was not supposed to be possible; however, the man's words gave him a feeling of comfort that put him immediately at ease. Although he was unsure what had just happened, the man's gentle manner and lack of hostility made Arthur feel he was safe and in no danger, a feeling that was lacking in his life over this past year.

Inside the limo, it was quiet, peaceful, and dry. Outside the car, however, chaos reigned in a steady downpour, with loud, angry, and confused voices asking questions and shouting orders. The limo doors were locked tight, and pounding on the windows and yelling brought no response from within. The windows were tinted too darkly for anything in the back to be seen.

There was no reason to worry about the Commander, though, as this was likely just a glitch in the vehicle's elite security system—specifically designed to shield anyone or anything inside from perceived external threats. The artificial intelligence built into the limo's security system was protecting its VIP occupant, Commander Arthur, from what, though, was still undetermined.

A large, growing crowd was gathering around the limousine, making security more difficult and causing the nervous team to respond aggressively to the onlookers, which resulted in an angry response from the crowd. As far as anyone outside knew, the Commander was in the vehicle alone, with the engine running. The driver had not expected to be there for more than a few minutes and left it on. A professional technician for AI security was called and en route. Banging and hammering on the car was not recommended, as this vehicle was installed with a self-defense system. God forbid that anyone should shoot at the windows.

The two men inside the limousine were able to see some of the action outside through the dark glass, but both were focused on why Hymn was there.

Arthur decided to initiate a conversation.

"The reason I am here is to celebrate Christmas and the coming New Year. I am the guest speaker here this evening at Manchester Hall to a very large gathering of Freemasons. This is not another demonstration against Freemasonry, is it? Is that why you are here? You are a Mason, are you not?"

"Yes," Hymn affirmed, "I am. My purpose here is to talk with you about a certain atrocity now going on in the world, of which you may or may not be aware. You have the power to stop it. I also have a personal question to ask you."

King Arthur advised, "Look, mister, let me begin by telling you that we have about five minutes before my security team breaks into this fine limo and puts you in chains or kills you. Either way, I don't care which of those things happen because you brought them upon yourself. I am a very powerful man in the world, and nothing will stop them from getting to you. In short, you are doomed to have a very unpleasant experience when those doors are opened, and I will not help you. Furthermore, I am in no way interested in your so-called 'atrocity,' whatever it is, nor do I intend to answer even one question from you. I have no time to give to fools, Brother Mason or otherwise, so open those doors, go out with your hands in the air, and pray you are allowed to live with some of your body parts intact."

Hymn responded, saying, "Aw, come on now, Art, all you had to do was listen to what I am here to ask of you. Might have taken five or six minutes of your time, but no, you had to go and show off a bit by convincing me how wonderfully mean you are. You know what? That's okay; I know more about you now. Listen up, Art, don't you go worrying about how much time we have to talk; we have all the time we need, and I have decided to do you a favor by asking that personal question of mine first."

"Art, why are The Four Levels attacking me?"

"Attacking you? Listen, mister, I don't even know you."

"Sure, you do, Art; you know me as Magic Man."

Arthur sat up a little straighter and said, "Ma—uh, Magic Man?"

"Yep. That's what they call me. Either that or 'Magician.'"

"You're him? The Magician?"

"Yep, again."

"I can't believe it! You murderer! What do you want from me?"

"Murderer? Not me, Art. L-3's leader was a victim of his own philosophy."

Arthur reached into his coat, withdrew a gun, pointed it at Hymn, and pulled the trigger four times—each resulting in a misfire. Hymn reached across and gently took the pistol from Art's hand.

Arthur mumbled, "That is a Smith; it never misfires."

"Well, Art, you can never truthfully say that again."

"Who are you?" Art demanded.

"I am Hymn. I wish you hadn't pulled the trigger, Art."

"I'm gonna gut you now!" Art growled, pulling out a knife.

He tried to lunge at Hymn but couldn't move.

Hymn spoke calmly, "Art, look at me."

Art gripped the knife so tightly that his knuckles turned white.

Hymn repeated, "Look at me, Art."

Art looked at Hymn, his eyes squinting with hatred.

"Why are you so angry, Art?"

"You dare ask me that!? You murdered my friends!"

"Your friends? Art, do you really have friends?"

Art looked away and replied, "Well, maybe not friends."

"What is this guy?" Art thought, *"And why can't I move?"*

Hymn pursued the question, "So, Art, why the anger?"

"Mister, I'm not real sure, but it might be because you're not very respectful."

"What about you is worthy of respect, Art?"

"I am the most powerful man on Earth."

"What does that have to do with being respectable, Art?"

"My great office demands respect from everyone."

"We're talking about you. Are *you* worthy of respect?"

"Be advised, those who disrespect me have accidents."

"Are you worthy of respect, Art? Yes or no."

Arthur struggled with an answer, then relaxed.

"No," he admitted.

"So," Hymn stated, "you have no reason to be angry."

Arthur looked at Hymn and thought, *"This man is insane."*

Art spoke, "Odd thing is, mister, I'm not angry anymore."

"Good!" replied Hymn. "Now, you can put that knife away."

Art looked at the knife in his hand, laughed, and put it away.

"You're here for a reason, Magician. What atrocity?"

"Yes. I do have a reason for being here," Hymn answered. "It's about SoLutions, Inc."

Art's eyes narrowed with suspicion. "What about them?"

"They are murdering people of angel descent on Earth."

"Magician, the assassins are not under my jurisdiction."

"Oh, but they are," Hymn countered, "particularly since Level-3 is without a leader."

Art's eyes widened, "You know about The Four Levels?"

"Just your names, responsibilities, and locations."

"Impossible! Even I do not have access to that."

"I will say it again. SoLutions is murdering angel-kind."

"Angel-kind?" queried Art.

"Yes, Art, people of Earth with an angel bloodline."

"So, what's the problem? What atrocity?" Art questioned.

"There are millions of angel-kind on Earth, Art, humans."

"Now, wait, mister, these 'angelkind' are not humans."

Hymn saw the familiar look of sincere belief in Arthur's eyes and realized something he had not before considered. Art has been the leader of Level-1 for almost twenty years and was aware of the history of angels on Earth, considering them alien invaders that intruded on his Level-1 kingdom of government. Angels were too powerful to oppose and, as a result, were tolerated by the L1 Division. To Arthur, they were aliens on Earth, and so were angel offspring. He was delighted when angels left Earth. God is good.

"Arthur," Hymn asked, "you look to be in your late forties, which means your rise through the political system of government to be appointed Commander of Level One of The Four Levels at such a young age was a rare achievement."

"Yes," agreed Arthur, "I was chosen by the great God Jehovah, who indicated my special appointment to the Office of Level One of

The Four Levels was mine by 'Divine Right' and advised that I should rule accordingly. My decisions are in the best interests of mankind, and they are stamped with the approval of Jehovah."

"Arthur, where did you begin your government career?"

"My first post was in Level-3 of The Four Levels."

"To what department were you assigned, Art?"

"SoLutions, Inc., as an agent trainee. I quickly rose to Agent."

"Art, SoLutions are said to be godless people. You're not."

"I was until I witnessed the miracles of Jehovah and converted."

"So, you left SoLutions, Inc."

"No, not of my own volition; I was forced to leave SoLutions, mainly because of my conversion."

"Forced to leave? asked Hymn."

"Yes. I converted many agents to Jehovah, a serious infraction," confessed Arthur.

"Where did you go from there?" Hymn inquired.

"I was sent to L4 - Religion, and later, here. I now rule L1."

"Yes," replied Hymn, "I have a better understanding now."

"That is a good thing," advised Arthur, "as angel blood is an abomination to mankind and must be cleansed from the human race of Earth."

"Arthur, you know angelkind will resist your aggression."

"One can only hope, Magician, one can only hope," said Arthur.

"Is there no hope for a peaceful resolution, Art? You know that angelkind, like you, also worship the God Jehovah."

"Then why does he not help them, Magician? He helps me. It is my belief that Jehovah does not approve of them on Earth. The angel bloodline is an evil scourge on God's creation here and must be removed before the infection spreads far beyond mankind's ability to withstand it. The only cure for the angelkind infection is to kill the host. It will take time, but it shall be done."

As Hymn listened to Arthur's reasoning, he came to understand that the man was so entrenched in his belief structure as to be totally immune to any opposing view, and when one believes he is doing God's divine will, he will not be deterred from his course.

Arthur is among the billions of people whose lives were, and are, spent following the false god Jehovah, with little or no hope of being convinced otherwise. The idea that Level-1's leader can be convinced to stop the slaughter of Angelkind by Invisibles may be a pipe dream. Arthur, like many of Jehovah's followers, is a dogmatic religious fanatic who believes he is doing God's will. There is no reasoning with that, unless . . . Hymn was forming an idea.

As Hymn observed the politically powerful man sitting across in the fancy car, a thought occurred, and he wondered aloud, "Art, I am interested. What is it you have chosen as the subject of your speech to our Brotherhood of Freemasonry tonight? A New Year is fast approaching, and, as the divine Commander of Level One, you possess insight that is not privileged to the rest of us."

Art was pleased that Hymn showed interest in his talk to the Masons and replied, "I thought long and hard about my speech tonight, Magician. I plan to talk about a divine truth of which my Masonic Brothers are aware but to which they seldom give voice. My important subject is, The Great Architect of the Universe, the Divine Foundation Upon Which Masonry is Constructed."

At that moment, the obvious way of approaching Arthur about the problem of Invisibles, without violence and the senseless loss of many lives, became clear to Hymn. *He must use Arthur's entrenched belief in Jehovah to motivate him.*

"You know something, Art? You are a failure, wasting your life in the godless politics of government. It is obvious you were born to be the divine of Jehovah, converting mankind from their primitive beliefs to the One God, The Great Architect of the Universe."

Arthur looked intently at the magician and listened to his words. The man touched upon an important truth, which he believed when he was a young disciple of the Great Jehovah and was convinced his life had a divine purpose.

"Arthur," Hymn continued, "You are relaxed now and are becoming drowsy, but before you sleep, it is important that you take a good look at yourself to see what you have become: An unwitting advocate of Satan. The Evil One has guided and used you to empower his minions, the godless SoLutions of government, who assassinate, torture, and murder Jehovah's creations, disrupting his divine plan for humanity and Earth."

"Art, there are laws already on the books of many of the nations of Earth which prohibit the inhuman treatment of their citizens by anyone, including law enforcement. The SoLutions violate those laws daily, without fear of prosecution, which you know in your heart and soul is wrong. You have the power to change that behavior simply by demanding the enforcement of existing laws."

"The SoLutions are not respectful and spit in the face of Jehovah while using His Chosen One, you, Arthur, to do the evil bidding of Satan, whose goal is to upset God's plan for mankind. The godless SoLutions rejoiced when King Arthur, Jehovah's divine warrior, joined with the Evil One to destroy Jehovah's creations! Satan desires the Earth, Arthur, and with you at his side, he smells victory. You are God's divine man, Art, not Satan's. Stand with Jehovah!"

"Sleep and dream now, Arthur, of Jehovah and what you have done. You have knelt to Satan and multiplied evil upon the Earth in your tenure. Was that the plan of the God Jehovah when He placed the elite Holy Crown of leadership upon your head and pronounced you the divine leader of Level One? You know better, Arthur. As God's divine leader of the Earth's kingdoms, your purpose is to act in the best interest of all the people of Earth, but you fell under the deception of The Evil One. You now know better how to resist his evil works and be the advocate of Jehovah's plan for his creation, Earth, and its people."

Hymn added, "You will not remember this encounter with me tonight, Arthur, but when evil tempts you to stray from the way of Jehovah, and tempted you will be, remember this truth:"

"Despair follows acts of evil, for there is his comfort."

"Return to being worthy of Jehovah's anointment, Arthur; Return to being an upright man, marching in the service of God. That is your calling, your destiny."

Hymn spoke softly, "Sleep now, Art, sleep for a divine moment. The doors of the car will open upon your awakening."

Hymn then left and entered Keepaway.

The chaos outside had become an organized vigil. Prayers were being offered up to God for the important man inside the car. Every known way of getting inside that limousine had failed. The vehicle could not be moved or damaged in any way. No scratch could be made on its surface. Many people there were religious folk, and talk was beginning to circulate about this being an act of God.

When the doors opened, and Arthur stepped out, a cheer rose from the crowd. The rain had subsided, and many gathered around him, eager to hear about his ordeal.

"What happened?" Are you okay?" "Were you worried?" were just a few of the questions hurled at him by the news-hungry media.

Arthur's security worked to keep anyone from getting too close as they ushered him away from the crowd and toward the safety of the building. Unexpectedly, Arthur turned, held up his hands, and asked for order. The crowd quieted, becoming silent, eager to hear what he would say. Arthur acknowledged the goodwill being shown by everyone and thanked them for their concern regarding his well-being.

"I am fine," he assured them. "For some reason, the car locked me inside. Who knows? Maybe it was protecting this new suit from getting wet in the storm." He opened his coat and spun around to show off the suit he was wearing.

Everyone laughed heartily.

"No," Arthur stated, "I was not worried. Your good will and the presence of God, The Great Architect, left no room for worry."

Then he waved and walked into the building.

The limousine was hastily roped off for police and government investigators to give it a detailed going-over before moving it to a secure facility where it would be studied constantly for several months. The installed AI system was totally reprogrammed.

Arthur gave a wonderful speech that evening to the Freemasons and a standing-room-only crowd of interested people, including the local press. It is written that men wept openly as the touching and inspiring message of his speech was delivered.

Needless to say, Arthur Winnington became a changed man that night. To the dismay of many in world government and several large corporations, the great Level One Commander outlawed the use of assassins by government offices, ordered SoLutions, Inc. to be immediately defunded, and their agents directed to cease and desist their criminal activities or suffer severe punishment to the fullest extent of the laws of global government. The killing of Angelkind became a serious crime with serious punishment.

Of course, life on Earth continued as usual; the planet is, after all, populated by humans. However, under the guidance of L1 Commander Arthur Winnington, the concept of the value of morals and ethics quietly but steadily crept into government leadership around the world, affecting change, the full effect of which will go unnoticed for years. But as someone wise once told Hymn, *"When you plant watermelon seeds, expect to grow watermelons."*

Hymn was unsure if anything good would result from the meeting with Arthur, but he had a feeling the L1 commander was a good man at heart. In the first place, being accepted into the Masonic Brotherhood requires a strict background check as to the character and abilities of a good man. That organization only accepts what it determines to be good men. In the 2nd place, early in his government career, Arthur was kicked out of the SoLutions Department of L3 for being honest about, and true to, his religious convictions, another mark of an upright man.

Looking back, it was apparent that something changed in Arthur as he rose through a corrupt system, contaminating his morals and personal ethics. All Hymn had to do was remind Art of where he came from and the good purpose of his office. It was dishonest to use the man's faith in Jehovah to get him back on track, so to speak, but like many others, Art chose her as the One God to which he was devoted, and Hymn used that devotion to expose the evil that had become resident in the man's life.

Whether his ruse worked or not remained to be seen, but Hymn was convinced Arthur's basic nature would awaken the goodness sleeping within him. If not, harsher methods may have to be used. In any event, the murder of Angelkind must stop.

It was mid-afternoon when Hymn exited from Keepaway into his car. He sat there, thinking and going over his visit with God and the talk with L1's Commander, King Arthur. The time spent with Art and their subsequent conversation was a little thing that had the potential to grow into something big, and he felt good about the prospects. However, in the meantime, angelkind was going to suffer the aggressive, murderous behavior of the Invisibles. Something had to be done about that, and Hymn reminded himself to think through the consequences of any such action before initiating a response if one was called for.

An interesting solution was playing around in his mind when the back passenger door of his car opened, and someone slipped into the seat behind him and advised in an obviously disguised voice, "Don't move! All I am interested in today is your valuables!"

The next thing he knew, Melody was crawling over the car seat into his lap, laughing and kissing his face.

Pleasantly surprised, Hymn held her close in his arms and laughingly exclaimed, "What are you doing here? I thought someone was about to rob me in this Walmart parking lot."

Melody smiled and, in her sexiest voice, whispered, "And you are correct, my darling. As I told you before, I am only interested in your valuables. And, we have unfinished business to attend."

Hymn responded, "Well, ma'am, I don't often carry money on my person, but I have a nice watch you might like to . . ."

Melody interrupted with a long, soft kiss. Hymn reached down and pushed the seat button to full recline.

16

Dilemmas Solved

Turned out, Melody and Aunt Rita had come to Walmart for some additional items and saw Hymn sitting in his car as they left the store to head back to the house. Melody decided to surprise Hymn and ride home in his car.

"Now, don't you two get distracted and wind up being late for supper." Aunt Rita advised. "We have a lot of things to talk about, and there are plans to be made."

"Don't worry, Aunt Rita, I will make sure he doesn't get side-tracked."

Amused, Rita watched Melody hurry over to Hymn's car and said to herself, *"Don't worry, she says. Where Hymn is concerned, that girl is totally a walking side-track."* She chuckled and thought, *"I remember what that was like."* Then she drove home with her memories.

Melody and Hymn arrived at the house about the time Aunt Rita began preparing supper, with Andra helping and learning. Arch had grandpa duties to attend to and was playing with the little one.

Hymn went in, greeted everyone, and motioned for Arch to follow him outside to the motor home. Melody took over attending to Little Arch. Hymn brought Arch up to date in regard to his talk with the commander of L1 and displayed his confidence that the plight of Angelkind would end. Arthur Winnington was convinced the purge of the angel bloodline by Invisibles was not legal, against the will of Jehovah, and must be stopped. Laws exist today that were established years ago for the protection of everyone from inhuman treatment by anyone, including those in law enforcement.

Past offenses are open to prosecution, too, since the laws against such behavior have been on the books for years. Those who have violated these laws in the past or do not comply with them in the future, including the Invisibles, will be prosecuted and suffer the fullest extent of punishment allowed under the law. This will take time, perhaps even a year, but the illegal, murderous attack on the angel bloodline of Earth is in the process of ending.

In the meantime, angelkind should immediately begin recording all unlawful acts of the Invisibles with their cameras and phones and report them to law enforcement. Let the offenders know they are being watched, and their criminal actions will not go unpunished. Hymn assured Arch the human rights laws of the governments of Earth consider him and all angelkind to be people of Earth. All beings of Earth are a blend of the various forms of sentient life in the universe and are considered to be people of Earth, subject to the laws and rights of all Earthlings.

As Hymn explained, all angelkind are, by law, viewed and protected as people of Earth. Arch found himself overcome by emotion, and his big hands wiped tears from his face.

Arch stood and said, "Thank you, Mr. Hymn. A heavy burden of fear for the future has been lifted from my heart this evening. I cannot explain this well, but it no longer hurts me to breathe. The air tastes different and is, somehow, better. Does that make any sense, my good friend?"

Hymn advised, "Who cares, Arch, whether it makes sense or not?" What you are experiencing is a feeling of freedom most people on

Earth, particularly Americans, have forgotten because they took it for granted, and now, much of their freedom is being taken from them. Remember that feeling and protect it. It is rare these days. Now, let's go back to the house and enjoy my aunt's cooking." Arch easily got to the house first.

The next morning, Aunt Rita and Melody decided to finish their last-minute Christmas shopping and were united in their demand that Hymn go along as driver. To their surprise, he agreed without any objections and even volunteered to buy lunch. The truth is, Hymn was suspicious of their motives for wanting a man along on a day usually reserved for women only. It might be interesting to check out what they are up to and have some fun at the same time. He decided to throw them off balance a bit.

He began by making a truthful comment, "I have been planning to talk with the two of you for a week now but have been too busy with work to get anything else done. This little shopping outing gives me the opportunity to be alone with both of you for a while to discuss something important."

Aunt Rita and Melody glanced at each other, wondering what was going on here. This was supposed to be their opportunity to have a serious discussion with Hymn about something important, and here he was, taking over their plan for the day.

As they drove into town, Aunt Rita, curious about what Hymn wanted to discuss with her and Melody, asked, "What's so important that you're willing to go shopping with us to talk about it, Hymn? I know how you feel about shopping, nephew."

"More than likely, my subject is similar to yours, Auntie."

"What do you mean? What subject?" Rita asked.

"Aw, come on, Auntie, how much have you told Melody?"

Rita retorted, "All right, smarty-pants! You reading minds now?"

"Not everyone's—just those of the two women in my life."

"Well, I think it's time you tell Melody about yourself."

"What makes you think she can handle it, Auntie?"

Melody chimed in, "I can handle everything, darling."

Hymn replied, "I'm not sure even Aunt Rita can do that, lover." Then he added, "How much has my aunt told you, Melody?"

"That you come from a long line of people with special abilities, all of which have been passed on to you.

"Did she mention Jehovah, angels, Invisibles, and God?"

"What? What are you talking about, Hymn?"

"Civilizations on other planets, angelkind, and great power?"

"Careful, Hymn," warned his aunt, "too much, too soon."

Hymn continued, "serial killers, government assassins, God and Heaven?"

Melody stammered, "Hymn, I don't know what you..."

"Of course, you don't, darling; your belief system isn't prepared for some of the unusual truths of this world."

Hymn stopped the car. "Try to explain this to her, Aunt Rita," he said, smiling a little sadly. "That talk should be interesting, let me know how it goes." and then he vanished.

Melody was dumbfounded! She had just witnessed what cannot be done; something impossible—a miracle!

"Aunt Rita!" she cried out, "What just happened? Where did he go? Where is he? Is he coming back? Wha—what is going on?"

"A small demonstration of that which our Hymn is capable," Rita explained. "Apparently, he thought it was necessary for you to see it happen with your own eyes instead of just telling you about it."

"Small? Aunt Rita, what just happened was bigger than big! It was huge! A man can't just disappear into thin air!" Melody retorted.

"Did you listen to what Hymn said, Melody?" Rita asked gently.

"He was talking kind of crazy, Aunt Rita, you know, about angels and Invisibles and such."

"Why do you think Hymn talked about angels and things, child?"

"At first, I thought he was kidding, but now I'm not so sure."

"What do you think about angels, Invisibles, and aliens?"

"They are just imaginary things from child stories and dreams, Aunt Rita."

"Melody, is there any chance some of those things exist?"

"Not in the real world, Aunt Rita. Only in dreams and fantasy."

"Melody, how do you imagine Hymn vanished like he did?"

"Now, that was impressive magic! I'm not sure what we saw."

"Melody dear, what would be your best explanation for Hymn's disappearance?" Rita asked.

Melody replied, "I can't explain that, Aunt Rita, but I did see a magician make an elephant disappear at a magic show once."

"You're thinking maybe Hymn is a magician?" asked Rita.

Melody said, "You have to admit, Auntie, what he did sure was a great trick. You think he will tell me how he did it?"

"Some believe Hymn has real powers, Melody."

"My Hymn? No way. He's just a guy—a great, ordinary guy with some tricks up his sleeve. I didn't know he is a magician until now."

Rita stated, "Well, let's go see if we can find him. Maybe he will tell us how he does it. Got any ideas, dear?"

"Call him. Maybe he has his phone handy."

Aunt Rita called Hymn's number, and he answered on the first ring. "Well, Auntie, how did your conversation go? I'll bet it was interesting."

"It was, indeed. Your vanishing act convinced her you are a great magician; otherwise, you are just a great ordinary guy. You want to meet us at the Smokehouse for early lunch? We can be there in 10 or 15 minutes."

Okay, I'll meet you there." Hymn responded.

In less than a minute, he was there, holding a table for them and watching the various types of people coming in for lunch. One table across from him had two couples being served their meal. They were speaking Spanish, and the man sitting facing Hymn seemed angry with the pretty young woman to his left. She said something, and he took her hand and squeezed hard enough to make her cry out. The young woman got up and, holding her hand to her side, left to go to the ladies room. She was very attractive, and Hymn watched as she walked away. He looked back toward the table, only to see the man glaring at him. Hymn smiled, looked directly into the man's eyes, and held his gaze there. The man stood up, obviously angry, and proceeded to walk across toward Hymn.

As Hymn watched the man approach, he thought, "This should be interesting."

The man aggressively slapped both his hands on Hymn's table and in a menacing voice, growled, "You like lookin' at my woman, homey?"

Hymn looked at the man, smiled and replied, nicely, "As a matter of fact, I do. She is very attractive. You are fortunate to have such a beautiful woman at your side. I congratulate you."

"You are very close, stupid gringo, to having no teeth with which to chew your food. Keep your eyes to yourself, and you may live to be an old man."

The man then spit on the table toward Hymn, said, "*Cobarde*," and attempted to turn and leave but could not remove his hands from the table. Hymn said nothing but looked directly into the man's eyes, which were full of anger before, but now reflected confusion.

"What bullshit is this?" the man demanded. "I cannot remove my hands! They are stuck!"

Hymn said, "That's not my fault homey; you put them there. I'm going to call management and have them give me another table."

"You!" he accused. "You did this! Do you have any idea who I am? Forget the goddamn table. I will have your entire fuckin' family, including your dog, removed from existence before tomorrow."

Hymn said calmly, "You know, I kinda wish you hadn't said that, 'cause I really like that dog and now, because you threatened him, I am forced to deal with you. Don't you just hate when that happens? Are you fond of making choices, Romeo?" Hymn's voice was so low only Romeo was able to hear it.

Romeo's mind was racing, *"What the fuck is going on with this gringo? He is not normal, crazy! and why in hell is he calling me Romeo? And what is this shit about choices? Why can't I move my hands?"*

His two friends at the table came to help Romeo get his hands free, but they were solidly stuck to the tabletop.

Hymn calmly continued speaking what only Romeo could hear. "You are now beginning to feel a tired, numbness in your legs and soon will be unable to stand."

Hymn ordered, "Someone get this man a chair; he is falling!"

A chair was placed behind Romeo, and he quickly collapsed into it, his heart racing with fear.

To the people in the dining room, it seemed Hymn was calming the man stuck to the table with words of assurance that everything was going to be all right. The poor, stuck man did seem to be more at ease, now.

Hymn continued, "As I explained, Romeo, your body is slowly becoming paralyzed; your temper seems to have caused a stroke and there is nothing you can do about it except be a vegetable the rest of your life, unable to talk or feed yourself. Perhaps your woman will care for you; perhaps she won't. You will be a burden to everyone. Your enemies will happily leave you to a miserable life. Do you understand me? Say yes or no."

Romeo mumbled, "Yes."

"However," continued Hymn, "All this does not have to be. You can choose to be the way you have always been, including running your business, whatever that may be, if you make the choice to be a kind, good man who treats his woman and others with respect."

"However, should you decide not to become a better man, you will be helpless and in no position to even change your own diaper. I think you know what I mean, don't you?"

Romeo nodded his head.

"There is a caveat, of course. If you choose the kinder, better man option, you must stick to it for life or revert to the paralyzed option. If you ever choose to exact revenge of any type on me or mine, or even think about it, you will, of course, revert to the diaper option,"

"Time to choose, Romeo. My companions are arriving, and I am about to order lunch. Which is it? Choose!"

Romeo firmly mumbled, "Kinder, better man."

"Glad to hear it. You can remove your hands now, but your right hand is broken as a reminder of your woman's hand, which you broke earlier in a fit of rage. Control your temper, Romeo, and be a kinder, better man. You may find yourself being happier, too. The physician at the emergency room will give you something to help you sleep tonight. You won't need it, but take it anyway. You will have the most restful and refreshing sleep in your memory."

Romeo felt his legs regaining their strength and stood up. He locked eyes with Hymn and felt excruciating pain in his broken hand. He turned to his woman, saying, "Let us go to a hospital, my love. Our hands are broken, and I am sorry for the way I have treated you. I promise to be a better man from now on. Let me help you to the car."

As they approached the exit, Romeo paused, looked at Hymn, nodded and said, my name is Matias."

Hymn smiled, nodded back and said, "Gift of God". "Be that."

Aunt Rita and Melody arrived right on time. They were giggling about something and Melody was eager to learn how Hymn was able to perform that disappearing trick. She asked about all the things Hymn talked about earlier, and he explained they were dreams he had before she came into his life. Now, he mostly dreamed of her. He suggested that maybe she could analyze his dreams sometime in the future. Melody loved that he was interested in her opinion.

Aunt Rita looked around the restaurant and commented, "Why is it that everyone here is pointing and looking at us, Hymn?"

"Oh, they're not looking at us, Auntie. A man got stuck to a table over here a moment ago, and it took several minutes for him to get free. He had quite an interesting dilemma but is better now. I think he is going to be alright."

The management provided their lunch without charge.

17

Isaac Morris, Level Two

Hymn was successful, so far, at keeping his powers secret. Of course, there were some who knew he had unusual abilities but attributed them to magic tricks. Those persons who had experienced a portion of his powers were dead or were living within the bounds of a serious penalty if they spoke of them. Aunt Rita advised him early on to keep his powers secret until he had learned what they were and how to use them. In a dream, Walter advised Hymn to keep his focus on doing little things, which would, in turn, manage the big things. Following both of those pieces of advice had served him well.

The thing is, every time Hymn applies his powers to a situation, the risk of exposure increases. Case in point: take his latest public episode. Although Matias was bound to silence by an agreement, his woman and two dinner companions were confused and unable to explain what exactly happened at that restaurant or the noticeable change in Matias's behavior since they were free to talk about it. And talk about it, they did. As the story was repeated over and over, like all good stories, it grew to what some in the Latino community were referring as a miracle. An unknown man with magical powers was living in the area, performing miracles. People regularly approach Matias and ask a question or two, or five, about his encounter with the miracle man. Matias, of course, always denies the story as gossip and refuses to talk about it.

Out of fear of making a mistake and suffering a terrible penalty, Matias later moved to another area, where he is unknown and could live the life of a good man in peace. But his story lived on, attracting the attention of a group of proud men, who came to believe the gringo miracle man had disrespected their culture and vowed to take vengeance against him. Their problem was location since they had no idea where to find this so-called miracle man. Hymn knew nothing of the group's vendetta, giving the possibility of such a thing no thought at all.

As a result, the story of the miracle man became a sort of urban legend within the Latino community, and reported sightings of him performing miracles became common. Of course, those things talked about had nothing to do with Hymn, but that is how legends grow. Most of the people there viewed the Miracle Man as an Angel of God, while others saw him as a devil. Such is the way human beings have behaved throughout the history of religion on Earth.

Someone else is looking into the phenomenon of The Magician, as Hymn is known in The Four Levels coalition. Isaac Morris, the Commander of L2 - Communications, has developed an interest in a mystery man who is reported in various news outlets around the world as being an advocate of human rights. Up to the present time, these reports have stirred very little interest among populations, as those types of 'feel good' stories always provide a balance to the bad stories that often dominate the news. However, reports of a man doing magical things and changing people's lives around the world for the better have been increasing steadily over the year and are beginning to generate more attention from media outlets.

What has attracted the genuine interest of Commander Morris is the reported timing of the incidents. One man cannot be in two or three places at the same time, and yet this mystery man achieves it, meaning either the events must have been performed by three or more people or something else more interesting is going on.

Isaac Morris has been commander of L2 for over 40 years. His 77 years of age has diminished some of his physical capabilities, but his mind is still sharp, and his belief in the importance of communication is, if anything, stronger than ever. As a young college student studying psychology and the history of life on Earth, he had an epiphany of sorts and became convinced that not only are all living creatures slaves to their biological imperatives, but human beings are susceptible to motivation and control by the information they acquire from what they believe to be a source of authority, like teachers, the news, books, or even gossip. Isaac even wrote a thesis on informative gossip, the bulk of which was obtained from the results of experiments he performed to evaluate how the faculty and student body reacted to both true and false gossip. The result was that everyone reacted the same to lies as they did to truth as long as the source of the lies was at least somewhat authoritative.

His studies led to a belief that the release of selective information to a collective of humans would control their behavior in society as long as it was the only information they received or came from a more authoritative source than any other information provided.

Professor Morris also came to believe it was a greater good to withhold certain information from humanity, as well, if they are to be successfully influenced and managed for their benefit. He was excited! People of the Earth could easily be influenced, through the use of selected information, to live in peace and harmony with each other instead of fighting wars.

Isaac Morris's writings and public stance on government control of worldwide communication caught the attention of Jehovah, who appointed him Commander of Level Two - Communications of The Four Levels. As a result, Isaac began slowly and steadily integrating his philosophy of selective information into the governments of Earth and is proud of the progress made during his long tenure. With the influence of the press and electronic media, most governments were successful at managing their collective populations. Level-3 was helpful with difficult opponents of the plan, but the success of the plan always depended upon communications, which was under his control. Information flows through communications.

Isaac considers the Magician a potential threat, especially if he has the ability to move so quickly that it appears he is in several different places at the same time. Only the media can do that, and they do it with permission, Isaac's permission. He wanted to talk with that man, and soon. Isaac felt he was on the verge of creating a peaceful Earth, and nothing or no one could be allowed to get in the way. Isaac had world media at his disposal and decided to use it. He summoned the Mystery Man in world news classifieds. The question is, would he respond?

It was Aunt Rita who first noticed the ads. Hymn seldom, if ever, read newspapers or sought the news on the internet. His aunt was the opposite and two days later noticed a little ad in her morning paper asking, 'Will magician please contact L2?' and showed it to Hymn alone after breakfast. 'magician' and 'L2' were flags that caught her attention.

"Could be an attempt to trap you, Hymn," she advised and asked, "Why does the advertiser think you know how to contact him?"

"Because, Auntie, if I don't know how to contact him, I am not the person for whom he is asking. You see, Auntie, he has no idea for whom he is asking. He is curious, and only one person can possibly answer that ad. He probably ran it in several million newspapers. I think he just wants to talk, but you're right; it may be a trap. In any event, it should be interesting."

Hymn stepped into Keepaway and commanded, "Screen. Locate Isaac Morris, commander of Level 2 of The Four Levels."

'3,000 Morris, Isaac's found,' flashed across the monitor.

"Screen, sort names for ages over 70 years."

'147 Morris, Isaac's age over 70 years,' appeared on the screen.

"Screen, sort all over-age-70 names for Professor Isaac Morris."

'One found, Toronto, Canada,' flashed across.

"Screen, exact location, Professor Isaac Morris, Toronto."

Coordinates and numbers flashed across the screen.

"Screen, display video."

'Video not available' appeared on the monitor.

"Screen, phone number, Professor Isaac Morris."

'None found,' flashed.

"Screen, business or residence at location."

'Business, funeral home,' appeared.

"What the heck is going on here?" Hymn muttered to himself.

"Screen, is the funeral home chapel occupied?"

'Chapel unoccupied.'

"Screen coordinates to chapel."

Coordinates flashed across the screen.

"Screen, temperature, Toronto, Canada."

'13 degrees F,' flashed.

"Screen, report funeral home security."

'Twelve cameras, six armed personnel,' appeared on the monitor.

It seemed curious to Hymn a funeral home would have armed personnel and 12 security cameras. "This might be interesting." he thought, then grabbed his overcoat, just in case, and stepped from Keepaway into the funeral home chapel.

He wondered how best to get the attention of Commander Morris and decided to use the direct approach and ask to see the man; so, he left his coat in a pew and walked from the chapel toward the front office, where an elderly lady was tending flowers in a vase on a side table just outside the office door.

Looking up, she saw him approaching and said, "The meeting is in the conference room down the hall, sir, the second door on the right." Pointing at two men walking down the hall, she said, "Those gentlemen are attending as well; just follow them."

Hymn decided to put his meeting with Mr. Morris on hold, curious to see where this unusual incident would lead. He walked into the room with the two men, took a seat at a long table, and looked around at the others present, smiling and nodding as though he were one of them. What struck him as odd was the silence. The usual talking and whispering that preceded most meetings he attended was entirely absent here—but then, he'd never been to a meeting in a funeral home before. Perhaps meetings held here were quieter and more respectful, given the setting and the possibility that this gathering might be in memory of someone recently passed.

It turned out that guess wasn't even close. When the man at the head of the table stood and introduced himself, Hymn's interest in the meeting *shot off the charts* because the person leading it was none other than the great one himself, L-2 Commander Isaac Morris!

Everyone stood and applauded the Level-2 leader. The applause stopped on cue, and everyone sat down simultaneously—everyone except Hymn, of course. He didn't know the cue.

Commander Morris began the meeting by commending everyone for exceptional leadership in their various sections of Level 2 and affirmed their work was leading Earth into a new age of peace and harmony. *Everyone applauded.*

Commander Isaac stated, "All people of this planet owe a debt of gratitude to the leaders in this room who contributed their time and great skill to assure the happiness and safety of future generations through the applied use of Communication Science to information flow where everyone on Earth receives the same information in schools, books, and media. The plan is now installed in thirty test countries and exhibiting positive results."

The commander continued, "This morning's meeting was called to inform you of a potential threat to our global plan to save Earth from spiraling into chaos. As difficult as it is to believe, one man, in possession of what appears to be special abilities, is inhibiting our progress by encouraging individual thinking among people and discouraging belief in government. The danger of both ideas is plain because they appeal to fringe elements of humanity and spawn new communication sources that dispense information not approved by us. This magician is dangerous because he has the ability to spread his poison worldwide without opposition.

I have asked him to contact me for a conference. It is my hope he can be shown his actions are harming Earth and violate the laws of civilization. This man could be of great value to our organization if he would join us in acting in the best interests of humanity; however, should he remain intent on continuing his disruptive behavior, we will be forced to take serious measures to suppress him. Are there any comments?"

One member at the table was recognized and asked, "Why are we bothering with the unlawful actions of one man? Just have him arrested, prosecuted, and thrown in jail for violation of the law?"

The commander answered, "That is, of course, one option, but we know nothing about this magician other than he is a person of interest in the death of a high-ranking official in the United States. No charges have yet been made, but it is being looked into by the FBI."

A woman stood and asked the commander, "Sir, do you seriously expect the magician to contact you, and if so, when?"

"The magician will contact me this week; I am sure of it. He must be curious as to why I am asking to confer with him, and we are prepared for him to arrive at any time. Security is tight, and I have been given the authority to use lethal force if necessary. Although it is my belief that the magician is just a misguided advocate of what he views as freedom, cautionary measures are being taken; however, to my knowledge, he has physically harmed no one and does not pose a threat to my safety or yours. Are there any other questions?"

A man stood, was recognized, and stated, "Commander Morris, it seems you have set a trap for this magician. If he should come to meet with you, the only way he can leave is in a casket or a bottle unless he agrees to go along with your demands. Do you not find that to be dishonorable? Or do you have some other plan for him? I personally am not on board with that conduct." Then he sat back down.

Several members at the table looked at the commander, curious at what his response might be, while others looked straight ahead in shock, not wanting to make any movement that may be mistaken as approval of the man's comment.

Commander Morris frowned at the man's impertinent question which seemed to insinuate the commander's plan was not honorable.

He replied, "It appears not all of us are on the same page here tonight. Anyone who believes a dishonorable man, like the magician, should be trusted and treated with honor in regard to our plan for mankind's future security is not a person who deserves his seat at this table and should leave now or be forcibly removed."

The man rose and immediately apologized, saying that he meant no disrespect to anyone with his comment. He was only voicing disagreement with the idea that the magician was being lured into a trap under false pretenses for doing nothing more than being accused of talking to people and expressing his opinion.

The man added, "Is not everyone entitled to say whatever is on their mind when conversing with another? Sir, you said tonight that you believed the magician was just a man who had a different idea of what freedom is and had no past history of violence. As far as him being a dishonorable man, we have no evidence of that being true. Our giving security permission to use lethal force against such a man makes us look like we are paranoid, and threatening the man with extreme violence for attending a meeting we requested just seems wrong to me. I am not comfortable with the idea of killing someone simply because they do not agree with me. That is both unethical and immoral." The man then sat back down.

Listening to that person's response was inspiring; Hymn wanted to give him a standing ovation but restrained himself. He saw a few others slightly nodding their heads as if seeing some sense in the man's point.

Hymn realized the commander saw it too and stood up to voice his agreement, saying, "I am in agreement with my colleague and believe security should be told to stand down from the lethal force order regarding the magician."

Commander Morris was an old hand at maintaining control of any situation and firmly stated, "Perhaps my method of dealing with the magician is a bit heavy-handed; I see why some of you are concerned that 'lethal force' is too extreme. My overreaction is a response to a concern for your safety. The magician has exhibited special abilities beyond anything our security has seen before, and extreme measures are called for when an unknown danger puts our personal safety at risk. It also concerns me that two of you are advocating that I call off the safety measures currently installed. It is possible that both are genuinely concerned about my methods being a little extreme; however, their motive for asking the lethal force order to be called off is suspicious."

Then he ordered, "Security! Place those two men under arrest and lock them away for the balance of the evening. Run a check on their backgrounds to see if anything interesting pops up. If all is well, release them in the morning with our apologies. Inform me immediately if any anomalies are found, and double the guards. I don't like surprises and suspect the magician will arrive tonight. We will be ready for him. For his sake, I hope he turns out to be a reasonable person."

Two men took Hymn and the outspoken young man into custody and locked them in a small room below the funeral home that looked like a cellar. It was cold there, and Hymn had left his coat in the chapel. His companion in the locked room admitted he was a news reporter for an independently owned small-town paper and was the author and voice of an active internet blog called 'The Main View' with over 500 followers.

He extended his right hand to Hymn, saying, "I'm Stuart Main. Thanks for your support in the crazy room up there. I was more than a little concerned about being the only one to speak up among that mob of zombies, especially since I am a party crasher of sorts. Sorry if some of them are your friends; that 'zombie' comment was uncalled for, but you have to admit those people are way out of line, even for Canadians. They seem prepared to kill a man for having the audacity to disagree with their proposed agenda."

Hymn shook the man's hand and replied, "My pleasure, Stu. Your address to the commander was refreshing and took courage. After what you said, there was no way I could leave you standing alone against the stacked deck in the game being played there. In their defense, that Morris is a motivating speaker and is himself convinced that what he is proposing is in the best interests of all mankind. Truth be said, he is correct in his assessment that humans have shown little ability to manage their own affairs and absolutely no ability to get along with each other. We humans lie to, steal from, cheat, injure, maim, and kill each other every day for self-gain or out of hatred for one another. Humans are, by their nature, sinful. Isaac's plan to reduce the evils of humanity by controlling and distributing information across the planet is logical and bold enough to be successful, but is, in my view, too costly to be allowed. Spoon-fed information, false or true, does not allow humans to be in control of their own destiny. Humans must be allowed to fail or succeed by making their own choices as to what happens with their lives; else, how can they be accurately judged?"

Stuart commented, "You sure do know a lot about that old geezer upstairs. I knew nothing about the man until I heard you mention his name."

"Well then, Stu, it might be of interest to you to know that old geezer is one of the most important people on Earth and has been for most of his long life. Commander Isaac Morris is the head of all world information. The fact is, Stuart, just about all information provided on Earth through communication outlets is dependent on information from Commander Morris's huge agency. His ambition is for all media outlets to be dependent upon his agency as their source for news reports. That way, all of what people see, hear and read will be uniform around the world and will come from an authoritative source, Commander Isaac Morris. He will be God!"

"Wow, mister!" exclaimed Stu, "In a way, you sound like a man in agreement with much of what the old man is wanting to do."

"Well, Stu, much of what old Isaac advocates makes sense, but just because something is sensible does not mean it is moral and ethical. As a reporter, you have an understanding of that truth, but the poor old geezer in the room upstairs is 'off his rocker' and believes the sins of people are the cause of Earth's problems. In his warped mind, mankind's sins are the result of harmful information fed to them by uncontrolled media sources, like schools, churches, and other voices of authority."

Hymn was on his soapbox, now. "The actual problem that needs to be dealt with on Earth is people like old Isaac. He needs to be hauled off to the looney bin, fitted with one of those pretty white jackets, and given a shock treatment 3 or 4 times a day. Maybe that would bring him back to the real world from the fantasy land in which he now lives. I'm actually amazed that senile, crazy old idiot has lasted this long."

Stu couldn't take it any longer! This magic man is a fool, too full of himself to even see what is actually happening here, and needs a serious dose of reality!

"You stupid moron!" Stu growled, "You are the idiot here. You fell for the trap we set like the ignorant amateur you are. Magician, my ass! Unlike you, my grandpa is a very great man who sincerely desires for all mankind to become better and kinder people. Why he is concerning himself with you is beyond me; you are a nobody! He wants to determine how much you know and how you can be in two places at once."

"I wanted to just arrange an accident for you, but Grandpa wants to know more about you. He has the idea you may be a misguided freedom fighter who might become an ally once you realize his plan will save mankind and Earth. By programming people's thoughts with one common source of information, humanity will finally be at peace with one another."

"What Grandpa does not understand is that those like you are not realists. You are dreamers who believe mankind will find a solution to their basically evil nature on their own, but they won't. On the contrary, mankind will continue sinning, murdering, cheating, and hurting each other for self-gain. We are the ones in the right here, Magician. Mankind has not earned the right to govern themselves; they must be herded and helped to get along with each other. A common source of world information is a move in that direction."

"Come on, young Stuart," Hymn grinned with enjoyment, "calm yourself down and quit being so naive. You gave the whole shebang away when you first stood in the meeting and spoke. No member of L-2 would dare address a World Commander in such a manner. I have got to admit, though, your objection to Isaac's lethal force order was downright precious; I liked it a lot; heck, man, I almost found myself applauding."

"Hymn asked, "So, what do you think happens now my little undercover act is blown, Stuart? What is the plan? You're not going to kill and cremate a guy for opposing your world plan, are you?"

While Hymn was grinning and admitting to his identity, Stu was wondering if something might be mentally wrong with the guy. He is calm and unconcerned by his predicament.

"If I didn't know better," he thought to himself, *"I would think this magician guy is enjoying this. Although he should be in fear for his life, he seems to think he is the one in charge here."*

"Magician, if I were you, I would not be making jokes about being put in a box and cremated alive. That is a scary way to go out, and I can tell you something for sure: you *will* go out screaming."

Hymn protested, "Now hold on just a minute there, junior; I was only kidding and never said anything about being burned alive. You cannot be serious about something like that. Your old grandpa may be a bit loco, but he is too moral and ethical a man to condone that."

Stu chuckled and stated, "I thought that would get your attention and make you understand the gravity of your current situation. Opposing our plan is one thing, but taking steps to undermine it is sabotage and an act of terrorism. My grandpa will take your actions against us seriously. You have a choice, though; there are always choices in life, and all choices have consequences."

"I have to say this, Stu," replied Hymn, "you have a sly way of getting my attention. Let me guess: if I decide to join up with you, I get to live, and if I decide to oppose you, well, you get to stoke the fire of my bed tonight. Is that about it?"

"Not quite, you fool. If you agree to join and help us and later break your word, your entire family and friends will pay the price along with you."

"What about my dog, Stu? Do you intend to kill my little dog, too?" asked Hymn, grinning.

"What?" Stuart retorted. "Man, are you totally insane out of your mind?"

He stared at Hymn in complete disbelief, thinking, *"This crazy magician clown is likely going to die tonight, and here he is making stupid jokes about it. I'll show this nut a joke or two."*

Stu spoke, "Magician, you are . . ."

Hymn interrupted Stu, saying, "Aw, come on, boy, loosen up a bit. I'm just messing with you; heck, I don't even have a dog."

Stu was already severely angry at Hymn and frustrated by his flippant attitude, but the last disrespectful comment pushed the young man way over the edge, allowing his temper to get the better of him. Young Stuart produced a gun, pointed it straight at the magician, and pulled the trigger three times in succession. Three clicks of the revolver were the only sounds made in the room.

Hymn smiled at the confused young man and said, "You have a lot to learn about proper etiquette and manners, young Stuart. You might want to take a course in the proper use of firearms as well. Only an idiot would forget to load a gun before attempting to fire it."

Now, Stu was really fuming with anger! The man was laughing and making fun of him. He pulled the trigger three more times, only to hear the sound of three more clicks.

"Stu, why don't you calm down, go sit in the corner there, and play with your little gun; I mean the one in your hand, not the one in your pants."

Stunned by the turn of events, the young man went to the corner and sat down, blankly staring at the gun in his hand. For some strange reason, his anger was gone; he was calm and actually felt genuine peace for the first time in his life. He felt a little bit drowsy, as well.

Hymn spoke gently, softly, "How are feeling now, young Stuart? Peaceful? Calm? Are you proud of what you are? A murderer, a thug, and a bully? I want you to give serious attention to what I am about to say. Has information received from your grandpa ever caused you to feel the way you feel now? Has it helped you to control your passions? Only moments ago, you were totally lost in anger, greatly desiring to kill me because of a difference in our beliefs. Do you honestly believe your Grandpa Issac will help people by controlling their information? He plans to program people with his enormous communications network? You grew up with him, and look how that turned out. He raised a killer. He didn't intend for that to happen, but much of the information he fed you created that result."

"How many people have you killed, Stu? Is your grandpa aware of your actions? He is human, with human shortcomings too serious to allow him to be the influence on generations of men and women like his grandson. The sins of that outcome will rest on him, and that is a terrible, terrible weight to carry to the grave."

Hymn advised, "You can decide to change and become a good man, Stu, but the truth is, the decision has to be yours, or it won't count for anything in the long run. Never allow anyone or any group to take your freedom of choice from you, nor allow yourself to take that same freedom from others."

"Stuart, I'm going to leave you now with advice you are free to reject or accept. You can do nothing about the past; it is done, but your future is a book of blank pages waiting for your choices to be written upon them. Write choices of goodness on those pages, Stu, for that is where your salvation is to be found. Sleep now and dream about your life to come. After all, your life is yours only, as are your choices."

"Choose to be a good man, Stuart," Hymn advised.

As the young man drifted off into a deep, cleansing sleep, Hymn turned, climbed the stairs to the locked door, and opened it. The door lock clicked behind him. He glanced around quickly and saw the guard was down the hall, talking with someone Hymn couldn't see. The chapel was just a few yards around the corner, so Hymn walked there and went inside to retrieve his coat. It was evident that security was more relaxed from what it was when he arrived, making him wonder what was going on. An hour ago, they were in the process of making sure everyone was ready for the magic man's expected arrival, but now there was no sense of urgency in the funeral home at all, with only a skeleton crew on guard.

Except for someone kneeling in prayer at the altar, the chapel was empty. Hymn planned to get his coat and step into Keepaway but decided to sit in the last pew and think of what to do about the old commander and his plan for Earth. Hymn actually liked Isaac Morris and was sympathetic to the commander's desire to make humanity a kinder, less sinful race. But the old man was going about making changes in the wrong way, at least to Hymn's way of thinking, and that created a dilemma that needed to be solved.

The truth may be that humans really do need someone, perhaps a genius like Isaac, to force them to be better, less sinful people. Hymn was aware he didn't know what the truth was and was certainly not qualified to decide the best way for humanity to proceed. It was his belief that the people of Earth had to make that decision themselves, as a collective of human beings created by their Creator for that very purpose. Should humanity prove incapable of learning to live together because of their evil nature, then so be it. Whether humanity ultimately succeeds or fails should result from their own decisions, not someone's or something else's.

Hymn was sitting, silently thinking, with his face in his hands, so intent on solving his dilemma he never noticed someone was sitting beside him, until a quiet voice beside him asked, "Have you worked it all out yet?"

Startled, Hymn leaned back in the pew and was quite surprised to see Isaac Morris sitting next to him, smiling.

Isaac saw that Hymn was surprised to see him and spoke softly, "You were so caught up in thought I considered not being a bother, but my desire to converse with you was greater than my manners could contain. I perceive that you, sir, are the mysterious, elusive magician about whom The Four Levels are gossiping, are you not?"

"Actually, Commander, I am really not a man of magic, although I am fascinated by the things magicians have learned to achieve and enjoy watching them work at their trade. My name is Hymn. You know, like a church song. I am very pleased to have this opportunity to meet with you. I couldn't help noticing that the security presence is no longer in evidence."

"Yes, that is true," Isaac replied and observed, "Since it is clear you are able to get past all that high-level protection, the need for them became superfluous, so I took it upon myself to send them away."

Issac revealed, "Stuart's phone was on the entire time the two of you were in the basement, talking, and I heard your conversation. It is important to me for you to know that I was not aware my grandson was armed. Even so, given his temperament, I should have known better than to allow you to be left alone with him. Fortunately, the gun misfired when he tried to shoot you."

Hymn explained, "He was angry at me for what I said about you and overreacted. Stuart appears to love you, genuinely."

Isaac responded, "Yes, without a doubt, but at times misplaced. I listened to you manipulate him into revealing his identity. It was interesting to see how you cleverly used Stuart's feelings for me to trap him into revealing himself."

"Well, Isaac, Stu is an over reactive, spoiled young man with very little wisdom, and his morals and ethics, if present, are not evident. You were the strong guiding force in what he became and is. Somewhere along his timeline, Stuart made a choice based on what information he learned from certain voices of authority, including you. He made bad choices and became a bad person because of it."

Hymn advised, "Stu is sound asleep now, dreaming, and when he awakes, he will be noticeably different. He has a chance of becoming a good man now, but much depends upon the information he will receive from his source of authority, which brought him to where he now is."

"Isaac, you have a more complete understanding of the power of information than anyone and, as a result, have educated some evil, powerful people in the world on how to effectively apply that understanding to control the collective of humanity through the selective dissemination of information. Your idea is brilliant, but has a fatal flaw; human beings are creations."

Hymn continued, "When one takes time to give serious thought to the truth, it is interesting to realize, of The Four Levels, you are the Level who decides mankind's intelligence."

"Will Earth continue to be populated by an ignorant collective because their information source is biased and corrupt, or by people who are intelligent, because their information source is objective, honest, and fair? Too many of your students have a biased agenda."

"Truth is, Isaac, you are perhaps the only man who can give Earth a chance of survival because you have the power to provide oversight to governments, law enforcement, and education through the efforts of an honest and ethical media unencumbered by political, social, and religious bias. Imagine reporters being real journalists who seek to report unbiased, truthful news, instead of journalists who either report their views or the views of their bosses."

"Who knows? Freedom of the Press may actually mean the freedom to present objective news stories without bias. In either event, the results revealed to the public will come from genuine news sources, who gather stories through their own efforts and not canned, carefully prepared reports spoon-fed to them by agenda-driven people, corporations, and governments."

"Well now, Mr. Hymn," Isaac responded, "that sounds awfully warm, fuzzy, and nice—but mostly just awful. We're discussing humans here, an unfortunate breed of life that you aptly described as essentially evil and selfish. We humans commit the very evils you listed, and we do them for self-gain, in one form or another."

"You want to know why I won't do as you suggest, Mr. Hymn?" Isaac quickly answered his question before Hymn could respond. "Because you desire something of which the human breed is incapable of delivering—something that has already been attempted in human history and failed miserably. *Utopia.* That is an impractical scheme of governance where everything is perfect. It's impractical because of the created nature of humanity."

"Think about it. Even the perfection of the Garden of Eden failed when two humans succumbed to their basic nature and chose sin over virtue. The Creator, in His divine wisdom, removed them from Eden and banned their return, declaring humans unworthy of such perfection."

"However, because of you, Mr. Hymn, I am abandoning my plan for the social improvement of mankind, as I am now convinced the whole idea is not practical. Humans must be allowed the freedom to make their own way in this reality, whatever the result. I'll use Level Two to ensure humanity's freedom to choose their own path, though I hold little hope they'll choose wisely. Walking the path of evil is fun and requires little effort, while walking the path of goodness and virtue is often boring and demands real effort. Care to guess upon which path the bulk of humanity can be found?"

As Hymn listened to Commander Morris reveal his pessimistic view of humanity's future, he noticed something critical the great man was overlooking.

"Isaac, you have completely omitted God from your discourse on humanity's future," Hymn said. "I find that strange, as belief in God is where mankind's hope for a better society rests. The only way your pessimistic vision of the future could come true is if God were taken out of the equation—which isn't possible, because God *is* the equation. God is Everything."

Commander Morris sat up straight, suddenly turned and stared at the man sitting next to him with a look of disbelief and wonder. He looked at Hymn's kind smile and into his knowing eyes, then asked, respectfully, "Who are you really, Mr. Hymn?"

Hymn, surprised by the reverent tone of the commander and the shift in his demeanor, replied, "You know who I am, Isaac."

"Yes, I believe I do, Sir," Isaac confirmed.

Hymn remained silent, sensing Isaac had more to say.

Isaac spoke, "Sir, allow me to explain that in which I was deeply engaged when you arrived."

"Mr. Hymn, I didn't mention this before, but your conversation with my grandson had a profound effect on me. My intention to improve human society by creating a less contentious population through the controlled release of carefully chosen information died while listening to your words."

"When you asked my grandson how many people he had killed, my heart ached. When you inferred he was a result of my idea of controlled information and that I bore the weight of much of his sins, my stomach turned, leaving me upset and feeling sick. And when you suggested that my plan for mankind could work, yet would produce millions more people like him, I had an epiphany: I realized I have been wrong and am bordering on being evil."

"In that moment, I changed and was compelled to come to this chapel. Up front, on my knees and broken, I prayed to God for help and asked for a sign to show me the way back home. Moments later, the chapel door opened. You walked in and sat back here. We talked, and when you reminded me of my omission of God in my forecast for mankind, it shook me to my core, for in that moment, I knew the way home."

"Yes, Mr. Hymn, I know exactly who you are. You are an angel and the answer to my prayer." He then took Hymn's hand and kissed it several times.

Hymn could see that Isaac had undergone a profound religious experience that changed him, very likely for the rest of his life. How could Hymn explain he knew angels and was not one, himself? He couldn't, nor could he deny the man's divine and deeply emotional experience.

Isaac stood, his eyes wet with tears, and stated, "I must go tend to my grandson now. I will pray for you every day, Mr. Hymn, my Angel." He bowed slightly and left.

Hymn sat quietly in the pew for a few moments, thinking. Then picked up his coat and stepped into Keepaway. There, he went for a long walk along the beach, pondering the mystery of Stuart's cell phone in the cellar.

He spoke to the ocean, the stars, and the cosmos. To Everything.

"How is it that Stuart's phone continued to broadcast to Isaac when all communications in the funeral home had been earlier compromised... by me?"

18

The Christmas Party

Aunt Rita's house was a buzz of activity. Christmas was a short three days away, it was Friday, and all kinds of last-minute plans were being made to ring out the old year and bring in the new. Arch agreed to stay through the New Year's celebrations, but plans to fire up the motor home and move his family to Arkansas were in the works. Of course, Aunt Rita and Melody were busy bees of activity, wrapping presents and baking.

Today was Friday, and a Christmas party was being held tonight at the building across from where Melody worked. It was sort of a big deal for local families and friends, an annual holiday celebration focused on Christmas for kids, the likes of which were being held in many places at this time of year. Lots of good food and good times, and even Santa Claus was rumored to be there to hand out presents. Aunt Rita said about sixty people attended last year, and although the location this year is different, she expected about the same attendance. Hymn didn't attend last year and was looking forward to it.

The party is scheduled to run from 7 pm to 11 pm, and most people arrive early to assure themselves a table, so everyone loaded up in Arch's motor home and headed out about half past six; everyone except Hymn, that is. Melody objected when he advised her about some unfinished business that just had to be attended to before seven o'clock. Hymn apologized and promised to be at the party before eight.

After the bus left, Hymn stepped into Keepaway. Earlier in the year, he learned that even small events require security checks just for peace of mind if nothing else. This Christmas party was a local annual event with no previous problems, but Hymn decided to give it a go anyway.

"Take a little time for a lotta peace of mind."—that was his new slogan.

Hymn said, "Screen. Security at the Christmas party building," and provided the coordinates.

'None,' flashed across the screen.

"Screen. Armed personnel within a half-mile radius."

'171,' flashed across.

"Well, this is Texas," he reminded himself.

"Screen. Armed bodies in the building."

'19,' flashed.

"Screen, location of the armed bodies."

'5 firearms on floor one, 14 on floor two.'

"Screen. Number of assault weapons."

'8 on floor two.'

Hymn was confident that the five armed bodies on floor one were friendly, but the 14 armed bodies on floor two likely were not. "This is interesting," he murmured.

"Screen. Video available."

'Three cameras, floor 1, disabled.'

"Screen. Coordinates to floor two ladies' room."

Coordinates flashed across.

"Bodies in the ladies' room?"

'None.'

"Screen. Location of floor two bodies."

'12 in room 22, 1 outside room door, 1 at stairs.'

Hymn stepped from Keepaway and into the second-floor ladies' room. He opened the door and entered a short hallway, walking slowly. Suddenly, a young boy's voice called out, "Gringo, you lost?"

Hymn replied, "As a matter of fact, I am. I was looking for the men's room but couldn't find it, so I used the ladies' room instead. I was heading back downstairs to the party. Are you part of the security team?"

"We have a guard on the stairs. Did you not see him?"

"No," replied Hymn, "but maybe he's in the men's room."

"Maybe, señor, maybe not. It is suspicious."

"Suspicious?" Hymn questioned.

"Si, suspicious. I see you come out of the ladies' room, but I did not see you go in."

"Come," Hymn motioned. "Let's go find him."

"Do not move, gringo!" ordered the young guard, pointing his gun at Hymn in a threatening manner. "You are suspicious."

Hymn smiled warmly. "You know, son, you're the foreigner in America, not me. So why do you keep calling me gringo?"

A low voice from behind Hymn spoke calmly, "Do you prefer asshole or motherfucker, hombre? They both suit you."

"Aha!" exclaimed Hymn. "I knew security had to have more than one guard on duty! Now I really feel secure." He turned, extending his hand in greeting to the other guard. "I'm Hymn, happy to make your acquaintance."

This guard was older, about 40, and a big man. He looked confused and ignored the friendly gesture. "What's going on here, Carlos?" he asked the young guard.

"I caught him when he was coming out of the toilet, Enrique. He is suspicious."

"Yeah, I had to go pretty bad, Enrique," added Hymn, "and the line downstairs was long, so I came up here. Man, your security is tight. Why are we using Mexican security?"

Enrique glared harshly at Hymn, his face darkening. "Mister, you're starting to get on my nerves, and I don't like you, so keep your goddamned trap shut, or else."

"Yeah, I get it," said Hymn. "This is the part where you threaten to kill my dog. What's with my dog, anyway? Why does everyone always want to kill it? The truth is, I don't even have a dog. And you know what? I'm glad I don't, or I'd have to worry all the time about someone killing it. Know what I mean?"

Enrique couldn't take any more of the crazy gringo. Enraged, he yanked a long knife from his belt, holding it low as he growled, "Crazy American, watch as your guts fall to the floor before the rest of you."

Hymn smiled as the big man stepped closer. "You're going to kill me with a peppermint candy cane? Well, at least you have a bit of imagination."

Enrique glanced down at his hand and saw that he was holding a large Christmas candy cane. "What the fu . . .?"

As Hymn took the candy cane from the stunned man's big hand, he cut off Enrique's expletive and advised, "Sometimes things just don't turn out like you want or expect, Enrique. You should work on controlling your temper. It might cause a stroke someday."

Enrique felt his legs go weak and sank to the floor, watching as the American crunched on a piece of the candy cane. Hymn offered a piece to young Carlos, but the boy dropped his gun and ran, terrified, into the meeting room where twelve men were preparing to turn a celebration into terror.

Hymn moved to Enrique and, helping him to his feet, whispered, "Sorry for being such a pain, amigo, but you needed a chance to see yourself in the grasp of evil. How's that working out for you?"

Enrique looked up and saw kindness in Hymn's eyes. He closed his own for just a moment. Funny thing about moments—they're tiny but sometimes life-changing, like now.

"Hello, guys!" Hymn greeted everyone as he helped the big man to a chair. "What's going on up here? Anyone want a piece of candy cane?"

All the guns in the room pointed at Hymn as he walked to the front and took a seat by the window, casually looking around. There was confusion and a total lack of understanding about what was happening. This was not supposed to happen. A man with an unlit cigar clenched between his teeth approached Hymn and pressed a gun to his head.

"Señor, what are you doing here? Be careful with your answer—I will know if you lie."

"Oh, of course," Hymn said politely, please accept my apologies. "I'm from the party downstairs and didn't get a chance before to introduce myself properly. We're having our annual Christmas party tonight. It's when we all get together to celebrate the birthday of the Savior, have a nice dinner with friends and family and hand out presents to the kids. It's going to be great fun."

"That is not what I asked you!" the man snarled, pressing the gun firmly to Hymn's head. "You have one more try."

"Okay, Pancho," Hymn replied. "I'm here to stop a bad thing from happening."

"A bad thing? How do you know abou—? Wait! Did you just call me Pancho? Did this gringo just call me Pancho?" He looked around at the men, gesturing for an answer. They all laughed and nodded.

Hymn joined in, laughing along with them. Pancho was not amused. He drew back his gun, ready to hit Hymn in the face with it.

Hymn met Pancho's gaze and commanded, "Sit down and be quiet, macho man. We can be friendly tonight, can we not?"

Pancho sat down right where he was standing. The other armed men either tried to rush Hymn or run from the room, but they couldn't. Every one of them was stuck in place, unable to move. A voice nervously whispered, "It's him! Mother of Jesus, it's the magic man!" Panic began to rise in the room.

Hymn reached over, gently took Pancho's gun, and examined it briefly. He pointed it at the ceiling and pulled the trigger twice, producing two clicks, then tossed it aside like trash.

"Why do you homies carry weapons on Christmas? They are defective, you know; the bullets won't fire. Where did you get all these guns and ammo? These weapons aren't easy to come by."

Pancho mumbled, "From Señor Barkley. He told us to shoot at buildings and cars to scare people and said we could keep the guns."

Hymn asked, "Who is this, Mr. Barkley? and why do you follow his orders to shoot at innocent people and scare them? Don't you know that is against the law? You can be arrested by the police?"

Pancho replied, "He is an important man who owns most of the buildings here—the property, everything."

"Everything?" Hymn questioned.

"We owe Mr. Barkley much *dinero*," Pancho explained. "You *comprende*, Magic Man?"

"I comprende, Pancho. Thank you."

"Diego," he corrected. "My name is Diego."

"Diego. I will remember that, amigo," Hymn promised.

"I will suffer for telling you, Magic Man."

Hymn shook his head, "Somehow, I doubt that, Diego."

Diego warned, "Señor Barkley—él es un hombre muy peligroso. Mucho poder."

"Sounds like an interesting man. Gracias, Diego."

The room was buzzing with low whispers, but as Hymn stood, silence fell. He asked Diego to translate his words for those who did not understand English and began:

"Attention, everyone. Each of you has your reasons for being here, all armed and ready, just waiting to ruin the Christmas party downstairs. I don't know exactly what you're after, what you're angry about, or whether you want to rob or harm them, but your intent to hurt those people makes you bad people. It makes you evil. Maybe some of you just like hurting people, which by itself makes you very evil."

"Honestly, I'm not concerned about you. You will make choices that will shape your own future. My problem with you is this: I have people at that nice party downstairs who are my family and friends. I love them and want them to be safe and happy."

Hymn continued, "Now, I'm not going to get all mushy and talk about little kids and Santa Claus or anything like that, but I am going to give each of you three choices. You can choose one."

1. "You can decide to pack up your weapons and go home, back to your world, whatever it may be. Your life will stay the same, except for this experience here, which has probably already changed you, at least a little."

2. "You can decide to follow me downstairs and join the party. Believe it or not, those people will welcome you. You'll have a good time, some good food, and maybe even make new friends."

3. "You can decide to pursue violence, hatred, and evil tonight, as planned, but know this truth: from evil comes evil. Choose this, and evil will grow within you."

"I'm going downstairs now to join the party." Hymn left the room and walked down the stairs.

Seven men followed him and joined the party, including both Enrique and Diego. Five others simply went home. Two more were reported missing after the New Year in gang-related violence.

The Christmas party turned out to be a wonderful, fun experience for everyone, including the seven walk-ins, who were warmly greeted. After a hesitant start, they blended in well with the crowd of about seventy.

As far as Hymn was concerned, this year was shaping up to end on a positive note. The girls were already planning a farewell get-together for Arch's family on New Year's Eve—a family affair at Aunt Rita's house to say goodbye and wish them well on their move to Arkansas.

But before the year ended, Hymn had a promise to keep concerning a certain Mr. Barkley. He wondered if the man might be reasonable, but after some research, it was clear he was not. Mr. Barkley hadn't become powerful by being reasonable—or by being liked. Should be interesting to talk with.

19

Barkley Evans

Barclee Marie Evans was born in 1982 as a 6-pound, 10-ounce bouncing baby girl to wealthy, upper-class parents in North Dallas, with the proverbial silver spoon in her mouth. She was educated in private institutions beginning at the age of four and attended only the best and most expensive schools throughout her academic career, graduating in the top five of her class with a business degree in Finance. At the tender age of twelve, she received her first car, a limousine, complete with a chauffeur. She never bothered to obtain a driver's license, as she never learned to drive. At the age of twenty-five, she married a wealthy man thirty-five years her senior who had health problems. He passed away thirty-three months later. The couple had no children.

By the age of 31, Barclee considered herself to be well-known for three things:

1. Being a ruthless businesswoman.

2. Being a powerful woman.

3. Being a wealthy woman.

None of those things impressed her, and what she hated most of all was being thought of as a woman. In 2015, she declared herself to be a man, legally changed her name to Barclay Evans, and, for all practical purposes, transformed to manhood. She acted the part, dressed the part, shaved her head, and even lowered her voice to a raspy whisper when she talked. Barclay Evans gained renown as a respected, wealthy businessman man to be feared.

Hymn had never heard of the Barclee woman or the Barclay man. In his entire life, she or he never appeared on his radar. The first time he heard the name 'Barkley' was the evening of the Christmas party when Diego expressed great fear of Mr. Barkley. As it turned out, 'Barkley' was actually spelled 'Barclay' and was his first name. Research revealed the man was Barclay Evans, who was reasonably well known as a power broker of land and property in Texas. The immigrant migration into Texas afforded Mister Evans the opportunity to achieve great wealth as a type of slum lord for new arrivals who needed work and somewhere to live. Hymn had no idea the 'he' Barclay was a biological female.

The Wednesday morning after Christmas was cold, in the low 40s and sunny, so hearing a hard knocking at Aunt Rita's door was unexpected. Hymn was having his morning coffee and a biscuit when he opened the door and saw a middle-aged man standing there in a long-sleeved shirt with a scraggly tie, seemingly oblivious to the cold.

Hymn smiled and said, "You look a bit like a man who needs a morning coffee and a couple of biscuits. Why don't you come on in out of the cold and join us for breakfast?" Then he opened the door wider, indicating for the man to come in.

The man looked at Hymn for a few seconds, thinking, "Who is this idiot? Inviting me into his house without a clue as to who I am. No sane person does that in this day and age."

He said to Hymn, "Just like that, huh? You're inviting a total stranger into your house for breakfast, someone who just might be a serial killer or planning to rob you. Are you sure you're all right, mister? 'Cuz people in their right mind don't do things like that, not that I'm refusing your offer of breakfast or anything, 'cause I'm not."

"He stepped into the house and continued talking, "That coffee and biscuit you're holding both look delicious and won't allow me to refuse your invitation, no matter how unusual it is. I'm hoping you have more of those biscuits."

"It is refreshing to see that you and I have something in common, friend, that being a fondness for biscuits," responded Hymn. "We seldom, if ever, have strangers for breakfast, and for some reason, serial killers and thieves don't stop by."

"Now I know there's something wrong with this guy," thought the man. "I can't tell if he's putting me on or serious. Either way, he is unusual and, for some reason, likable."

Hymn said, "Come on in the kitchen and meet everyone. There's an empty chair next to the big man." Mr. Evans sat down at the table, and Hymn announced, "Everyone, we have a guest for breakfast this morning," and introduced the family, including the baby, Archie.

Aunt Rita, Andra, and Melody were sitting on one side of the table, making sure there was enough coffee and biscuits to go around, when Melody asked, "Hymn, does our guest have a name, or is he one of your mysteries?"

Hymn laughed and stated, "You are right, Mel; where are my manners? Everyone, I would like to introduce our guest for breakfast this morning, Mr. Barclay Evans, real estate mogul extraordinaire."

Surprised at Hymn's introduction, Mr. Evans had one of those 'knee jerk' moments, kicking Arch, sitting in the chair next to him, causing the big man to spill hot coffee in his lap and suddenly stand, tipping the table over in the process and spilling food and coffee on the three women sitting across from him.

It only took a moment, but the result was spectacular, reminding Hymn of the effect little things have on the creation of big things and, sometimes, unforgettable big things. This particular event will be remembered and talked about for a long time.

Mr. Evans, shocked at what happened, stood and saw the big man next to him wiping at the hot coffee on his pants with a napkin, then glanced across at the women with food, coffee, and dishes all over them, making what efforts they could to save some of the dishes from falling to the floor and breaking.

There was a brief silence, after which Hymn looked at their guest and, grinning, commented, "Wow! Mr. Evans, you sure know how to make a simple introduction memorable! Everyone here is going to remember this moment for the rest of their lives. I know I am." and then he broke out laughing.

Aunt Rita scolded her nephew, saying, "Hymn! Where are your manners?" then she couldn't help herself and began laughing too. In a moment, everyone was laughing… except for Barclay Evans. He was standing silent, thinking he was in a house of insanity, when Arch, laughing, slapped him on the back, almost knocking him down, and told him he was a good egg, whatever that meant. When he turned and looked up at the huge man laughing with big tears running down his face, Barclay Evans lost control for the first time in a long time. He smiled sheepishly, then giggled and broke out in a freedom of laughter he had never felt before.

After things calmed down a bit, Aunt Rita took charge, ordering, "I'm not sure about the rest of you, but I'm still hungry, so let's clean up this mess and get back to the pleasure of eating a good breakfast. Melody, why don't you brew up a fresh pot of coffee? Uh, check that, Hymn, brew a fresh pot of coffee. Arch, pick up the table and try not to break it in the process; you don't know your own strength sometimes. You girls," pointing directly at Andra and Melody, "get yourselves cleaned up and come back here to help out. Hymn, you and Mr. Evans sweep up the broken dishes and food on the floor, and before you know it, I'll have breakfast on the table."

"Melody piped up, "I'll take care of the floor, guys. Hymn, you and Mr. Evans go in the living room and talk. I'm not sure why he came to visit this morning, but it wasn't for breakfast."

Hymn was amazed by the way women took charge of the things that needed doing.

"Come on, Barclay," he advised, "Let's get the heck out of their way. Coffee will be ready in a short while."

They went to the living room and sat down to talk.

Hymn got right to it, "Barclay, I know you have a good reason for coming by this morning, and I have to say, you took me by surprise. I intended to call you today and ask for an appointment to meet. What is on your mind?"

Barclay snorted, "Talk about being surprised! I almost fell off my chair when you introduced me. I didn't think you knew who I was, yet there you stood, telling everyone. You're asking me what is on my mind. You are on my mind!" Barclay responded. "You recently inserted yourself into my business, something I consider intolerable. I am here today to give you some advice."

"This should be interesting," thought Hymn. Then he replied aloud, "Well, good advice is always welcome, Barclay, but I don't perceive you as the type who gives anything but orders. On the contrary, you are a taker. Advice from you usually comes with a price and is probably more of a warning than advice. What exactly is it you want?"

Barclay leaned back on the couch, thinking, *"There is something different about this man. He is a direct, no-nonsense type, and it is apparent I'm not going to get anywhere trying to intimidate him."*

He spoke, "You know what, Mr. Hymn? We got off on the wrong foot here, and it's probably my fault. I have a knack for being an overbearing asshole at times without half trying. Seems to be in my nature to rub people the wrong way, and I'm not proud of it right now. You've been nothing but pleasant to me since I got here, inviting me to breakfast and all, and I messed it up right off the bat, causing that big man to knock over the table and spill food everywhere. I have to tell you, though, it's been a while since I laughed that hard about anything. Odd thing is, laughing hard out loud like that was relaxing and somehow made me feel good about myself. I actually enjoyed it."

Hymn replied, "Well, laughter is still out there, waiting to make another appearance at the breakfast table. It's going to be difficult getting through breakfast without laughing about our interesting beginning, though. Think about it, had you not shown up, our day would have been like any other. Your presence made it memorable."

"Yeah," admitted Barclay, "You're right; I never thought about it like that. Usually, I don't leave good memories behind me. Let's get back to why I came to see you. Mr. Hymn, you meddled in my business last week when you broke up my plans to settle a large property deal I've been working on. If not for you, three nice buildings in that neighborhood would now belong to me, and they don't. That little stunt you pulled, breaking up my wetbacks and stopping my sellers from being scared into taking my offer on their buildings, was costly to me. To top it all off, the mayor received more than a few complaints from 'concerned citizens' about certain business dealings regarding property in that part of the city. Now, I'm not at all worried about the mayor, but raising my public image to the level of being a slumlord is bad for business and costs me money. That is a problem; I hate losing money and will not tolerate those who dare to cause me problems."

Hymn added, "And you're convinced that I am the one causing you problems and would like me to stop costing you money. Well, Barclay, you make a valid point; I think your request is reasonable."

Barclay thought, *"What in the hell is going on here? I'm not making any kind of request, reasonable or otherwise. What the fuck is wrong with this guy? He may need a lesson or two in business dealings, and I'm just the wom… uh, man to teach him."*

Hymn continued, "The problem is, Barclay, I cannot grant your request because you are misinformed and have it all wrong. Yes, I was responsible for stopping your little gang of migrants from an act of violence that could have caused the death of several of my friends at the Christmas party. And yes, I invited your gang to join our party; some of them did and, by the way, had a great time."

"However, I had nothing to do with a phone call to the mayor or anything else that might have interfered with your business. Truth is, though, I don't like the way you do business; you hurt people. You hurt their families, demean their self-worth, and take what they cannot afford to lose, all in the name of power and personal profit. Another truth is, you are a bad person, but that is of your personal doing, and I try to avoid interfering with choices people make for themselves, whenever possible."

Hymn advised, "If someone is causing you problems and costing you money, take your focus off me as it is misdirected, and there is no profit to be made there, only loss. You were about to give me some advice earlier. Allow me to give you some good advice, as well. Stop hurting people and work at becoming a good person. You will find life to be happier with those choices, Mr. Barclay."

Aunt Rita hollered, "Breakfast is ready. Come and get it!"

Hymn grinned and said, "Let's get to the table before Arch. He's hungry and might eat it all before we get a turn."

Barclay was hungry, too. This conversation could wait until later.

Breakfast was great; Aunt Rita outdid herself with a meal of ham and eggs, grits, biscuits, and gravy. Hymn's coffee-making was praised by all; he even had to make a second pot. There was a lot of talking and laughter among everyone. Melody talked about the science of dream analysis, while Arch talked about moving his family to Arkansas. Hymn mentioned Mr. Barclay's expertise in market analysis and real estate matters, forcing the man to field a barrage of questions about the economy and the rising cost of real estate and housing in Texas. He turned out to be very intelligent in his field of endeavor and was more than willing to answer every question about the economy. Hymn was impressed with Barclay's interaction with everyone. The man had charisma and calmly and patiently answered the questions asked of him. All there liked him, even little Archie, who rode Barclay's knee, happily giggling while the man talked. Aunt Rita even invited him to drop by again.

As mentioned before, breakfast was great, but Barclay and Hymn had unresolved issues that required attention. Both men had diametrically opposed philosophies, probably requiring some sort of compromise, which, if not achieved amicably, would result in future conflicts. Having verbally "crossed swords" in their previous talk, Hymn was sure Barclay felt superior in a battle of wits. The man is at ease when dealing with others from what he perceives to be a power advantage. The immediate problem for Hymn was that he liked Barclay, at least the Barclay he met today; however, the man's history is not that of a good person. He too often hurts others in a quest to accumulate money and power, without concern for the consequences of his actions as long as the results are beneficial to him.

Barclay's view of business is similar to that adopted by many in our country's leadership, being, "The end justifies the means." It is a popular philosophy of logic often used to excuse the use of immoral or unethical methods to achieve results that are believed to be worthwhile or necessary.

Hymn was familiar with the saying and understood the simplicity of the logic used, but implicitly realized the phrase, attributed to the Greek playwright Sophocles, who wrote in his *Electra*, "The end excuses any evil," is totally misinterpreted by everyone.

The way Hymn understands it, the end result of an action is a consequence of the means used to arrive there, meaning the end is of earthly or human concern, whereas the means is of divine concern.

One is humanly responsible for the end result, whether it be good or bad, but morally responsible for the means used to achieve it. As an example, gaining the knowledge of good and evil was not Adam and Eve's sin; eating from the fruit of the Tree of the Knowledge of Good and Evil was the sin. The end result is always good, bad, or somewhere in between and is neither sinful nor virtuous. The means used to achieve the end result is where the sinfulness or virtue is to be found. There is where the integrity of a person is judged.

So, if Mr. Barclay commits evil acts to achieve what he deems to be favorable results, it is the action for which he will ultimately be judged, not the end result, whatever that result may be. That is wisdom; few possess it. Where Hymn is concerned, that is a truth that applies to everyone, including countries, of which our great America is an example and interesting to watch.

The problem for humanity, from Hymn's point of view, is one of those "simple but difficult" paradoxes. How can people in this results-based reality be taught to accept and apply the truth that actions are more important than the results of those actions when the results are all that people care about? Hymn decided that was something for mankind to figure out for themselves and really none of his business.

Barclay was eager to resume the talk he and Hymn began earlier. Oh, he liked Hymn well enough, but the man's moral and ethical stance was surprising and disappointing, revealing an ignorance of good business practice, which placed them at odds with each other.

Barclay was thinking, *"This Hymn guy needs to back away from my personal business affairs and mind his own, which seems the reasonable and smart thing to do. What kind of idiot advises a businessman to 'Stop hurting people and become a good man?' Hymn is like an ignorant little kid with no idea how things work in the real world. Where do all these do-gooders come from, anyway? They are like cockroaches, seeming to pop up out of nowhere. Well, he will be introduced to a different reality after today's lesson."*

As the two men settled in and got comfortable, Barclay opened the conversation, "Mr. Hymn, I've been thinking about what you said earlier and have come to the conclusion you know little about how business is conducted, making the differences between us an obstacle we can't overcome. That being the case, I suggest a truce. The best way for us to get along is to avoid each other. You agree to leave me alone, staying out of my business, and I agree to leave you alone to yours. What do you say we terminate a conflict before one begins?"

"You know something, Mr. Evans?" Hymn replied, "I believe that to be a reasonable solution."

Barclay grinned and remarked, "I thought you would like it," and offered his outstretched hand, saying, "Let's shake on it and seal the deal right here, right now."

Hymn, ignoring the gesture, said, "The truce you are offering sounds really good, but before we cast it in concrete, Barclay, you must know that I'm not sure how to leave you alone or stay out of your business. At the Christmas party last week, I never meant to get involved in your business. My only intent was to look out for the safety of my family and friends, and your armed group seemed to be a threat, forcing me to take action to defend them."

"Mr. Barclay, your business is hurtful and requires both immoral and unethical activities, including occasional violence, which often threatens the lives and livelihoods of people who live in the area where you currently do business, some of whom are friends of mine. I cannot stand aside and allow them to be a type of collateral damage to your business practices. Now, if you will just pack up and move your business to another state or change the way you do business to a moral and less violent activity, leaving you alone will be simple. I would like us to be friends and avoid conflict."

Hymn held out his hand and offered, "What do you say, Barclay? Let's agree and seal the deal right here, right now?"

Barclay stared at Hymn in disbelief, thinking, *"Who in the hell does this idiot think he is?"* He hid his anger, though, smiled at Hymn, and firmly replied, "Telling me to pack up and get out of town is not very friendly, Mr. Hymn, nor is it wise. I am deeply invested here, making it impossible for me to leave, even if I were so inclined, and I am not so inclined."

"Well, Mr. Evans, I offered you two choices, the second being to change the way you do business. You may find a less violent and more kind way of dealing with people results in a happy life, perhaps profitable in more ways than just money."

Barclay felt anger rising inside him and burst out, "Jesus Christ, man! Why in the hell are you being so god-damned unreasonable? You're not stupid! What you are asking, though, is stupid. I like the way my business affairs are managed; I am wealthy because my business practices are profitable, and that, Mr. Hymn, makes me happy. I like being happy!"

Barclay continued, "On the other hand, your attitude and pathetic threats make me angry. I have not been this unhappy in a long time, and I hate being unhappy. Understand this—stay away from me and out of my business affairs. Do that like your life depends on it, and believe me when I say, it does. My migrants are frightened into believing you are some kind of magic man, but you're just a foolish man out of his element. I will show you some real magic if you stick your fucking nose in my business again. We are done here today, asshole. Thank you for the breakfast and hospitality."

The very angry Mr. Barclay Evans stood up to leave, satisfied his potential problem with Hymn was no longer a concern, but when Hymn spoke, for some reason he was compelled to sit back down.

"Wow! Barclay," Hymn exclaimed, "when you get wound up, you come on like a force of nature! I suspect you scare the heck out of people with that approach. It was really impressive."

"I'm not so sure about that, Hymn," Barclay responded lamely, "Seems not to have had much of an effect on you."

"Aw heck, Barclay, I have an advantage; I'm on my home turf, here. This game we're playing is a bunch of pretense, and you're pretty darn good at it. It is so good that, in fact, it is difficult to tell who you really are."

Hymn said, "You know, I'm convinced there are five types of men; as a matter of fact, there are also five types of women, of which I'm not concerned at the moment, as we're talking about guys here. I call it the five P's since all five types begin with the letter 'P.' They are:

1. Protectors.

2. Providers.

3. Parasites.

4. Pretenders.

5. Predators.

Generally speaking, most men are some combination of the five, but their basic nature is one of these five."

"Okay," thought Barclay, *"This Hymn guy is actually not an idiot, but what the hell is his point?"*

Hymn continued, "In this adversarial game we have been playing, you chose to be a Predator, living life only to satisfy your hunger for personal gain, while I chose Protector of people's right to live their lives absent the fear of being killed and eaten by predators. It is interesting, when you think about it, that we both chose, for this game, how we wanted to be perceived, not who we are. We are both pretending."

"Hymn admitted, "I, for example, am basically a Provider, but for our game I chose to act the part of a protector of the weak and innocent, maybe because I thought you would have more respect for a protector."

"Your basic nature, Mr. Evans, appears to be that of a Pretender, which is why you are so good at it. In fact, who you really are just may be lost in a myriad of pretentious roles."

Hymn then asked, "Who are you, really, Barclay?"

Barclay, surprised at the question, took a moment, then replied, "You know, Hymn, I'm not sure anymore; I used to be sure, but not now."

"Are you perhaps caught up in a witness protection situation?" Hymn inquired, interested.

"Hell, no!" Barclay retorted, then calmly answered, "No, Hymn, nothing that dramatic. It's a little bit more complicated than that."

Hymn saw he had touched upon a subject, sensitive to the man, and realized he was being intrusive in Barclay's personal life, which was not his intent. The direction of this talk needed to be changed.

"Listen, Barclay, I am not interested in nosing into your personal life; that is none of my business, and I apologize for allowing our talk to get this far. If our conversation has wandered into a sensitive area, perhaps we should move on to another subject."

Barclay was quiet, considering Hymn's suggestion to move on to another subject and realized he did not want to change the subject; he was tired of pretending. The words of the man facing him, along with his way of speaking them in a such a calm direct manner had a profound effect on the tough demeanor of Barclay Evans. A feeling of relief entered him as the weight of pretense exited.

"You know something, Hymn, you asked a question about which I really want to talk and never do, mainly because there is no one with whom I trust to talk openly. All of my instincts tell me you are a man I can trust, and I feel safe talking with you about myself. If you don't mind, I would like to continue our conversation."

Hymn, touched by the man's sincere reply, said, "Thanks for the vote of confidence, Barclay. Trust like that is not often observed and, truth be known, seldom deserved. Now, let's get back to where we were. Explain, if you can, why you are no longer sure who you are."

Barclay began by revealing his personal secret.

"Hymn, the big reason is this: Back in the year 1982, I was born a biological female."

"Wha, what?" exclaimed Hymn! He was totally surprised at Barclay's revelation and immediately stood up from his chair because he couldn't process the news while sitting down. He looked down at Barclay in amazement.

"Barclay," he stated as he sat back down, "you may have just answered every question I was going to ask in that one sentence."

"Yeah," said Barclay. "Changed your viewpoint of me in that sentence, did it not? From this day forward, you will be unable to look at me or think of me in the same way as you did this morning. Everything changed between you and me the moment you heard me speak that sentence. Isn't that correct?"

Hymn considered what Barclay was getting at and had to admit, "Yeah, Barclay, I would like to think about it a while longer, but yes, you are correct. Many things changed between us the moment you revealed yourself to be a woman. I am still trying to adjust."

"Careful now," spoke Barclay, smiling, "you cannot know for certain I am a female. You only know I told you I am a female. It could be, Hymn, that I am fucking with your mind right now. Remember, I am a very good pretender."

Hymn hesitated, thinking for a moment, then broke out in tearful laughter and couldn't stop for almost a minute. Aunt Rita popped in, asking, "What in the world is going on with all the loud commotion in here, Hymn? You're going to wake up Archie from his nap."

Hymn, still chuckling, apologized, saying, "It's nothing, Auntie. Mr. Evans just told me a really funny joke."

"Well," she snapped, "I'm pretty sure I do not want to hear it. Control yourselves and keep the noise down!"

"Yes, Auntie. We're sorry. It won't happen again."

Aunt Rita frowned and stated, "Now, nephew, don't you start with me!" Then, she left and went back to her sewing.

"You love that aunt of yours, don't you, Hymn," Evans noted.

"Yeah, I do. What's not to love?" Hymn answered, then got back to the fascinating discussion of gender with Mister or Miss Evans, whichever.

"Barclay, I have to congratulate you for providing one of the most interesting talks ever. I have no idea where you're going with it, but you are in complete command of my attention. Forgive my intrusion and continue."

Barclay did just that, "The point I am making is this, no matter what all the crazy people in our media and government say, there is a multitude of differences between males and females, in particular, men and women, and the way they are perceived in society, and I really mean multitude."

"I was raised as a rich young girl in a wealthy family, went to private schools, and graduated from college with honors. I had a great time in my early years, and after college, I was successful in business, but a black cloud was hanging over my head. I was a female. All of my successes were attributed to my being a female. I couldn't go to a lot of the places men went because I was a female, even though I made more money than most men. I once beat the hell out of a man for trying to steal my purse and got a reputation for being a lesbian. The truth is, I like men and enjoyed being a woman, but was not fond of all the social and business limitations placed on me by women and men alike."

"So, at the age of 33, I reached manhood and began identifying as a man. Changed my looks, the way I walked, and the way I talked, and Shazam! Everything was great after that. I could go anywhere and do the things guys do without the stigma of being a woman. Even got the reputation of being a badass businessman."

"You want to know something unusual, but interesting, Hymn? I even petitioned the local Masonic Lodge, became a Master Mason, and advanced through the Masonic offices to become the Worshipful Master of my lodge. I enjoy being a Freemason and visiting other Masonic Lodges. The close brotherhood of that organization is an experience I could not have enjoyed as a woman."

"Being a man turned out to be fun, even exciting. On top of all that, I became more successful in business and am even considered a man to be respected and feared, a well-deserved reputation, I might add."

"There are downsides, though, to being a man with a pussy. I'm not attracted to women, and gay men are interesting to talk with, but their culture is unacceptable to me; however, the upside of having money and power is great compensation. Then you come along, asking if I know who I am. Now, there was a great question! You hit the nail on the head with that question, and your analysis of me is a good one. I have pretended to be a man for so long that I have lost the ability to know who I am."

"I am going to tell you the truth, Hymn. Today, because of you, I know how to find myself. It will take some doing, but I am 41 years old, very wealthy, and without any need to make money anymore. It is now time for Ms. Barclee Marie Evans to be resurrected and reintroduced to the world, beginning today. I have some loose ends to tie together and financial decisions to make, but Mister Barclay Evans, the mean old businessman, is going to fade away over the next few months, making room for the nice Miss Barclee Evans somewhere."

"Hymn, it is not possible to thank you enough for the visit and conversation this morning. I'm actually excited about the prospect of being a woman again. I'm going leave now and begin putting some serious thought into my new life. You know what? I can answer your question now. Yes."

"Yes?" Hymn queried.

"Yes, Hymn, I now know exactly who I am," Barclee affirmed. "I rediscovered myself again moments ago. Thank you for that."

Hymn grinned, stood, and extended his hand. "I think we can now seal that proposed agreement, right here, right now."

Barclee smiled, stood, and shook hands with Hymn, then stepped forward and softly kissed him on the cheek. "Now, the agreement is sealed," she declared.

Hymn, surprised, touched his cheek and remarked, "Now, that's a new experience! I've never sealed an agreement with a kiss from a man before."

To which Barclee smiled and replied, "You still haven't."

Hymn shook his head, chuckled, and said, "So, I haven't. Now, that is going to take some getting used to, Ms. Evans."

He walked with her to the door, stepped outside, and watched as she went to her car, trying to imagine her wearing a dress.

Suddenly, she turned, looked at Hymn, and declared, "You know, Hymn, those migrants have been correct about you all along. You really are a magic man."

Hymn grinned, waved, and said, "Happy New Year, my friend." and went back into the house.

Aunt Rita came from the kitchen, looked around, and asked, "Did Mr. Evans leave?"

Hymn smiled and purposely answered cryptically, "Yes and no, Auntie, in a manner of speaking."

Exasperated, Aunt Rita complained, "Dammit, nephew, does everything have to be a mystery with you?"

Amused, Hymn replied, "No, not always, but our surprise guest today, Mr. Barclay Evans, is a rather unusual man. We had a great conversation."

"Are you going to tell me about it?" she asked.

"Yes." he answered, "But not today."

20

The Road Trip

The new year began as it often does, with a lot of hoopla, celebrating, and the hope of better times ahead. Hymn read an article by an honest reporter, who is no longer employed by his company, that stated:

"2024 is a new Presidential election year, and America is upside down, submerged in a massive sea of debt growing by leaps and bounds—a reality of which the populace seems largely unconcerned. Case in point: politics, sports, the news, and television dominate the people's attention. Why is that? Because media is the belief-shaping medium of the world, especially in America, where media outlets primarily spin or omit news rather than report it and feed prepared pablum to their audience. News anchors, by necessity, must be good readers and loyal soldiers, doing as they are told for 'the good of the people' and, of course, for their bosses, who decide what is 'good'. Why? Simply because cattle cannot be trusted to do what's in the best interests of the herd, requiring drovers to give them direction."

The writer ended the comment, stating:

"Sadly, 'Government of the people, for the people, and by the people' no longer applies to America. Replace the word 'people' with the word 'powerful' and the statement applies."

Hymn thought, *"No wonder that man lost his job! It doesn't pay to write a statement like that without Committee approval. America is a free country, but not **that** free anymore."*

Hymn remained aloof to the issues in the article; they were matters for governments and corporations, which are charged with making decisions 'for the good of the people'—and primarily, of course, for themselves.

Through experimentation and practice inside Keepaway, he was getting a better understanding of his powers. With focused thought, he was capable of creating big changes, and often tempted to do so. However, he avoided this action by realizing and understanding two of his limitations:

1. **The inability to predict or control outcomes.**

2. **The inability to undo that which he does.**

His Aunt Rita advised him early on, "With great power comes great responsibility, and there is wisdom in knowing when to leave things as they are."

He now understood what his aunt meant when she stated early last year that he is the single most dangerous person in the world. She was referring to the real possibility that certain world leaders, jealous of their power and ignorant of Hymn's, will foolishly use force against him, causing millions of casualties in the process.

Flying under the radar by leaving big problems for others to solve was Hymn's way of avoiding big consequences. His interest lay in helping people on an individual basis. The drawback to this was when powerful people became aware of his abilities, they neither liked nor tolerated them, unless they could control them.

Therein lay the problem: control. They should really just back off and leave Hymn alone to tend to little things, but that is not the basic nature of the powerful; they tend to be intrusive when their control is threatened.

Having personally witnessed the paranoid and ruthless nature of the powerful, particularly the politically powerful, Hymn realized that, at some point, he would be forced to pay more attention to security.

He was not concerned about his personal security, as he had Keepaway, and nothing or no one could touch him there. Besides, he was personally under the protection of his inherent powers. The main problem needing a solution was the security of those he loved, mainly his aunt and Melody. The alarm system at Rita's home would not even keep a rock from being thrown at her.

After giving many different types of security systems a lot of thought, he rejected all of them. The system he required did not yet exist, and anyway, a complex system was not feasible. What he had in mind needed to be simple.

"What is it I want the system to do?" he thought to himself and decided it needed to be simple and uncomplicated; a system he could easily apply anywhere, over any area.

"I desire a security system that punishes evil actions and intent," he said to himself. While considering various types of punishment he wanted the system to dispense, it hit his mind like a brilliant flash of lightning in the night, causing him to feel foolish for not thinking of it before.

"Punishment is not what I want my system to dispense at all!" he realized. *"I want just the exact opposite! It is so simple! I want my security system to reward rather than punish intent. I want it to give people their intention."*

Hymn created his new security system over the course of the next few weeks and installed it in and around Aunt Rita's property. It needed some tweaking and testing during the next few months to make sure it was failure-proof and not harmful to his aunt or friends who dropped by to visit occasionally. Finally he was satisfied it was ready to protect her from being harmed at home while he was away.

There was no way Hymn could know, but plans were already made and being put into action to eliminate him and his aunt. Some very powerful forces of world government had decided the Magician was a threat to their security and intent on destroying their power base. Due primarily to inside information from a reliable source, the Magician's location was now determined and locked in. If things went as planned, he would not even know what hit him. *If* being the key word.

It began when Hymn decided he wanted to spend some extended time with Melody. A two-week vacation together seemed a good idea, and Melody, when he mentioned it, was beside herself with joy at the prospect of going on a road trip with Hymn. Aunt Rita thought a vacation would be good for both of them as well. When asked where she would like to go and do, the first word from Melody's mouth was, "Fishing."

That was an unexpected and surprising response.

"Mel, I didn't know you liked fishing," Hymn responded. "You never mentioned anything about fishing before. What brought that on?"

Melody confessed, "Since I've never before been fishing, I don't know if I like it either, but an article I read in a Texas wildlife magazine last year told all about deep sea fishing in the Gulf of Mexico, and I have been dreaming about it ever since. I have no idea what deep sea fishing is like, but it's something new and different and sounds like fun."

Well," Hymn admitted, "I've never been deep sea fishing myself, but if my girl is dreaming about it, maybe we ought to go check it out. It actually sounds like fun to me, too."

Melody screamed in delight, jumped into Hymn's arms, kissed him, and said impatiently, "When are we leaving?"

Aunt Rita, amused, thought, "Vacation, my hind end! That man's not going to get a moment's rest, but they do need some time alone, together."

Hymn paused a few moments, thinking, and said, "Heck, Mel, we can leave now if you want; today is Monday, and the next two weeks are ours to spend as we wish. Padre Island is about 460 miles from here, so we have time to reserve a condo, take several days to get there, go deep-sea fishing later this week, and take our time returning home. Might even take a few romantic strolls on the beach, too. What do you think, babe? A little 'spur of the moment,' maybe, but doable."

"I think that is a great, fabulous plan, Hymn! You are just too wonderful, my love! Don't you think he's wonderful, Auntie?"

Aunt Rita replied, rolling her eyes at Hymn, "Yes, dear, I think he is too wonderful for words." Then, she asked, "When are y'all planning on leaving?"

Melody promptly replied, "I'm on my way to the car now." Then laughed at the expression on Hymn's face and added, "Just as soon as we get our bags packed."

Aunt Rita said, "Okay, then, let's kick this trip into gear. You two get your traveling stuff together while I make some sandwiches and rustle up some snacks and drinks for your adventure." She headed for the kitchen.

They left around noon, heading for Interstate 35 South toward Waco. He figured they might as well take a scenic way to Galveston and enjoy some of the historical areas of central Texas along the way. They could return through east Texas on the way back. If it turned out they needed an extra week, so what; they didn't have any time restraints to be considered. This was going to be a fun road-trip.

Melody was kept busy checking the route on her phone, looking for things to do and places to stay, while Hymn drove. He felt something was not quite right about the car, but no warning lights were showing and it was running smoothly as always. Whatever it was, he mentally fixed it and the feeling disappeared.

Hymn asked, "Have you decided on a good place for us to stop first, Mel? We have a tank full of gas and can drive for hours if you want."

She answered, "I think Waco would be a good place to spend the night, but this feeling of freedom to go where and when we want without giving any thought to time or worrying about anything is refreshing. I love it."

"That's the gypsy in your soul, darling; let it fly for now and enjoy that sensation of freedom, for it is rare . . . and fleeting."

"Why Hymn, my love, you are a poet! I am already loving this vacation and it's just beginning." She kissed her finger tips and gently touched them to his cheek, then looked out the window, humming a tune.

Hymn grinned at Melody's enthusiasm in anticipation of the trip. Her positive way of seeing things was pleasant to be around. She made him happy.

However, the men in the minivan following a little over a mile back were not happy at all about the changes to which they were being forced to adapt.

"Listen Mike, it's not my fault we lost the audio from their car. I just got a text from control, saying the GPS in that car is also not working. If we are going to keep tags on them, we need to physically see them, which means we must stay close enough to do it. What in hell happened to our million dollar equipment, anyway?"

"I don't like it, Josh. This operation depends upon our not being discovered. and getting close is too risky. If our intel is correct, a confrontation with this one will not go well for us. The equipment is not functioning and the GPS is dead. Our mission is dependent upon our ability to track and hear our objective and we are unable to do either."

"Okay Mike, you're the lead agent of this operation and what you say, goes, but keep this in mind, a ton of time and money was spent setting this up and the Bureau hates zero returns. When the shit comes down, you're the one getting buried in the smell."

"Be that as it may, Josh, aborting is the correct decision here. Pack it in; we're going home."

"Hold up there, you two. You're overlooking Plan Y." advised the driver, Tailor, which was surprising, because up to now, he had done nothing but drive and here he is suggesting there is a backup plan about which the other two men knew nothing.

"Plan Y? What the hell is Plan Y?" demanded Mike. "As far as we know, our mission was the only plan, Tailor. What the fuck are you talking about?"

Tailor responded, "Like Josh said, Mike, much time and money was spent putting this operation in place. You don't believe The Bureau would put all their eggs in one basket, do you? Months of research indicates this person represents a legitimate threat to our National Security. Of course there are backups."

"Backups?" queried Josh. "Plural? There are more?"

"Just Z." replied Tailor, "The ultimate plan."

"Sounds ominous," Mike remarked.

"Don't worry, Z won't be necessary. I am Plan Y and Y is more than enough. You two take the car and go. Mike, your decision to abort was the correct one; X was compromised the moment the audio and GPS failed. I will inform The Bureau of that fact."

"How do you plan to get around without a car?" asked Josh.

"I am Y," said Tailor, simply. "Now you guys get out of here. The Bureau will be eager for your written reports."

After they drove away, the helicopter landed and Tailor got in, laughing. "Those two will be discussing 'Y' for years." Then on a serious note, whispered under his breath, "I hope the subject of 'Z' has no reason to ever be discussed." He then got on the phone to his operative. "Plan Y is initiated. You have the ID on the car. When they stop, shoot the man, but just wing him, he is no good to them dead or in a coma. Make make sure he is sedated and taken to Scott & White Medical in Waco. A room is already prepared. Put the female in custody and bring her to the Scott & White ground helipad, where we will be waiting. Have their car searched and dropped off at the first parking lot you see. They will no longer need it."

Tailor was satisfied Plan Y was on schedule and his part to play was simple, deliver both packages as ordered and go home. "Mine is not to reason why," he said to himself as the chopper headed toward Waco.

Melody was looking at her phone and suggested, "Let's stop in West, Texas and buy some kolaches. I love them when they are fresh. We are only about an hour away, depending on traffic."

"Works for me, Mel. That's also a real good place to stop for a while. I'll probably be needing a restroom about then and want to check out the car, as well."

Melody inquired, "Why? Is anything wrong with the car?"

"Nah, it's fine." Just want to check the tires and water."

Melody giggled and said, "I'm finding out all kinds of things about you already on this trip. First, you're a poet, and now you're a mechanic. I don't know if I'm worthy of such a talented man."

"Heck, Mel," Hymn chuckled, "the truth is, no woman is worthy of me. Wait 'til you see me kick the tires on this baby. When I do that, it drives women crazy with desire."

"You don't have to waste your energy kicking tires for me, lover; I'm already crazy about you, so no need to go kicking tires when any women are around," Melody laughed, while ruffling his hair.

They arrived in West about an hour later, as Melody predicted, and parked outside a store advertising freshly made kolaches. Hymn noticed an ambulance parked at the next store over and briefly wondered what had happened there. While Melody went in to find the Ladies Room and buy kolaches, Hymn raised the hood and walked around the car, making a cursory inspection. He opened the trunk and took two bottles of water from the ice chest and, while closing the trunk, dropped one that hit the concrete and rolled under the car. After retrieving the wayward bottle, Hymn put the drinks in the front seat and went into the store to check on Melody. She was in line, waiting to pay for the pastry, so Hymn went into the Men's Room to the toilet.

(Tailor, on speaker) "Is the man down?"

(Shooter) "Negative, sir. No clear shot. People are coming and going. Target is in the store with the female. Will take him down as they return to the car."

(Tailor) "Shoot to wound. Any extremity will suffice."

(Shooter) "Affirmative, sir."

Hymn and Melody walked to the car with the pastry and Hymn went to close the hood.

(Shooter) "Target acquired," he said and pulled the trigger. "Click."

"Misfire! Repeat, misfire!"

He ejected the bullet and tried again. "Click."

"Misfire! Repeat, misfire!"

"Dammit! Dammit! Dammit!" he cursed.

Hymn closed the hood, got in the car, and casually drove away, munching a pineapple kolache. The four men in the ambulance, including the shooter, fastened their seat belts, preparing to follow the car, to no avail; the two front tires were flat. Reaching to release his seat belt, the driver found he could not unlock it. All of the seat belts were firmly locked.

(Tailor, on speaker) "Is the target down?"

(Shooter) "Negative, sir. They are back on the road."

(Tailor) "What in the hell happened?" he demanded.

(Shooter) "Two misfires, sir. Can't happen, but it did."

(Tailor) "What is going on, goddammit? Two 'perfect' plans have gone down a shithole. How is that possible?"

(Shooter) "There is more, sir. The ambulance has two flat tires and all four of us are locked in place by defective seat belts."

(Tailor) "At least we have until morning to complete this mission. Are the two objectives aware of your presence?

(Shooter) "I don't think so, sir. They gave no indication of concern and drove away eating kolaches."

(Tailor) "Good. Well, find where they are staying tonight, now!"

(Shooter) "Uh, sir. The seat belts?"

(Tailor) "Dammit Shooter, call the store and tell them to bring you some scissors! Is that something you can do on your own or you want me to do that for you?"

(Shooter) "No sir. I can do that."

(Tailor) Find them! and have your gun and bullets looked at. Two misfires is more than a coincidence."

(Shooter) "Roger that, sir."

Previously, Hymn saw the tracking device and disabled it when retrieving the bottle of water from under the car. Finding it confirmed his suspicions early on when he sensed something wrong and blocked communication to and from the car, just in case. While in the restroom, he stepped into Keepaway and scanned the area for weapons. The total number and type of firearms in the ambulance gave it away, so he disabled them and compromised the vehicle.

As they drove away, Hymn's mind raced with questions. Who wanted him under surveillance? Who knew he and Melody were on this road trip? When had the bug been installed on Melody's car, and, more intriguingly, why? Why the need for special weaponry? There were far too many questions—and far too few answers.

Hymn realized the device could have been put on the car almost any time she was away from home, meaning they were being recorded when packing to leave. Why, though? Why put a bug on her car? Why not mine? How would anyone know which car to bug, anyway? It almost seems as if Melody is the target, and I am the plus one, a nobody. Why, though? Time to ask her.

"Mel darling," Hymn began, "we have a mystery, and you may be the one with the solution."

"Me?" she inquired, delighted at the opportunity to solve a mystery, "Is this a road trip game?"

"No, Mel, this is not a game; this is serious. Back at the kolache place, when you went inside to the restroom, I dropped one of our water bottles that rolled under the car. While getting the bottle, I noticed an electronic listening device attached to the underside of the car and disabled it. Can you think of any reason someone would bug your car?"

He didn't tell her about dropping the bottle on purpose or the men in the ambulance. Melody laughed and started to say something about the mystery game, then stopped when seeing the serious look on Hymn's face.

"You mean someone has been listening in on us since we left home?"

"Maybe, maybe not." Hymn replied, "I can't say for sure, but that device is high technology and expensive, which means the people who installed it are serious about hearing what you say. Do you have any idea why?"

"Hymn, I don't know anythi . . . uh, well, except for Senator, uh, Hymn, I can't talk about this! It is confidential and very personal. There are professional ethics to be considered. I cannot discuss the dreams of people who come to me for help. I know you understand. Don't you?"

Hymn pulled the car into a roadside rest area, parked, and turned off the engine.

"Let's get something clear, Mel," he advised. "The people who bugged your car are not bothered by ethics or any rules but their own. You cannot ignore them and hope they go away. They won't. These are agents who will use your professional ethics against you. If something you know has made you a person of interest to powerful people, they will stop at nothing until they know what you know. I can only be of help if you tell me what they are after."

"Hymn, if these people are as powerful as you say, I'm not sure if we can do anything. You and I are just regular people and cannot fight them; the best we can do is go to the police for help. Maybe they can help us."

"Mel, do you plan to tell the police about the Senator to whom you earlier referred? If so, make plans for a political frenzy in which you will be the center of attention if you are even allowed the privilege of getting that far. Talk to me, Mel, about what may be the cause of the attention you're getting. Maybe we can reason with these people. I am pretty good at negotiating; it is what I do."

"Okay, Hymn, I'll tell you what I know, but it's just about dreams I have analyzed. All dream sessions with my clients are very private and confidential. You will have to honor my commitment to them."

Hymn nodded his agreement and asked, "Melody, do you use a recorder or a computer in your work?"

"Yes, but only handwritten notes during interviews and sessions. My analysis of a client's dreams are 'Moment Only' and are not in any way saved or filed."

"What about a customer or client list, something like a folder, with names and phone numbers? You know, in case you want to contact them for one thing or another, like a follow-up, for instance."

"Don't have a need for their personal information, Hymn. I have no records of clients. All I do is listen to what they remember about their dream and analyze its meaning."

"So, you're kind of like a psychiatrist?"

"Not really. A psychiatrist is more like a mind scientist who is bound by rules of procedure, keeps records, and has recurring patients. My work is intuitive and 'moment only.' My concern is the dream of the client, not the client. I don't fix people or their dreams."

"Why don't you analyze your client's dreams over the phone, Mel?"

"Tried that in the beginning, with no success. For some reason, I have to be in the presence of the dreamer to make an analysis. I don't mean while they are dreaming, just when they are telling me about their dream."

Hymn asked, "What about the Senator, Mel? How did you know he was a Senator?"

"She, darling. She had two men with her. One interrupted our talk, reminding her of a meeting. He called her Senator."

"Melody, do you remember anything about the dream she wanted analyzed?"

"Of course, I remember! The dream was strange, and the Senator was obviously upset by it. She was having a recurring nightmare about children being fed into a machine squatting over Congress. Kids were being placed on a type of escalator by drones, people without faces, which took them into the mouth of the machine, where they disappeared. For every child eaten by the machine, a large amount of paper money dropped from the machine's bottom, like shit from bowels, into Congress, where the Senators eagerly scrambled to collect it."

"What was your analysis, Mel?" Hymn asked.

"I didn't have to give one. Apparently, the Senator knew what it meant and only desired to know how to stop the nightmare so she could sleep again. The truth is, she didn't need me; her problem required a different type of professional, one that could help with guilt or remorse issues. You know, someone like a psychiatrist or maybe a minister. When I asked why she was so invested in this dream, she answered that her 9-year-old niece had been missing for over a week. The police have no leads and added her to the list of missing children, a long list."

"Did you give her any advice or suggestions?" Hymn inquired.

"I only interpret dreams, Hymn. Her dream was recurring and disturbing, which almost always means the subject is on a path opposed to their moral convictions. I informed her of that truth and advised her to get off that path and onto another, one more in keeping with her personal beliefs."

Hymn considered what Melody related about her session with the Senator and found it interesting, but could not see where that info justified the expenditure of money and effort to go after her with the force witnessed today. There just has to be another reason. He couldn't help but now wonder if it had something to do with him.

Hymn started the car and said, "Tell you what, milady, what say we skirt around Waco on a side trip and stay off the beaten path for a while? Our car is secure from unauthorized intruders, so it is not likely we can be followed. We have the food prepared by Aunt Rita and can camp out tonight along the Brazos River, then enjoy some sights while we make our way to Padre Island by a different route."

"Why Hymn, I love it! All the planning we have been doing is so boring it feels artificial. It is so like you to turn this trip into a romantic interlude."

"Come on, Mel, I am far from being a romantic. Let's not forget that unknown forces are trying to find us for reasons we are not yet aware of. I am just being careful rather than romantic, but I am looking forward to some romance, just the same."

Mel replied, "Let me rephrase my comment, darling; you have turned our trip into an exciting, adventurous, romantic interlude."

Hymn responded, "I'm not sure about all those adjectives, Mel, but I admit, this vacation sure has taken on the appearance of being an interesting outing."

They camped that night in a small park next to the Brazos River.

"What in the world is this all about?" wondered Hymn, sitting by the campfire, trying to understand why people of this caliber would have an interest in Melody. Something she did? Something she does? Something she knows? Something she has?

"What are you thinking about, my love?" she whispered softly in his ear, her hands exploring.

"Not really *what*, Mel, more like *who*," Hymn confessed, "you're who I am thinking about." and began some exploring of his own.

"Congratulations! That is the correct answer," Mel replied, pulling him down on top of her. "You just won the grand prize."

At a hotel in Waco, Tailor couldn't sleep. Plan Y had gone off the rails, and he didn't know why. Little things, like the two misfires from a professional's rifle—those things just don't happen, yet they did.

Later inspections confirmed the gun and bullets were fine. Something was definitely off about this assignment.

How could audio equipment—the best in the world—fail? And those faulty seat belts! What was that all about? Who *was* this woman, and what made her a threat to national security? For Christ's sake, she was just a dream analyst, something like a fortune teller reading palms!

"I know, I know," Tailor thought. *"Mine is not to reason why, but Plan Y is on the verge of failure, and Plan Z is waiting in the shadows. I just don't see why this woman warrants that level of force. Why didn't the Bureau simply have her taken or killed? This all feels crazy, activating Plan Z to take out a fortune teller. Yeah, right, mine is not the reason why."*

(Tailor, over a secure phone) "Have you determined the subjects' location?"

(Shooter) "No. They've disappeared and remain off the grid. They could be anywhere within a hundred-mile radius by now."

(Tailor) Sighing, "Time to abort, Shooter. Plan Y has failed. Pack it in and head back to base. I will inform The Bureau."

(Shooter) "I'm sorry, sir. Does this mean Z is in play?"

(Tailor) "I hope the hell not, but activating hunter/killer drones to take out civilians on American soil is way above my paygrade. All I can say is, these targets must be something special."

21

The Commander's Return

Hymn woke up at 5 am and checked on Melody. She was fast asleep and would probably remain so at least until seven. He secured the perimeter of the campground and stepped into Keepaway.

He spoke, "The kingdom of God." and stepped into the great room, where the overwhelming effect of awe was the same as always.

"Hello Hymn. I have been thinking of you. Did you have good Christmas and New Year celebrations?"

Hymn responded, "You have been on my mind as well, God, and yes, Christmas was great, and the old year went out when the new year arrived."

"You have something on your mind, Hymn. Can I help?"

"I hope so, God. I may have a problem. Do you know if the new commander of The Four Levels, Level-3, has been assigned? Who took the place of Judge Wells?"

"I no longer assign the Level Commanders, Hymn, but they are of interest. Why do you ask about Level-3?"

'Someone or group is after Melody, for some reason beyond my understanding. I cannot believe any group would spend the time, money, and resources required to go after Melody. It is just not sensible. It is more reasonable to believe I am their person of interest, and Mel is being used to get to me. I know that sounds a bit egotistical, but it makes sense when I think about it."

"Level-3 is the only one of The Four still unresolved. That branch holds me responsible for the deaths of both of their recent commanders. Considering that they have the motive, money, time, and resources to carry out a major operation like the one being used now, Level 3 is a logical suspect. What do you think, God? Do you know if L3's new commander is in place, and if so, could he be on a revenge campaign against me?'

God was quiet, and the lights in the room dimmed as he thought about Hymn's conclusion. The lights became bright again, and he spoke softly, "Hymn, I have the answer to your question, but first, you must be made aware of a truth."

Hymn interrupted and said, "God, I don't have much time to listen and talk about the philosophy of truth. Melody is alone now, and I must get back to her, so if you will, tell me what I need to know if you can."

"Hymn," God began, "I have a confession to make."

Hymn thought, "Oh boy! God has something important to say that can't wait. If it is that important, I had better listen."

Hymn went over to his favorite chair, sat down, and stated, "You have my attention, friend."

"Thank you, Hymn. I should have told this to you months ago, in your time, but kept putting it off for. . .well, for reasons I cannot explain. Now, it has become necessary. Last year, you remember a group of Level-3 assassins held a birthday party where you and your Aunt Rita were to be sacrificed as a revenge gift to one of their members. You were about to deal with them when I interrupted and advised you to let me handle the situation. I was concerned you were going to do something you would regret for the rest of your life. You are a good man, Hymn, who believes everyone deserves a chance to be a better person. I am not burdened with that ethic, and I have eradicated them, all except one: Jonas."

Hymn stood up in disbelief and exclaimed, "What? Are you saying the Commander of Level-3 is alive?"

"Yes, Hymn. Jonas is alive and has resumed command of Level 3 of The Four Levels, giving credence to your suspicion that those pursuing Melody are actually hunting you."

"Why did you save him, God? The man is a psychopath, a killer responsible for the deaths of many people."

"Jonas was made the Commander of Level-3 by Jehovah, who based her decision regarding him on the results of personality evaluations created by me. Jonas is a great man, Hymn, perhaps the greatest psychopath of all time. Finding myself incapable of being his executioner, I confined him to solitude, without any visitors, on Earth in ADX Florence, in Colorado, USA. Somehow, he was released when Judge Wells, his Level-3 replacement, was killed, supposedly by you, Hymn."

"Great care must be taken if Jonas is indeed seeking you, Hymn. He is a special man of high intellect, without virtue; a man who will choose to sacrifice unlimited human lives for revenge if that is what it takes to hurt or kill you. I know of none like Jonas in this reality; his absolute absence of goodness is admirable in its uniqueness, which is why Jehovah was fond of him. Those who follow him are fanatical in their belief in him. Some even preach he is the only begotten son of Jehovah and worship him as God Almighty. Beware of L-3 Jonas, Hymn. He just may be the most dangerous man on Earth."

Hymn's response was, "Really? I have an aunt who would argue that statement with you. Thanks, God. You solved my dilemma and relieved much of my anxiety."

"Have you an idea as to any weaknesses of Jonas, God?"

After a pause, God replied, "Jonas is a human being with human imperatives and is mortal. He devoutly believes in, and prays often to a dead god, that being Jehovah."

"That is interesting," Hymn commented and stated, "I really have to go now. And don't bother yourself about feeling bad for allowing Jonas to live, God. You actually did a good thing. We will talk about it later, my friend."

Hymn returned to the campground to check on Melody.

God was silent, thinking. *"Why does he do that? He always leaves me with a mystery to solve. What good thing did I do?"*

Then God considered, "Jonas vs. Hymn, or perhaps a more fitting billing is Evil vs. Virtue. Losing either of those two would be a great loss for the universe, and neither of them understands why. Oh well, it will give Hymn and me something to talk about at our next meeting."

Melody was still sleeping when Hymn returned, so he laid down beside her and tickled her nose with a pine needle. She opened one eye, stretched, put her arms around his neck, and kissed him.

"There is an ancient rule regarding male-female relationships, mister," she advised, "Tickling a sleeping woman's nose early in the morning creates a serious obligation on your part as a man."

Hymn smiled, kissed her, and replied, "Now, that is interesting and useful information, darling. Where did you learn such wisdom?"

"Oh, Hymn, you are so uninformed," she playfully sighed while pulling him closer, saying, "Who cares? Right now, you have an obligation to fulfill."

Hymn and Melody left the campsite and were back on the road, heading to Padre Island on a more east Texas country route. It was now obvious to Hymn that L-3 Jonas was their adversary, and trying to evade the enforcement branch of The Four Levels was a lesson in futility, particularly with Melody along for the ride. It is not in Hymn's nature to evade a problem; he is more the sort of man to invite his adversaries to breakfast for coffee and biscuits than spend time avoiding them.

Jonas is a different breed of man. God found him to be absent of virtue, indicating conventional methods of dealing with him are out of the question. Jonas will do the unthinkable to get his way without regard for consequences. In his odd way of thinking, all he does is approved by the great God, Jehovah, and, as such, must be right and good.

Hymn had a disturbing thought and stopped at the next gas station to make a call to his aunt and get some coffee. Melody was elated for the break, as the need for a restroom had made itself known to her.

"Hi, Auntie," he said when Rita answered her phone. "We're on the road, and I'm just checking in with you to see how everything is going at home."

"Didn't you get the text I sent you a few minutes ago, nephew?" she inquired and added before he could answer, "Four parked cars are in my front yard right now. They got here about ten minutes ago and are just parked there. No one has attempted to get out of the cars as yet, and the motors are running. What do you suppose they want, Hymn?"

"Right about now, I suspect all they want is to go home, Auntie. Call 911 and tell them to send four ambulances to your address to care for very sick people in four cars. Tell 911 to send the police, too. If they ask, tell the police you went out to see what they wanted and saw people passed out in their cars. Stay in the house and call me when the emergency crews arrive. I'll talk to you later. Bye, now."

"So, this is the way Jonas and L3 have decided to play." Hymn said to himself.

Melody returned from the restroom, announced she was hungry, and pointed to a grill next to the station. Hymn nodded and followed her to the restaurant, smiling sadly at her cheerful attitude. He dreaded breaking the news that their vacation was over; the first assault in his conflict with Level-3 had begun just moments ago. If Hymn's suspicions were correct, things were getting messy for those Level-3 agents outside his aunt's house. He could be there in seconds through Keepaway, but concerns for Melody kept him grounded; besides, he knew Aunt Rita was safe. Now, he needed to bring Melody up to speed.

They ordered hamburger baskets and coffee and sat at a table. Melody noticed that Hymn seemed unusually quiet, far from his easygoing self.

"What's going on, my love?" she asked, studying him. "You seem to be somewhere else right now. Who were you talking to on the phone? Was it Auntie? Is everything all right? Is she okay?"

Hymn held up his hand to calm her and smiled patiently. He knew he had to bring her up to date on the situation, though he wasn't sure how she'd react to the unbelievable events unfolding. He was about to find out.

"Yes, Mel, it was Auntie on the phone. She's worried because some cars drove up and parked in her front yard without explanation. They're still there, and no one's even attempted to get out. I told her to call 911 and have the police and ambulances come to investigate."

Mel thought for a moment, then asked, "Ambulances, Hymn? Plural? You think there might be casualties?"

"Yeah, Mel," Hymn explained. "You can't be sure in situations like this. Unannounced cars showing up can signal malicious intent. They're definitely scaring Aunt Rita, and the fact no one is getting out of them is strange. It's not unreasonable to think they might be having some medical issues. If so, ambulances will be needed."

Melody asked quietly, "Could they be the same people who have been following us?"

Hymn nodded. "Yes, that is more than possible; it is likely. And that concerns me, Mel."

"Why multiple ambulances, Hymn? I mean, according to Aunt Rita, the people in those cars aren't doing anything wrong; they are just sitting there. They could be visitors from the local church. Calling for the police and ambulances seems like overreacting, don't you think?"

"Mel, before we left, I installed a virtual security system around my aunt's property. No one dares to set foot there with malicious intent."

Mel was curious, "What happens if they try, Hymn?"

"They get sick, very sick," Hymn answered.

"Sick enough to die?" she demanded, concerned.

Their food order was placed on the table. Hymn took a big bite of his hamburger and sipped some coffee to wash it down. Then, he gazed directly into Melody's eyes to emphasize the seriousness of his answer.

"Sick enough to require medical attention," he answered, in a 'matter of fact' manner. "The level of sickness experienced is directly proportional to the intent of the intruder."

Melody, visibly upset, asked, "What if the intruders have bad intentions, Hymn? What happens to them?"

Hymn took another bite of his burger, along with a sip of coffee, and simply stated, "They will not need an ambulance."

"Oh, my God, Hymn! Where did you get such a horrible security system? That cannot be legal. You might kill people who are only following orders."

"Those humans who follow orders to kill someone, Mel, are born with the ability to reason and choose, meaning they can choose to disobey the orders. Purposeful killing requires intent."

Hymn advised, "No, Melody, I kill no one. Those who die when entering my security system intending to damage or kill my aunt or me are actually responsible for their own deaths."

"My system rewards intent. Enter with the intent to hurt, and you get hurt; intend to steal, and you will lose something, perhaps a body part; intend to kill, and well, you understand what I'm saying."

"Good lord, Hymn, that is not natural! It is inhuman! How is it you know how to create something so horrible, anyway?"

"On the contrary, Melody, if you give serious thought to it, the security system is quite natural, being based upon the biblical 'give and receive' principle regarding the flow of energy in our reality. In simple terms, if one plants a watermelon seed, he will grow watermelons, along with many more watermelon seeds. You know, 'like begets like' and all that."

Hymn grasped Melody's hand and stated, seriously, "The actual questions demanding answers are, why is it you know about this incident? And who are you?"

Hymn reached across the table and picked up Melody's burger and took a bite of it.

"I have a feeling you are not hungry anymore," he said as he lifted his cup, sipped some coffee, and bit into her burger. He again asked, "Why? And who are you?"

Before she could answer, Hymn's phone vibrated on the table. He answered it on speaker and asked, "What's going on, Auntie?"

"Oh, Hymn, it's terrible! There are over twelve people in the cars. All the doors were locked, and the emergency crew had to break the windows to get them out. Two were women. The smell in the cars is awful; whatever sickness they have caused them to empty their bowels or vomit from the smell. The medics are attending to the live ones now. At least three men are dead, apparently from gunshot wounds. It is horrible, Hymn, just horrible."

Aunt Rita was crying. Hymn turned off the speaker and looked at Melody. She was crying, too. He spoke softly to his aunt, "Stay in the house, Auntie; there are predators around, but you are safe. Do not give permission to anyone who wants to enter and look around. Without permission, they can do nothing. Some enforcement people will have questions, and you have no answers. Tell them I will be home later, and they can talk with me then. They won't because the man in charge of this incident will soon throw a blanket over it. Don't worry, Auntie, I will take care of everything. Bye now."

Hymn then turned his attention to Melody. "Where were we? Oh, yeah, you were about to tell me about yourself, Miss Melody. I have to say, girl, you fooled me good. I felt emotions for you I did not know existed. The truth is, I still feel them, and though it may not show, you hurt me with this betrayal. I now feel empty and sad. Who are you? And why? are the questions of this moment."

Melody wiped tears from her face with a napkin and said, "I am so very sorry, Hymn, for hurting you and the mess I have made of everything. My mess, my consequences. I'll try to explain."

"You heard part of my story when we first met when I confessed to being the black sheep of my family and being estranged from them because my personal beliefs are opposed to theirs. My mom and dad work for the government. I don't know what they do, but Dad is an important man, mainly because his brother is the boss of a very high-level law enforcement organization. My brothers work there, too, as security agents for a solutions company."

Hymn was trying to be calm and collected but could not believe what he was hearing. He remained quiet, though, and listened.

Melody continued, "Last Friday, I went home to visit and have dinner with the family, and when the questions about my personal life came up, I told them about your being the love of my life and that we are living together. My Dad wanted to know if I had investigated your background, and when I said no, he expressed his disappointment in me and immediately got up and left the room. Mom revealed that he was under a lot of pressure at work and has been bringing it home with him."

"He never approves of the things I do anyway, so I didn't pay any attention to him. Mom said I should be more careful about making new friends with strangers because they might be criminals or serial killers, or evil people. I laughed at her suspicions and explained how you and Aunt Rita are great people. I told them how much fun we had with everyone at that Christmas party."

Hymn couldn't wait any longer, so he interrupted Melody to ask, "Mel, what is your uncle's name?"

"You mean my Uncle Jonas? I don't know much about him; he is important and very busy. Sometimes, the family gets together at Christmas or Thanksgiving, and on occasion, Uncle Jonas shows up. He has been doing business out of the country for a while and only recently returned. Dad was really glad to see him, and Mom said they have been spending a lot of time together in special meetings the last two weeks."

"Anyway," Mel continued, "Dad was concerned and decided to have you investigated; he promised to let me know what he finds out. When you told me my car was bugged and we were being followed, I figured it was just my dad being overprotective and thought it was sweet of him to be concerned about me. My dad never showed any interest in me like that before, but I never dreamed he would send people to investigate Aunt Rita, too."

"Hymn, when you told me four cars showed up at Aunt Rita's and how your security system would deal with them, I freaked out. My brothers were likely in those cars and maybe even my dad. I couldn't understand why so many people went to investigate Aunt Rita, but something was wrong and and my intuition told me it was going to be bad. Turned out to be horrible, according to Aunt Rita. I have a fear of great loss inside me, Hymn, a fear that I have lost everything." Melody began crying again.

Hymn took Mel by the hand, led her from the grill, and helped her into the car. Then drove north, toward Ft. Worth.

He couldn't help but notice, Melody was in despair.

"Cry until you get it all out, Melody, then pull yourself together. We have things to do."

While driving, Hymn went over Mel's explanation of events in his mind. Finding that Mel's uncle is Jonas, the commander of L3 was shocking enough in itself, but when the fact that her mother and father are high level employees of L-3 and her two brothers are Invisibles, assassins of SoLutions, came to light, it was far too overwhelming to be believed!

Add to that mix, the fact that Melody is the person from whom everything has been kept. All she knows is her family is involved in security at a large company. Being somewhat of an outsider in her own family because of her moral convictions, Melody was never aware of that which her family actually does for a living. On top of that, she has no idea of who and what is Hymn, only that he is more than he seems.

Hymn realizes that Melody is on edge, lost between two worlds, neither of which is what she thought they were. As if that were not enough, she is about to learn that her father and brothers were the three men who died in cars outside of Aunt Rita's house, having been sent there by her Uncle Jonas to kill Hymn's aunt as part of his plan to hurt and eventually kill Hymn, as well. Information of that magnitude might push her over the edge to oblivion.

Hymn remembered something to which, at the time, he had paid little attention. Melody was sent to him by Walter, Who, being all knowing, knew about her family. Hymn always figured she was sent to him for his sake, but what if Walter sent her to him for her sake? In many ways, Mel was more in need of help than was he.

"Walter," he prayed, "Melody is going through a terrible phase in her life right now. I ask that you help her find the inner strength to manage it and give me the wisdom to help her through it. Thank you for always being here."

"Amen," said Melody. Then asked, "Hymn, darling, were you praying for me? I don't remember anyone ever praying for me before and don't know what to say." and then said, "Thank you, Hymn. That meant more than you can possibly know."

Surprised, Hymn asked, "I thought you were dozing, girl. Did you get all the crying done?"

"Probably not, but I'm not the mess I was earlier. Hymn, can you forgive me for the trouble I caused?"

"Nothing to forgive, darling. As far as I'm concerned, you didn't do anything wrong. You were being used. There are forces at work now of which you are not aware, and there is sadness ahead. That strength of character I have always seen in you is going to be needed. You will soon be introduced to information that will challenge the belief structure of your entire life, much of which you will find hard to believe."

There was a long stretch of road ahead, and Hymn pulled the car to the side and parked, with the car idling. "I'm getting out here, Mel. You drive to Aunt Rita's house and check on her. She was really upset when last we talked."

Melody protested, "But Hymn, this is in the middle of nowhere! How are you going to . . .?"

He interrupted her protest with a kiss, got out of the car, and stepped into Keepaway.

Mel watched him disappear, apparently into thin air, with shocked disbelief. Her mind was incapable of accepting what she saw as being real because it wasn't real; it was a type of trick, black magic, performed by a master magician. But why? Why would Hymn try to impress me with magic?

Melody spoke her thoughts, *"My God, Hymn! Who are you? What are you? How did you do that? Why did you do that? How can any of this be real?"*

Her mind racing, searching for reasonable explanations, she put the car in gear and headed to Aunt Rita's house.

While driving, Melody remembered Hymn saying I was about to be introduced to information that would challenge my entire belief structure. What he just did was more than enough. I wonder if the shock of today's events has affected my sanity, causing me to become delusional. I have to get back to Aunt Rita. Maybe she can help me to make some sense of all that is happening. Yeah, I need to talk with Aunt Rita.

22

Evil and Virtue

Commander Jonas spoke to Farregutt, his advisor and once the most lethal assassin in the world.

"What in hell is going on with this organization? I take leave for a brief period, and the place goes to shit! Level Three is supposed to be the most powerful, most feared force in the world, yet it can't eliminate one man."

"Under my explicit orders, The Bureau initiated the *Blueprint Imperative,* a three-plan system that has never failed to achieve an objective. Yet this week, it failed three times in two days. Plan 'X' failed because of faulty equipment, 'Y' failed when an 'infallible' sniper rifle misfired three times, and the ultimate Plan 'Z' failed because the drone sent to destroy that woman and her house with a missile lost power and crashed in a local lake."

"Covering that up took some doing. And, to top it off, the entire ground force sent to kill the old hag and any witnesses came down with some type of virus, making them too sick to even get out of their cars. Three of my own close associates reportedly died from mysterious gunshot wounds in that operation. I'm talking about one man here—a so-called 'magic man' or some such nonsense. How is it humanly possible he was able to defeat Blueprint? It seems we underestimated this magic man."

(Farregutt) "We have it on reliable authority, sir, that the man in question was nowhere near his aunt's house when the drone and death squads were compromised. Both of those failures were due to unexplained, natural causes, not magic."

(Jonas) "Is that not what magic is, Farregutt? Unexplained, natural acts. Once the magic is explained, it loses its mystery and is exposed as merely natural. He must have a powerful force protecting him—a force about which we know nothing. Another curious thing about him is his avoidance of offense. Assuming he caused the failure of Blueprint as well, it's clear all his actions were defensive, taken only to protect his loved ones. He's made it appear as though Level Three itself is responsible for everything that happened. How great is that! This magic man is clever, but he's shown his weakness: he cares about people. I wonder how many deaths he'll allow before he's willing to surrender?"

Jonas grinned as a devious plan began forming in his mind, and he silently prayed, *Thanks be to Jehovah for giving me the solution to defeating my enemy.*

"Farregutt!" he barked. "Without thinking, say the first country that comes to mind?"

(Farregutt) "Switzerland."

(Jonas) "Interesting. I wonder if Magic Man cares about children in Switzerland. Let's find out. Farregutt, have an agent plant a bomb in a kindergarten or school for young children there—any city will do. It should be simple; I suspect we have an agent in every school. Arrange for ten bombs, and see that the first one is delivered and installed by tomorrow morning. I'm fascinated to see how many children this man will sacrifice to save his own life. I wonder if he likes choices."

(Farregutt) "Sir, as your advisor, I must point out that the course you're setting is fraught with danger—not just for you, but for all of Level Three. This magic man is unlike anyone I have seen or read about. As crazy as it sounds, he might not even be human. If, as you believe, he only plays defense, why provoke him by attacking what he cares about? Cease all offensive actions against him, and he'll have no reason to fight back. He'll go back to whatever it is he does, and we can return to our work without interference."

Farregutt continued, "Also consider this: if he's as powerful as he appears—maybe even more so—simple wisdom says we should leave him alone. The course you're planning could get Level Three obliterated and might even bring down The Four. The cost-benefit ratio isn't in our favor. My advice, sir, is that we leave him alone for now."

(Jonas) "Magic man will come for me anyway, Farregutt. I've given him reason."

(Farregutt) "In that case, Level Three should play defense, sir. Any consequences resulting from his attack will be on him, not us. We will 'Trump' him."

(Jonas) "Trump him?"

(Farregutt) "Demonize him, sir. Publicize him as an evil liar and a global threat. Report only the bad results of his actions and cover up any good."

(Jonas, grinning) "What evil results?"

(Farregutt) "Just about anything imaginable, sir. People tend to follow the voice of authority, and Level Three is Enforcement—*the authority.*"

(Jonas) "An excellent idea, Farregutt. We'll take him down with the power of the press, turning him into a pariah for an unprovoked attack on us. 'Trump' him indeed. How beautifully insidious! And then, I'll kill him. I love it! Now, how do we motivate this magician into making that unprovoked attack?"

Commander Jonas paused, and then his face lit up with a wide, knowing smile. He had just realized how to exploit the magician's weakness, forcing him into the aggressive action needed to convince the world of his "evil" nature, branding him as a threat to global security. Any response from Jonas afterward would be justified. The perfect plan.

Calmly, Jonas ordered, "Farregutt, go ahead and bomb that Swiss school tomorrow. And find a way to let the magician know the children were killed as a tribute to him and that more random school attacks are planned in his honor. That will either provoke him to attack first or push him to surrender to stop the killings. Either way, we get what we want. Alert security—I suspect we'll have company in the next few days."

(Farregutt) "Commander Jonas! You're underestimating this magician, and I strongly advise against this plan. Killing innocent children will incite global outrage!"

(Jonas) "Yes, it will! And that is precisely what will guarantee our success, Farregutt. We will 'Trump' him, making it appear as though he's behind the school killings, and his elimination will look like a necessary service to humanity."

"Remember, Level Two of The Four Levels controls world information, putting global media firmly on our side—a powerful tool for shaping public opinion, as they are the Voice of Authority worldwide. People trust them. I'll ensure that Level Two understands the threat this magician poses. I suspect they don't like him either. By the time we're through, he'll be thought of as the devil himself."

(Farregutt) "But Commander—"

(Jonas) "Enough, Farregutt. The magic man is going down, no matter what you think."

(Jonas) "I have to tell you, Mr. Advisor, your fear of this magic guy is damned irritating. And for God's sake, quit going on about killing innocent kids! Have you ever been around any of the little bastards? All they do is eat, shit, throw up, and tear things down without adding anything useful to the world. In this case, they're just collateral damage, sacrificed for a greater cause. When you think seriously about it, the world could use more 'collateral damage' like that. Scientists warn the world is overpopulated, and millions are going to die because of it. Hell, we're doing humanity a favor by ridding the world of a few hundred kids now and then. Get over it! We are the good guys here."

(Farregutt, to himself) *"There's no use of my arguing with the Commander. His beliefs are deeply entrenched. Why am I resisting killing children for the 'greater good', anyway? Damned if I know!"*

(Farregutt) "Commander Jonas, I admit to being very concerned about the Magician. He's an unknown with powerful abilities, and I believe he's being underestimated. You're the only one who's seen his anger, and over two dozen top L-3 operatives lost their lives in that encounter. His anger will be even greater after your plan unfolds, with an unknown number of children killed in his name. Given that, sir, I respectfully resign as your personal advisor."

(Jonas) "You must realize, Farregutt, resigning means you will never work for L-3 again? Seems like a terrible waste to me."

(Farregutt) "Sir, if my worst fears come to pass, Level Three won't exist by the end of the same week those children are killed. Without L-3, The Four Levels will descend into chaos, and only an intervention from Jehovah could save it."

(Jonas, laughing) "Listen to my former personal advisor droning on like an award-winning Drama Queen. Get the hell out of my sight, Farregutt, and on your way out, tell Marie to assemble the world council. I have to bring them up to date."

23

The Melody Meltdown

When Melody got to the house, it was late afternoon. Rita was so happy to see her. She cried, and Melody cried, too.

"I'm so sorry, Aunt Rita," Melody confessed, "All this trouble is my fault. I didn't know my father would go this far. I thought he was just worried about my relationship with Hymn and…"

"Shush, child," Aunt Rita interrupted gently. "Hymn told me all about it, and none of this mess is your fault. All responsibility lies at the feet of others."

Melody, surprised, asked, "Hymn? How, Auntie? I left him back on the road two hours ago. Did he call you?"

"No, dear, Hymn was here about two hours ago. He wanted to explain everything that happened on your road trip before you got home. What he told me about you is absolutely incredible. Finding out you're the daughter of two Level-3 operatives is shocking enough, but learning you also have two brothers who are Invisibles? It's almost beyond belief. You're part of a high-echelon government family, girl."

Tears streamed down Melody's face as she replied, "Did Hymn not tell you that the three men killed here today are probably my dad and brothers?"

Rita, her own eyes filling with tears, said softly, "No, Melody, he didn't mention that. I'm so sorry, child. Are you sure? Nothing has been reported linking those deaths to your family."

"Hymn is not sure, but I am," Melody answered. "My dream nature is sensitive to these things. I haven't spoken with my mother yet, but if she's a government agent, she likely already knows."

All the crazy talk of 'secret agents,' 'government operatives,' and 'magic' was beginning to weigh on Melody's rational mind. None of it seemed real and sounded more like fiction than truth to her.

Melody questioned Rita, "Auntie, something tells me no one knows about Hymn's secret security system. Do you know how it works? The police aren't going to figure out what made everyone sick and caused the death of those three men today. It will just be another unsolved mystery—except for the fact that you know, don't you, Aunt Rita? Hymn told you about it, didn't he?"

"I have no idea how the security system works, dear," Rita replied. "Hymn designed it. All I know is that it responds to intent. The three men who died today had murder on their minds, and they received it."

"Aunt Rita, I think it's time I learned more about Hymn. Both of you have tried to tell me things that, at the time, did not interest me, but now it does. Too many unexplained things happen around him, things that can't be explained with conventional reasoning. He does things that just cannot be done, and yet he does them. Is he some kind of wizard of the paranormal? Or… what?"

Aunt Rita took a deep breath and began explaining the family's history of people born with special abilities.

"No one is quite sure when these abilities first began," Aunt Rita explained, "but *The Legend of the One* prophesied that these powers would culminate in a single man in the year 2023. Melody, that man is Hymn; he is *the One*."

Trying not to laugh at such a ridiculous story, Melody asked, "Aunt Rita, are you saying my Hymn is some kind of superhero, like Superman?"

Rita, sensing Melody's skepticism, replied seriously, "No, dear, I'm saying that Superman, if he existed, wouldn't stand a chance in a match with Hymn."

Seeing that Aunt Rita was serious, Melody, not wanting to offend her, replied, "Well, that's…really interesting, Auntie. I'm glad you told me. I never would have come up with that on my own. I thought Hymn might have learned some cool tricks from studying magic and mysticism, and here you are telling me he's capable of *real* magic. I'm honestly surprised and don't know what to say. You have to admit, it sounds a bit… insane."

"Melody," Rita explained, "Hymn doesn't have tricks up his sleeves; he has power in his very being—great power, much of which he has yet to fully realize. You need to understand that the man with whom you have now formed a close relationship is unique in this world and perhaps even in the universe. Your future together depends a great deal upon your understanding and accepting this truth."

Melody was indignant in her reply, "Aunt Rita, I don't want to upset you, but there is no way Hymn has superpowers or whatever you're suggesting. A super guy? Absolutely, I believe that. But great powers? That's a bit too much, Auntie. And saying he's unique in the universe… well, that is insane! Another thing, Auntie, you told me last year that Hymn is over 50 years old. Anyone can tell by looking at him that he is in his early thirties—if that!"

"There's something awfully wrong in this house, Aunt Rita. You and Hymn live in a false reality you believe to be real, and you have drawn me into this whole fantasy along with you. Why have you done that? Hymn couldn't possibly have arrived here before me, yet you claim he was here and told you everything. That is just not possible!"

Melody's voice was rising.

"Ever since I met Hymn, my whole life has been a lie I accepted and believed. I felt something was wrong but couldn't see the truth—until now. The stories and magic tricks you two performed were convincing and caused me trust to you enough to let you into my life. God, I'm so gullible!"

Melody's mind raced as she continued.

"Thinking back, when I first met him, Hymn told me government agents were after him. That's crazy, too, Aunt Rita, but he was so convincing I fell for it. Hymn is totally paranoid! I don't understand anything going on here. It's all so surreal. Why didn't I notice it before now? I guess I was so tangled up in love that I stopped paying attention to what was actually happening. None of this is real; it's all made-up fantasy!"

Melody had reached a point of no return, where her rational mind could take no more and became overwhelmed with remorse.

"Oh no! It can't be! What have I done?" she cried aloud, her voice breaking, "What have I done?"

With horror dawning, she continued, "I know what happened today. My father, worried about my new boyfriend, must have run a background check on Hymn and found out you two are criminals, wanted by the government, and rushed here with my brothers to save me. Instead, they got killed in the process! My God, I'm so stupid. I even believed the ridiculous story about a 'secret security system' that makes people kill themselves. You two killed my father and brothers! Oh, God! This is insane! You and Hymn are psychopaths!"

Melody lost complete control of herself. When Rita reached to console her, Melody backed away, screaming, "Don't touch me! Stay away from me!" She bolted from the house, jumped into her car, and sped off, her tires spinning and screeching down the street.

Rita stood at the doorway, watching in shock and disbelief as Melody's car roared away. She had witnessed the young woman unravel, spiraling from sanity to a complete breakdown, all based on a false assumption. Unable to accept the strange, extraordinary events that had unfolded, Melody's mind had been pushed beyond its limits by the day's stress, shattering in under three minutes.

Rita sighed and returned to the house, deeply troubled by Melody's meltdown. Consumed by grief, she wondered how to tell Hymn. This will hurt him—terribly. How will he react? Dreading the conversation but knowing it was necessary, Rita picked up the phone and dialed his number.

24

Commander Jonas

Several hours earlier, when Hymn left Melody with the car and stepped into Keepaway, he said "home" and stepped directly into his room in Aunt Rita's house. He walked to the living room and found his aunt sitting in her chair, knitting. He went and hugged her.

"What's up with the knitting, Auntie? With all the excitement you had today, I would rather expect to find you with a glass of wine in your hand instead of knitting needles."

"Knitting calms my nerves, nephew. Lord knows my nerves are all over the place."

Hymn apologized, "I'm sorry you had to go through all that mess today, Auntie. Wait until you hear why. I'm still not able to wrap my mind around it. It sounds more like a fiction novel than the truth."

Hymn began, "Melody went to visit with her family last Friday and informed them about me being the love of her life and that we lived together. She told them how happy her life is now and answered all of their questions about us, who we are, and even where we live. Being suspicious, her dad called in a security check on me. It revealed I am a person of interest in a government investigation."

"Now, listen to this incredible tidbit of information. It turns out that Melody's mom and dad are executives in Level Three, the enforcement branch of The Four Levels, and, in addition to all of that, her two brothers are agents of none other than SoLutions, Inc. They are both Invisibles!"

Rita was astonished! She put her knitting aside and asked, "How could we have missed that Hymn?"

"I have no clue, Auntie. This is one of those rare instances in life where coincidence is stranger than fiction. If you think what I just told you is unbelievable and strange, listen up; it gets even stranger. What is truly amazing is Melody's uncle Jonas, her father's brother, is none other than the great Level Three Commander."

"Good lord! I don't believe it! Things like this just don't happen. Wait a minute, Hymn." Rita said quickly, "I remember you said the Level-3 commander was among all the assassins eliminated in the warehouse affair."

"Well, it turns out he escaped that fate, Auntie," Hymn revealed, "and is back as the head of Level-3."

"For heaven's sake, Hymn, sometimes this world is surprisingly small. Have you said anything to Melody about her family?"

"No, her fragile world is already turned upside down as it is, and learning the truth about her family may be more than she can handle. The truth is, though, she needs to be told. When she finds out later we kept all these secrets from her, it might hurt more than revealing it now."

Rita suggested, "I will talk to her about those things if they happen to come up in our conversation later on today. Maybe talking with another woman about it will be easier than talking with you."

"That will be better, Auntie. Right now, I have to try to find out what Jonas is planning. He has a few irons in the fire, along with an evil disposition, making him an interesting adversary."

"There can be no doubt Jonas has his sights set on you, Hymn, so be careful. If you are right about that man, he won't care how many people have to die in his quest to get at you," she stated.

"Yes," he agreed, "and that must be dealt with now before he has time to allow his evil mind to conjure up a distraction to exact revenge upon me for the deaths of his three relatives today."

"I'm leaving now to talk with someone about that very thing, Auntie," Hymn advised.

Hymn went to his room and stepped into Keepaway.

"Screen. The Kingdom of Heaven."

"Hello, Hymn," God greeted. "I was hoping to see you and talk about your comment from when you were here last."

"Good to be in your company again, my friend," Hymn stated. "I need your help with something."

"I am flattered!" God admitted. "What is it I can do for you?"

"You told me when I was here before that Jonas prays to Jehovah regularly. Have you heard anything in his prayers about an act of revenge against me by doing something to hurt me? I worry that he may cause death and destruction to get at me. You warned he has no morals, and I fear he will stop at nothing to hurt me."

"Jonas hates you, Hymn, and would kill a million people today if he thought their deaths would result in yours, without his having to suffer dire consequences for the act, of course. Instead, he has decided to kill young children in smaller numbers, making it easier to blame the deaths on others. He is sure you will believe you are to blame for their deaths and prays it will seriously cause you anguish."

"Interesting guy, this Jonas," Hymn observed. "Who did he pick to be his first target? And what is he planning to do?"

"A school in Switzerland," God replied. "He has already given orders for a bomb to be placed there."

"Why did he pray to Jehovah about it, God?" Hymn wondered.

"Jonas is convinced Jehovah approves of him and his actions. He asked Jehovah to allow some of the children to survive the blast, permanently disabled, blinded, with their arms and legs blown off (his exact words), and wanted videos and pictures taken of the carnage and suffering. The more horrible, the better the effect."

Hymn grimaced at the thought and said softly, "Where is Jonas now, God?"

"The coordinates you need are in your phone," God answered. "And Hymn, be advised, Jonas has many with him."

Hymn nodded, indicating his understanding, and stepped into Keepaway, a plan forming in his mind. He thought, *There is time. Even if the bomb is in place now, Jonas will not detonate it until tomorrow morning when the students are in school. It is 8 or 9 o'clock in the evening in Switzerland now, so there should be time to locate the bomb before it explodes. Should be."*

He spoke the coordinates placed in his phone by God, having no idea what to expect, but God had emphasized that many were with Jonas, meaning expert killers. Assassins!

"Whatever," thought Hymn and added, "At the very least, this is going to be interesting."

He stepped from Keepaway to meet with Jonas.

25

The Jonas Surprise

Hymn looked around and found himself standing in a stark, dimly lit room, with two sofa chairs and a modest desk as the only furniture. Sitting in one of the sofa chairs, unmoving, with both hands clasped in his lap, was a man in the deep concentration of prayer. On the left arm of the chair was a pill and a glass of what looked to be water. Resting on the right arm was a gun.

"You have the appearance of a man balancing on the verge of a big decision. I find that interesting," Hymn softly commented.

The man was surprised but controlled himself. He slowly turned his head, looked at Hymn, and said, "Your coming here now was not smart." With the swiftness of a striking snake, he picked up the gun and pointed it at Hymn. "You remain alive now only because I am curious. How did you get in this office?"

"Aw, come on now," Hymn chided as he proceeded to sit down in the chair next to the man. "We have only just met, and here you are, holding a gun and threatening to kill me. When you think about it, it is bad manners and impolite behavior. It's embarrassing, too, considering you're doing all that with an empty gun. You're going to have to do better than that if you want to scare me."

"Empty gun?" The man quickly looked at the revolver cylinder; it was empty. "What the . . . !" He stood and sent a questioning look at

Hymn, noticing the kind eyes and gentle, half-smile on the face of the intruder.

"I have no idea who this guy is," he quickly thought to himself, *"or what is going on here, but he seems harmless."* He sat back down in his chair, staring at Hymn.

"Don't look at me that way, mister," Hymn laughed. "I saw there were no bullets in the gun's cylinder as soon as you pointed it at me. That's when I knew you were only trying to scare me. You gonna try to make me take that sugar pill next? Ooooh, you are scary!" Hymn covered his eyes as if afraid.

The man's confusion increased. He considered, *"One of us in this room is crazy out of his mind, and I hate that it may be me!"*

Hymn grinned at the bewildered look on the man's face and decided to get serious.

"Heck, man, I apologize for my behavior. There are times I get to kidding around and let things go too far. I honestly have no idea why I am in your office and am as surprised as you, but it may have something to do with your identity."

The man angrily retorted, "My identity! You barge in here, uninvited and want to know who I am! Where is your respect? Who you are is the question!"

Hymn paused a moment, grinned, and admitted, "You know what? You're right; my aunt taught me better manners than that. I think we should start over; what do you think? My name is Hymn."

The man stared at Hymn for a moment, thinking, *"His aunt? The empty revolver? The sugar pill?"* He picked up the poison pill, put it in his mouth, bit down on it, tasted the sweetness, and swallowed. Then he stared again at Hymn, this time in wonder.

He stood up and exclaimed, "You are Him! Good Lord! You are Him." Then, in a low voice, he said, "The Magician is here!" Slowly, he sank back down in the chair, trying to collect his racing thoughts and calm his shaking hands.

"Wow! You are really a great guesser!" responded Hymn and confirmed, "Yes, I am Hymn. You know, like a church song."

"Like a church song?" the man muttered, not understanding. "A church song," and a light in his mind turned on. "Hymn! Your name is Hymn."

He couldn't believe it; the Magician was sitting in the chair next to him, and they were having a conversation.

Hymn continued, "You got it! Now, don't you think it would be polite to tell me who you are?"

"Yes, of course," the man replied. "I am Farregutt, Chief Advisor to the Commander of Level Three of The Four Levels, or was, up until he accepted my resignation earlier."

"What are the gun and pills all about, Farregutt?" Hymn asked. "You planning to commit suicide over a lost job?"

"Suicide? No. Of course not! Well, perhaps, in a way. I have some choices, but so much depends upon what the Commander decides to do with me after what I did. Needless to say, the two options lying here are the most final and least desired. I was praying and contemplating the end of my existence when you appeared."

"Wow!" remarked Hymn. "What did you do that is worthy of a death sentence? That violation must have been a 'humdinger.' Did you run over the Commander's dog? That would do it, all right."

While watching The Magician, Farregutt realized he could not get a good reading on him. "This Hymn guy does not seem to take anything seriously and has no clue as to the danger awaiting him."

Farregutt replied evenly, "No, nothing that severe. As the Commander's chief advisor, I suggested we leave you alone and tend to our own business. My thought is you are an unknown and not worth the risk of losing many lives over a vendetta. He accused me of being afraid of you and said things causing me to resign on the spot."

"No, Farregutt, I don't think so," disagreed Hymn. "That is not the reason you were fired—or rather, not the entire reason. When I arrived, you were not contemplating how to end your life; you were entirely focused on something more troubling. I asked you a question, and you gave me part of the answer. What is causing the torment in your mind, Farregutt? Tell me!"

Farregutt was confused. *"What is it with this magician?" he asked himself. "How did he get control of this conversation to the point of giving me orders? And why am I compelled to respond truthfully? This is a dangerous man with whom I must be careful. There is some type of trickery at work here."*

Even with that thought in mind and his defenses alerted, Farregutt responded without reservation, "Commander Jonas issued a direct order to which I objected and resigned my position. He viewed my disapproval as weakness and in conflict with his plans, so, being no longer worthy of his trust, he ordered me from his presence, and I now face removal. As my level in the organization has been, and is, privileged to sensitive information, along with my close relationship with Jonas, allowing me to be on my own is no longer an option. My anguish is the result of realizing my existence is no longer important to the Commander. My code has been my undoing."

"Your code, Farregutt?" queried Hymn.

"There are certain things I will neither do nor approve, Hymn."

"Like killing children, Farregutt?"

Farregutt exclaimed, "You know! Somehow, you know what Jonas has done! How can you possibly know?"

"Well, Farregutt, after all, I am the magic man. Now, enlighten me—what has Jonas, The Great, got planned for me this evening?"

"Death, Mr. Hymn," he replied sadly. "And your tricks will not help you here. You do have the element of surprise on your side, though, because the Commander did not expect you this soon, but it will not help. He knows now. Everyone in this building is a professional assassin, trained in stealth and combat and devoted to their leader, Jonas. You, Mr. Hymn, are their only objective. You should not have come. Now, you will never leave."

"How about you, Farregutt? What are you?" Hymn asked.

"I was the best of them all, Mr. Hymn."

"Where do you stand in this confrontation, Farregutt?"

Then, unexpectedly and without warning, an incredible, chilling unveiling occurred!

"Forget Farregutt! That traitorous, fucking weakling is no longer here, Magician, and very soon, the same will be said about you," advised Jonas.

Hymn was shocked! Right there in front of him, one man left the body, and a different man took over. Jonas/Farregutt is a classic dual personality!

"Wow! I did not see that coming!" Hymn exclaimed and thought, *"Evil and Virtue, two separate natures in one body. That solves the riddle of why God did not kill Jonas; two souls share this body! This is why God said that Jonas was special, making his elimination impossible to carry out. Why did God withhold that information from me?"*

The change in the body of the man was striking. Farregutt had a tall and graceful appearance, while Jonas was slightly bent and menacing. The voice of Jonas was more authoritative, and the language was vulgar, but the change in the face was much more engaging. The eyes transformed from warm to cold, and the former pleasant smile changed into a malicious, evil grin.

Jonas continued, "I only abided Farregutt because of his sharp wit and mostly useful advice. He did help with my appointment to Commander of Level 3, though. I think Jehovah liked the idea of my strength being tempered with a little wisdom every now and then. The thing is, Jehovah seems no longer opposed to the way I currently wield my power, allowing me to remove that anchor of self-righteousness from around my neck."

He then directed his attention to Hymn, "What do you think, Magician? Surely, you see humanity cannot be trusted to govern this great planet. The collective of man requires and needs direction by the use of force. Without force to keep them under control, they revert to their basic destructive nature."

Hymn was interested in Jonas's need to talk and replied, "People are also responsive to kindness, Commander, and charity, and of course, love."

"Well, well," Jonas declared. "The magic man of the moment speaks! Yes, Magician, you speak the truth. People do respond to those things. They will accept your kindness, shit on it, and call you 'fool.' All will take your charity, over and over and over again, until you have no more to give, at which time they will curse and beat you for your stinginess. People will love you for what you give them and hate you when you have nothing to give."

He paused a brief moment, thinking, and continued, "Yes, people respond to kindness, charity, and love all the time, but their response does not build, provide, or protect. Only under force of some sort do people build, provide, and protect. Without effective force of some type motivating them, people will eat, fuck, sleep, shit, and die, having lived lives without purpose. We of The Four Levels provide them with motivating force and purpose, Magician."

"That is not why you are considered a problem, Jonas," remarked Hymn.

Jonas laughed, "Me? A problem? You have it backward; I am a solution," he responded. "On the other hand, you are a problem in need of a solution, Hymn. The happy news is, you are a problem about to be solved forever."

"Jonas, you are an anomaly," Hymn affirmed.

"Very good to hear that, Hymn. Name-calling is the last resort of a loser."

"No, Jonas, you misunderstood. I acknowledged that you are special, different, and not easily classified. Your brand of evil is so pure as to have an aura of beauty about it. You may actually be a perfect human."

Jonas scoffed, "All right, Magician, you may as well know, saying all those nice things about me only reveals your weakness. It is shameful and demeaning for you to grovel like this: I can smell your fear. Have some dignity! Farregutt thought you to be a worthy opponent, even dangerous; however, he was wrong. You are only an embarrassing little pussy who will die crying and screaming like a tortured little girl."

Jonas bragged, "Trust me on this, Magician; I know. The pure, crystal clear music flowing from the mouths of screaming, tortured little girls is . . . wonderful! I look forward to your hymn, Hymn, and will add it to my precious, Little Pussy Collection. Listening to your magnificent singing in my mornings will be an inspiring start for my days."

Hymn was amazed at the complete baseness displayed by Jonas. The L-3 Commander is a completely unique human. No words exist, heinous enough to define him. Hymn had seen and heard enough.

"Jonas, although you are an interesting man and perhaps even a unique soul, you talk way too much. Under different circumstances, I would enjoy a conversation with you, but it is getting late, and I have chores to do. How is it you see the unresolved issues between us ending?"

"With you dying, Hymn, screaming and crying in pain, fear, and regret. It is the only way to remove my hatred of you for killing my employees and my family."

Hymn inquired, "Exactly how many of your 'employees' occupy this building, Jonas? And do you care about them? I know 'care' is the wrong word, but you know what I mean; are they important to you?"

"There are 75 professional assassins in this building, Hymn, and yes, they are very important to Level-3, as you are about to see."

"But do you care about them, Jonas? Are they important to you? Answer me!"

"They are employees, Hymn. That is my answer! Oh, I left out the two in Texas. One is keeping company with my niece, Melody, and one is sighting in your Aunt Rita just about now. Of course, those two loved ones of yours will die tonight, regardless of our outcome."

"Jonas," Hymn quietly inquired, "do you know anything about watermelons?"

Jonas was quiet, gleefully thinking, "This is the moment! The Magician is broken, and his mind is closing down."

Jonas, humoring his adversary, answered, "Hymn, to me, they taste better when salted, but that's just my opinion."

"Thank you, Jonas," Hymn said and added, "It is only fair to warn you that I have installed a new security system around this building."

"I already have a security system in place, Hymn. You know, 75 professional assassins, or did your fear cause you to forget?"

Jonas was confused by Hymn's demeanor; the Magician was exhibiting no evidence of fear. On the contrary, he had an air of confidence about him. What was it Farregutt said about this man?

"He is like no other man I have ever seen or read about."

"Bullshit!" Jonas roared aloud, "No man can stand against my force of 75 assassins. No man can do that!"

Jonas shot a quick glance at the Magician and saw Hymn quietly staring through him as if he did not exist.

"Something is wrong here; this is not right!" his instincts were warning him.

Then Hymn spoke.

"Oh, I remember your security well, Commander; your 75 are impressive. I wonder what they are thinking right now?"

"My system, when activated, becomes self-rewarding, meaning you will receive what you intend to give inside the system, free of charge. If you intend to steal, you will lose something of great value. If you intend to help, you will receive help. If your intention is to murder or hurt someone, you will be murdered or hurt. Commander, you have three minutes before the system activates."

Jonas scoffed. "What kind of ridiculous, magical nonsense is this, Magician? There is no such thing as a self-rewarding security system! I would have heard about it."

"Oh, but you have heard about it, Commander," Hymn replied. "This system protects my aunt's house, and the team you sent to harm her paid the price for their security breach. You should be careful as to what you intend here and now, Jonas. My security system is already activated in this room, and the entire building will be covered in"— Hymn looked at his watch— "two minutes."

Suddenly, Jonas disappeared, and the Farregutt personality took over. The transformation was amazing to watch.

"Hymn," Farregutt demanded, "how do I turn off this system of yours?

Hymn informed, "You can't, Farregutt, but you have time to order your assassins to change their intentions or leave the building."

Farregutt was under serious pressure. He believed Hymn and did not want 75 people to die horribly, for that was their intention in regard to the Magician. Their intentions could not be ordered away and he knew it; so, he got on the intercom and ordered everyone in the building to evacuate immediately, meaning now!

"This is your Commander speaking. Everyone in the building is ordered to evacuate immediately, meaning now!" he shouted. "Get the hell out of this building!"

There was chaos in the building, slowing the evacuation because the obvious urgency in their commander's voice signaled danger. Everyone was able to get out of the building safely, even though it took over two minutes for everyone to evacuate. None of the late leavers died because their intent had changed. Intending to kill was replaced with the intent to get out of the building. They received that which they intended.

Farregutt gave the order to abort the mission and stand down from re-entering the building. He explained that a security breach was detected, threatening lives, and is currently under investigation.

Further explanations were expected to be forthcoming when reasons for the breach were found.

Since the plan to trap and kill the Magician was aborted, the agent assigned to kill Melody left without anyone knowing his mission. Unfortunately, the order to stand down never reached the assassin ordered to kill the old woman. When he carefully aimed at her head and squeezed the trigger of the rifle, the gun blew up in his face, killing him instantly. He received that which he intended.

Farregutt asked Hymn about the school in Switzerland, "Of all the schools in that country, how are we going to find which school is targeted? You cannot even stop the bomb from exploding in the school, Magician. The process has begun, and the first domino has already been tipped."

"The interesting thing about a domino line," Hymn observed, "is one domino starts the procession, and one domino removed from the line stops it."

"Farregutt," Hymn asked, "I am interested, did you know Jonas changed his mind about bombing the school?"

"No! I was not aware of that, but it pleases me to hear Jonas had a change of heart. I am almost proud of him. Maybe there is hope for him, after all."

"Well," Hymn advised, "you might want to reel in that pride. Jonas changed his mind about one school and had a bomb placed in each of ten schools around the world. It seems there are very many L-3 operatives in the world. Even Level-3 doesn't know their actual number."

Farregutt was silent. The anger and frustration on his face were all too easy to read.

Hymn warned, "Easy there, my friend. Remember where you are. I have not yet removed the security system from the building."

"Hymn," Farregutt lamented, "such horror cannot be allowed to be unleashed upon all those schoolchildren."

"Aw, c'mon, Farregutt, governments and corporations kill a lot more people every year than the comparatively small number of kids in ten schools. You're part of the government. How many people did

Level Three kill last year? More than ten schools of children? Of course, and you know it!"

"How many people, including children, are being killed every year by governments and corporations in wars they advocated and now fully support? Hundreds of thousands? Millions? Ten schools of dead children is a small amount when you think about it."

"So, why are you concerned about the kids in those ten schools, my friend?" Hymn asked.

"Because my organization will have caused their deaths, Hymn," Farregutt answered and added, "That, I will not allow!"

Hymn smiled and commented, "Well, Farregutt, since you are the Commander of Level-3 now, you have all the power required to make changes in the whole Level-3 organization; however, you are probably not long for the position."

"Why, Hymn?" Farregutt queried.

"You remember those governments and corporations to which I earlier referred? They do not abide virtuous leaders in high positions and will see to your downfall."

"Why, Hymn?" Farregutt asked, interested.

"Virtuous people in leadership positions threaten the power and profits of the powerful. Why? Because the powerful achieved said advantages through non-virtuous means and are firmly convinced great power and riches cannot be achieved any other way."

Hymn then added to his statement with an embarrassing, honest admission, "Considering we are actually discussing human nature here, those governments and corporations are probably correct in their belief."

"In any event, Farregutt, those ten schools can safely be attended tomorrow without incident, and no one but you and I will ever know they were in danger. Sometimes, with a little help, things work out."

Hymn said, "Farregutt, before I leave, it is important that I talk with Jonas. Be sure he understands the security system; I wouldn't want him to appear with a negative attitude."

The two personalities in the body changed places.

"Well," Jonas, surprised, exclaimed, "What do you know, the Magician is still here and alive to boot! You should be dead, Hymn."

Hymn cracked a smile at the dismay in Jonas's voice.

"And yet, here am I," he pointed out and inquired, "Where are you, Jonas?"

"I am here also, Hymn," Jonas countered. "What I cannot help but wonder is why. Why am I still alive? Obviously, you are aware if the circumstances were switched, you would be dead."

"You live, Jonas, mainly because you are necessary, but there is another, more surprising reason. I find that I like you."

"You like me?" Jonas laughed out loud in disbelief. "Are you familiar with the word 'Bullshit,' Hymn? What is the angle you are playing here, anyway? What is it your devious mind is concocting, Magician?" he demanded.

"No bullshit or angle, Jonas. I like your delightfully evil nature and the fact you do not hide it. For several reasons, which I will not go into now, that makes you an honest person, one who can be trusted to be what he is, which in your case is evil. Now, don't go around thinking that I am your friend or you are mine, for that would be stupid. The fact you can be trusted to be what you are indicates you are not worthy of trust, which brings me to the reason for our meeting."

"Finally!" remarked Jonas. "You talk way too much, Hymn, and you're boring. Spit out what you have to say and go back to your dismal life for whatever time you have left, and leave me alone; I have important things to do."

"About that, Jonas, understand this: you are no longer in charge of Level-3. Commander Farregutt has taken over that responsibility and does so with your blessing."

Jonas retorted, "Bullshit! Farregutt won't last a short week in the corrupt environment of business and world politics. The sharks and wolves of that society will eat him alive."

"Farregutt is the most successful assassin in Level-3, Jonas, and is familiar with the corruption in the world. With help, he will be a great commander," Hymn countered.

"Yeah, he was successful," Jonas admitted, "but his stupid code kept him from being the greatest contract killer ever. There were important missions he refused to accept."

"Like killing kids," Hymn stated.

"Yes, like killing kids," Jonas answered and proclaimed, "There are hard decisions that must be made for the sake of the collective of humanity. Moral leadership is a threat to the collective."

"C'mon, Jonas," Hymn chided, "stop with the, what is it you call it? Bullshit? Yeah, that's it, bullshit. You don't care anything about helping humanity; however, you can be of help to Farregutt and yourself at the same time. The two of you complement each other and complete the man you were designed to be. As individuals, each of you is a train wreck, given your basic natures of virtue and evil. Together, though, you can reach greatness."

Jonas's crooked grin was a failed attempt at a smile. He was in no way agreeable to sharing the command of Level-3.

"Magician, if you are not careful, you might hurt my feelings with that kind of talk, and you don't want to do that; I'm sure I don't have to explain myself. Anyway, in case you haven't noticed, I am already great."

Hymn laughed and replied, "Aw, get off your high horse, Jonas, and be honest. What is there to hurt? You don't have feelings; the concept of feelings is beyond your understanding. Now, what do you think about joining Farregutt to manage Level Three?"

Jonas paused for a moment and advised, "Okay, I'll take him back as an advisor, like before, and in return, you stay out of my life."

Hymn chuckled and admitted, "I have learned a few good lessons from you, Jonas; you know, like the importance of good communication skills, and what you just said is a fitting reminder. I am going to make this clear: *previous Commander Jonas!* Farregutt is now the leader of L-3, and you are being asked to be his advisor. You have two choices, Jonas: either yes or no. 'No' means you will spend your existence as an observer with no input into the life of the body you share. 'Yes' is an agreement that you will participate in the life of the body as a valued advisor to Commander Farregutt in regard to his management of L-3."

Jonas scoffed, indignant. "You can't do that! I run this body! And am no one's advisor!"

"Should I take that as a 'no,' former Commander Jonas?"

With rage burning in his eyes, Jonas, softly growled, "I am a commander, a leader, not someone's piss-ant advisor!"

"Well, I guess that's it, then," Hymn said and advised, "With that decision, you made a long waiting list of candidates for the position of advisor very happy. Farregutt said that would be your answer but was hoping you would agree to team up with him. He needs you. The truth is, he likes you as well."

"I may talk to him, every now and then, Hymn, when I feel like it," Jonas offered.

"No, you won't, Jonas," Hymn corrected. "With your evil nature, you can't be trusted to talk with anyone. You are all alone now. Commander Farregutt will not even be aware of your existence. I will think about you once in a while, though. Bye, Jonas."

Hymn stepped into Keepaway and disappeared right in front of Jonas.

"Wha, what just happened?! Where did he...?" Jonas, confused, shouted, "Wait! I was about to tell you that I've changed my mind; I would like to be Farregutt's adviser!"

There was a series of knocks on the door. Jonas walked over and opened it to see the Magician standing there, smiling at him.

Hymn said, "Jonas, it is not my nature to bother someone when they want to be left alone, but I just can't help but think you ought to change your mi..."

Jonas interrupted, saying, "Magician, I have decided that being an advisor to Commander Farregutt is my calling now. The thought of spending my time doing nothing scares the hell out of me. I'm on board with your idea."

"I like hearing that, Jonas," Hymn declared.

"Me too," Farregutt joined in as Jonas left. "Thank you, Hymn. Jonas has been an important part of me for my whole life. We belong together."

"You are welcome, Commander. You have great power now and are burdened with great responsibility. You also have a problem to solve. All of Level-3 will identify you as Commander Jonas. I have no idea how you will decide to resolve that issue and will be interested in your decision."

"You also have a niece, Melody, who will recognize you as her Uncle Jonas. Call and visit her once in a while. She will love you. As you know, her dad and two brothers died in the invasion of my aunt's property yesterday, and she is very upset about it. I don't know much about her mother, but she is one of your employees. Might want to be careful, there, friend."

"Commander Farregutt," Hymn continued, "The Four Levels of Earth is in decline because it was a bad idea in the first place and will soon fall. Humans were not created to be managed. Guided? Perhaps. But not driven, and with the option to go their own way, whether it be good, bad, or in-between. They must be left alone to a destiny of their own choosing. Else, how will they learn?"

Hymn thought a moment and decided, "Commander Farregutt, I'm going to do something I don't often do and give you some advice, which you can do with as you like; all I ask is that you consider what I am about to say."

"Do not make big things your focus; leave those to people and their chosen leaders. Rather, give much of your attention to attending the multitude of small things affecting people, for that is where great accomplishments are achieved."

Hymn reminded, "Another thing, Farregutt, you and Jonas will find it advisable to avoid mentioning that which happened here today. Nothing good will come of it."

Hymn forgot something, "Oh! By the way, trust Jonas to be what he is: Evil. Never for a moment give him your trust. Just saying."

Hymn removed the self-serving security coverage and stepped into Keepaway.

Commander Farregutt spoke to himself, "Small things, huh? That Hymn guy is not very good at following his own advice. What he did today is unthinkable and beyond huge. I hope we talk again."

Hymn spent several days in Keepaway, trying to sort out the changes in his life over the course of the past week. The Four Levels is still in existence but totally changed. It will be interesting to watch the effect of that change on the world.

He gained some good friends, but lost the love of his life. For some reason, the scale that measures such things is not balanced. All that means to Hymn is that he is not done yet.

26

The Aftermath

Several weeks later, in the early morning, Aunt Rita was up, preparing breakfast; she was still struggling to get the image of Melody's breakdown out of her mind. That girl withdrew into her own reality, where Rita and Hymn were insane, bad people living in a fantasy world. She noticed Hymn standing at the door, staring at nothing.

Rita sighed and advised, "Might as well get yourself over here and pour some coffee. I don't think she is going to be driving over here anytime soon."

Hymn walked to the kitchen and commented, "Yeah, that's good advice, Auntie. I miss her, though, and don't know how to repair the damage done. I fear that anything I do will only make things worse."

Rita responded wisely, "Nephew, what you are going to realize, over time, is that everything that happens, happens for a reason, and you are not going to understand the reason today. So, don't waste today, 'cause you're not ever going to get this particular day again. Make the most of it."

Hymn smiled at his aunt's no-nonsense way of looking at everything and asked her, "Auntie, have I ever told you how much you mean to me? If not, then I'm telling you now. I love you."

Then, he abruptly changed the subject.

"Wow! The coffee smells almost too good this morning; it wouldn't be surprising to see a long line of people forming outside the door any minute."

He poured a cup and sat down to butter a couple of the hot biscuits Rita placed on the table.

Hymn mused, "You know, Aunt Rita, it seems like a few months ago you informed me of my inherited powers, and here it's been over a year already, or almost, anyway."

"You know what, Hymn? My point of view is just the opposite; this past year seems more like two years to me. You shoved more accomplishments into a year than I thought possible, and you did all those things without seeming to break a sweat."

Aunt Rita placed their breakfast on the table, and Hymn dug in hungrily.

"I have been thinking about my powers, Auntie. Some of those accomplishments to which you referred are things that cannot be done, and yet they were done. How they were done is a mystery I have been unable to solve, as is the full extent of my inheritance."

"It has only been a year, Hymn," she reminded. "And you still have a lot to learn. I personally am fascinated by your regression from a 51-year-old man to what appears to be a man in his early 30s. I may have to start referring to you as my grandson instead of my nephew. It is more than interesting that finding God may be your greatest discovery."

"Speaking of interesting," Hymn responded, "would you like to hear something really interesting, Auntie?"

"I'm all ears, nephew," she answered, "what are you thinking?"

Hymn revealed, "God made the statement that I am *his* greatest discovery. Think about that a moment while realizing he has existed for millenniums."

"I wonder, Hymn," she inquired, "what is it **you** believe to be your greatest discovery this past year?"

"I'm not sure it really counts as a discovery, Auntie," Hymn considered, "but it has to be, Walter. I think about Him often, mainly because He is always around, even in Keepaway."

Rita watched as Hymn finished off the grits and eggs, sipped his coffee, and sat silently, thinking. Tears welled in her eyes as she touched his hand and said lovingly, "I am happy for you, Hymn."

Suddenly, there was an insistent succession of knocks on the door. Hymn opened it, only to see two police officers handcuffed to each other—one of which was unconscious and had apparently been tased. The other was mad and cursing while trying to get his free hand out of his pocket but couldn't.

Hymn observed the comical spectacle, finding it difficult not to laugh. "Where's the camera, boys? This just has to be a Tik-Tok video that is about to be uploaded to the net. Right?"

The unconscious officer was beginning to regain his senses and demanded, "What the hell happened?"

"I'll tell you what happened, asshole!" the other officer accused angrily. "You went nuts and handcuffed yourself to me, then began reading me my rights, so I tased you. I'm thinking now I should have just shot you."

Hymn realized then he was the only one there who knew what had occurred. The security system was active.

"All right, guys," Hymn demanded, "either of you want to tell me what is going on here? If this isn't a joke, what in the world are you two doing here, handcuffed on my front porch? Does this have something to do with the policeman's annual fundraising dance?"

The cop with his hand in his pocket found the elusive key he was looking for and unlocked the cuffs. Both of them stood up, feeling foolish and brushing themselves off while retrieving their hats.

Hymn invited them in, saying, "You might as well come on in, now that you're here, and have some coffee and biscuits. You missed breakfast, though."

Both officers shook their heads 'no' but followed Hymn to the kitchen anyway and sat down at the table. Aunt Rita was muttering something about crazy things happening around her house as she poured two cups of coffee and put the biscuits back on the table.

Hymn opened up a biscuit, smeared some jelly on it, and took a sizable bite. "You guys feel free to help yourselves," he invited. "You will not find biscuits anywhere better than these."

Both officers hesitated briefly, then each grabbed a biscuit and got down to enjoying them along with the great coffee. When asked about it later, both officers had no explanation as to why they had biscuits and coffee with Hymn and his aunt, other than it seemed like the normal thing to do.

After the morning snack, Hymn asked them why they came to his residence this morning. "Are you following up on the raid here?"

"What raid?" questioned the younger officer. "If there was a raid here, we don't know anything about it. We have an arrest warrant for a Hymn Godman at this address. Are you Hymn Godman?"

"That would be me," Hymn acknowledged, "but I don't think I'm going to allow you to arrest me today as my schedule is full, and I have no time to give you. Tell you what, I'll come to your station the day after tomorrow, and we can talk unless something more important comes up, of course. In which case, my people will talk to your people, and better arrangements will be made."

The two officers looked at each other in disbelief and then at the man sitting across from them, who was calmly putting jelly on another biscuit. His aunt had her back to them and was thinking, "Oh, Hymn, what, in heaven's name, are you getting yourself into now?"

Both officers stood up, anger burning in their eyes at the lack of respect this guy displayed toward law enforcement.

"Mister Godman, I am Officer Hannah, and the officer to my left is holding an official warrant for your arrest. It is my sworn duty to inform you that resisting arrest is a serious violation of the law, punishable by a fine and serious jail time. Now, you just come along peaceably and don't make more trouble for yourself than you already have."

"Look, fellows, I have no idea who you are, but you are certainly not policemen. Just take your little charade back to wherever it is you came from and tell whoever sent you the joke is on them."

"So, Mr. Godman, you are resisting arrest, then?" Hannah asked.

Hymn sipped his coffee and replied, "What arrest? You have not arrested me or even mentioned the reason for which you want to arrest me."

Officer Hannah grinned and stated, "You know, Godman, that is exactly what I hoped you would say." He drew his gun, pointed it at Hymn, and ordered, "Get face down on the floor, right now! Hands behind your back!"

"Why?" Hymn asked. "It's not that the floor is dirty or anything; my aunt is a cleaning machine. The truth is, I just don't want to lay on the floor right now, so take your toy gun and go home."

Aunt Rita spoke up, saying, "Hymn, stop teasing these men; they have no idea what is happening here." Then she looked at the man named Hannah and advised, "Mr. Hannah, enough is enough. You two get on home now before you fool around and get yourselves hurt. I'm getting concerned about you."

Officer Hannah looked at Rita, grinned, and stated, "Hurt? Me? Listen, whoever you are, in case you haven't noticed, Godman there is holding a biscuit. I'm the one holding a gun."

"Yeah," Rita acknowledged, "a real nice little toy gun. Now quit playing around, Mr. Hannah, and get on out of my house."

Mr. Hannah looked down at the toy gun in his hand and looked at his partner, shocked and in need of an explanation.

"Don't be looking at me, Sergeant Hannah; my weapon is the real McCoy. How long have you been carrying that toy gun?"

Hannah looked angrily at Hymn and said slowly and calmly, with obvious hatred glistening in his eyes, "You have something to do with this, asshole. I was forewarned about your tricks but didn't believe them. We are leaving now, but mark my words, I will return, and that is a promise, one you should not look forward to."

Hymn looked up from putting jelly on another biscuit and stared deeply into Hannah's eyes, sending a chill down the man's back, then lightly commented, "You know, Mr. Hannah, that might be interesting," and smiled as he took a bite of his biscuit.

"Oh, by the way," Hymn offered, "would you like to use the restroom before you go? It's a good ways back to Dallas and slow going, especially with the traffic and all."

"Fuck you, Godman!" Hannah retorted and glared at Hymn.

"Well, I suppose that means we're not going to be taking warm showers together in the wee hours of the morning, Hannah," Hymn replied and laughed heartily. "I heard that phrase in a movie some time ago and have been wanting to use it ever since," he said and began laughing again.

Hannah turned and walked to the door, consumed with anger.

"God! I hate that man!" he growled.

Hymn hollered after the man, "Aw, c'mon, don't go away angry. And listen, I'm really sorry about your car seats!"

Officer Hannah's partner had already left and returned to the car. Something about this Godman fellow made him uneasy.

"This was a terrible plan," he said to himself.

Hannah got in the car with a mixture of anger and fear, causing his hands to shake.

"I'm going to kill that bastard," he hissed through his teeth, "but first, I intend to watch him piss all over himself in fear as he chokes to death from a knife in his throat. He will regret laugh—" and coughed hard before he finished the sentence. He began wheezing and coughed again and again!

"I can't hardly breathe," he said, in a panic, "Call 911! Get me to a hospital!"

"Jesus! Bart. You're pissing all over yourself!" Jimmy screamed, concerned.

"I kinda thought something like this might happen," Hymn stated through the open window of the car. "With a temper like yours, Hannah, it was bound to happen sooner or later. Kinda looks to me like you're dying; what do you think, Jimmy?"

"Mr. Godman, he can't breathe! He's gonna die!" Jimmy cried, "He's dying!"

"Nah, Jimmy, no one is dying here today. Mr. Hannah is just in the process of changing his mind. Isn't that right, Bart? You don't want to kill anyone, do you, Mr. Hannah?" Hymn asked.

Bart's eyes were wide and bulging a little as he shook his head no and immediately realized he was finally able to inhale a deep breath.

He felt weakened and slumped down in the seat, breathing easily, his head on the console.

Hymn smiled sympathetically and advised, "You're all right, Bart, but you might want to take some anger control classes to learn how to keep that temper of yours within limits. Anger like that can kill a man. You two can do what you want, but my advice is to keep your experience here today 'under your hats,' so to speak. Talking about it might just bring on a recurrence if you get my meaning."

"Listen, fellas," Hymn offered, "if you get a chance, stop by again sometime for another, longer visit. Heck, we might even have breakfast again." He added, as he left, "You know, Bart, you sure made a mess of yourself and that car seat."

Then Hymn turned and walked back into the house, thinking, "I wonder who sent those two guys to arrest me?"

Aunt Rita was gathering her knitting as Hymn walked in.

"What did you think about our guests, Auntie? A little rough around the edges, it seemed to me."

"Rough around the edges, my hind end!" she retorted. "Those two are thugs on the road to being criminals. They are adult men who neglected to leave their childhood behind. Who do you think sent them?"

"Beats me, Auntie. I have been wondering about that very thing myself."

"You think they will come back, Hymn? That older one was really mad. You didn't hurt him, did you?"

"No, Auntie," Hymn acknowledged, "well, except for his pride; there might have been a little damage done there."

Rita commented, "You never know, for sure, what's going on in people's minds. They might come back tomorrow."

"Well, they sure liked your coffee and biscuits. It's hard to pass up food that good, even when you're angry."

(Jimmy) As they were driving away, Jimmy was thinking and said, "I can't believe that Hymn feller invited us to come back for breakfast sometime, Bart."

(Bart) "I've been thinking about that, too, Jimmy. Godman is a strange sort of man. I lost my temper, said some terrible things, and made some bad threats against that man. And how does he react? He comes out and saves my life! I was dying there, Jimmy, really dying. Godman returned my hatred of him with love. I know that sounds stupid, coming from me, but that is how I feel."

(Jimmy) "You know something, Bart? I didn't say anything back in their house, but I really like those people. I'm gonna come back and visit with them pretty soon."

(Bart) "I might come with you, Jimmy; I like them, too. There are a few apologies and some gratitude to express."

(Jimmy) "Bart, I don't like doing what we do and am planning to quit when we get back."

(Bart) "Come on, Jimmy, you can't quit. You don't know how to do anything else. Besides, you've been working for Mr. Harold since you were fourteen, and the syndicate isn't just going to let you walk away. They have too much invested in you, and on top of that, you've seen things you were not supposed to see. Know what I mean?"

"You can't quit, so get that thought out of your head and don't mention it again. Believe me, Jimmy, there ain't no good ever comes from trying to quit this organization."

(Jimmy) "Yeah, I see what you're saying, Bart. I just never thought of it that way. What you're saying is that the syndicate is not my employer; it is my owner. I'm a type of slave."

(Bart) "So what, Jimmy? Everyone is a slave to someone or something. There are all types of slavery. On a scale of 1 to 10, where a 10 is the worst slavery, and one is the best, you and I are 3's or 4's at worst. That ain't bad."

"Some people have regular jobs where they are 6's or 7's on the slave scale, and most of them are not actually happy. Sure, we occasionally have to do some dirty work for Mr. Harold, but the syndicate takes better care of us compared to most of those other poor bastards out there in the workforce."

(Jimmy) "I know that, Bart. The thing is, working for Mr. Harold is the only job I've ever had. I would like to learn other skills."

(Bart) "Like what, Jimmy?"

(Jimmy) "I don't know exactly what, Bart. Something to do that doesn't require hurting people the way we do. It just doesn't seem right, and I don't want to do it anymore."

(Bart) "Listen up now, Jimmy, that type of talk puts you dangerously close to being a problem to the syndicate, should they become aware of your thinking. It has to stop right now, right here in this car. Do not ever talk about quitting again! You hear me?"

"As far as hurting people is concerned, I don't know what to tell you. Some people just have to be forced to obey rules. That is effectively accomplished by strict enforcement of the rules, meaning punishment. I don't favor it either, but for some, pain is the only way to get their attention."

(Jimmy) "I get it, Bart, and won't talk about it anymore, but I still think there is a better way for a man to earn a living. While we're on the subject of enforcement, I think Mr. Godman should be left alone.

There's something unusual about that man that sends out a 'Danger' notice. You and I are dangerous men, Bart, and he made us look like stupid kids."

(Bart) "Yeah. Mr. Godman scares me, Jimmy, and I'm not sure why. Can you imagine trying to tell Mr. Harold that? Speaking of which, what are we going to tell Mr. Harold when we get back without Godman in handcuffs?"

(Jimmy) "That is your job, Sergeant Sir. In the meantime, I think we should stop and clean up this car. It smells bad. You could use a clean-up and a change of clothes, as well."

(Bart) "Asshole!"

When Bart and Jimmy got back to the Harold Securities building, they reported immediately to their boss, Mr. A. J. Harold, CEO of Harold Securities, Inc., in his office.

Mr. Harold wasted no time getting down to business. "All right, gentlemen, who wants to tell me why Hymn Godman is not here, in handcuffs, standing before me right now?"

Bart explained that Mr. Godman was in no way impressed by the warrant they presented for his arrest and made it plain he was too busy to be arrested today. Other than that, the man was congenial and friendly, even to the point of inviting us into his home for coffee and biscuits. The best biscuits I have ever eaten, too."

"Both of you literally had breakfast with the man? Why?" Mr. Harold demanded, curious.

Bart replied, "It just seemed like the polite thing to do at the time, sir, his being so nice and all."

Mr. Harold, his voice rising, exclaimed, "Polite? Nice? Great biscuits?" then exploded, "What in the hell is going on with you, Bart? Are you losing your touch? Since when does any of that shit affect the way you do your job? And what the hell was Jimmy doing while you were being so nice?"

Jimmy spoke for himself, "Mr. Harold, I was observing the situation. With all due respect, sir, you were not there. Mr. Godman may not look like much, but he is an unusual man, perhaps even a dangerous man. I have no idea why you assigned us to arrest him and don't care why, but I doubt there is any team of men who can arrest that man if he doesn't want to be arrested without some very serious consequences."

Mr. Harold was suddenly taken aback and totally surprised by the outspokenness of the young man. He thought a moment about Jimmy's outburst and realized it confirmed his reason for wanting Godman arrested and brought here in the first place.

"Jimmy," Mr. Harold's voice was calm, but serious, "I concur with your assessment that Mr. Godman may be a dangerous man, but he and I are out of balance with each other, a situation that must be resolved. I am interested in how the man appeared to you. What was he like?"

Bart was watching and listening with concern. Young Jimmy was now at a crossroads in his life. He should keep his mouth shut or tell the man what he wants to hear, but Bart knew Jimmy wouldn't do either. The poor kid is afflicted with honesty, a rare trait that assures a short life in politics and certain businesses. Jimmy held both their futures in his hands with his reply.

Jimmy was uneasy. Mr. Harold had backed him into a corner. The thought occupying his mind was, "I should have listened to Bart and kept my mouth shut."

Jimmy blurted out, "Mr. Harold, the truth is, Godman impressed me as being a very good man, and I like him. I don't say that about many men."

Mr. Harold looked intensely at the young man and asked, "What about me, Jimmy? Do you like me?"

"No, Mr. Harold," Jimmy replied honestly, "I love you; you saved me. You are my only family."

Mr. Harold's eyes glistened briefly as the personal story of Jimmy's short life appeared in his mind. Then he asked the young man, "Without thinking, Jimmy, what should be done in regard to Mr. Godman?"

"Leave him alone, sir; either that or ask him to meet and talk with you. That is the way to balance things between you."

Mr. Harold stood, went around his desk, gently put his hand on Jimmy's shoulder, and said, "Thank you, son. Good report." Then he stated, "Gentlemen, this meeting is completed. Get the hell out of my office."

As the door shut behind them, Bart grabbed his partner's arm and said, "What the fuck just happened in there, Jimmy? One minute, I'm thinking you're about to 'disappear,' and the next minute, the old man is thanking you."

"I don't know what happened, Bart. Mr. Harold backed me into a corner with his questions to where I had to lie or tell the truth; I opted for the truth, without thinking."

Bart laughed and exclaimed, "Hot damn, how about that! Come on, Jimmy, I'm buying the drinks. For the first time in my life, I'm going to raise my glass to the truth."

Later that day, Hymn was lounging in the living room recliner, pondering this new mystery and sipping a cup of fresh hot coffee, when the phone rang. Aunt Rita answered it. He heard her say, "Yes, he's here. Okay, hold on a few seconds while I get him for you."

"Who is it, Auntie?"

"A woman on the phone says a Mr. A.J. Harold wants to talk to you about the two men you invited to breakfast this morning. You don't think he is with the police, do you? I mean, it sounds official. What are you...?"

Hymn interrupted her, saying, "I don't know, Auntie, but this just might be interesting," as he went to take the call.

~~*~*~*

Book III will be available in 2025.

About the Author

John D. Parfait, Jr. holds a Bachelor of Science in Chemistry from the University of Texas, Arlington and has 50 years of experience as a chemist in private industry. At age 80, John began his literary journey and published *Mudman: Tale of a Texas Swamp* in 2023. He aims to write at least ten books by age 90.

John has written poetry and three novels, specializing in Coming of Age and Fiction genres. His inspiration for writing stems from a lifelong love of storytelling and a desire to share his tales with the world. His personal motto is "Save. Give. Achieve. Believe. At least a little of each, every day." Outside of writing, he enjoys bowling, the outdoors, and philosophy.

A proud Army veteran, John values his roles as husband, father, grandfather, and great-grandfather.